Praise for *Crooked Hallelujah*

"In her more than promising first novel, *Crooked Hallelujah*, Kelli Jo Ford summons the details of minimum-wage life in the last quarter of the 20th century . . . This is a novel in stories, a dread form in the wrong hands . . . But *Crooked Hallelujah* has a supple cohesiveness . . . [Ford's] book reads like a series of acoustic songs recorded on a single microphone in a bare room with a carpet. There are times when you might wish for more boldness, but she never puts a wrong foot. This is a writer who carefully husbands her resources. Small scenes begin to glitter." —Dwight Garner, *New York Times*

"Ford has drawn characters who are earthy, honest and believable in how they resolve or reconcile to difficulties—money, jobs, relationships with men. There are so many passages in this book that are moving." —*Minneapolis Star Tribune*

"Ford, a citizen of the Cherokee Nation of Oklahoma, offers a novel in short stories, allowing her to move with ease through perspectives, history and time. Each heartbreaking chapter slowly adds to the reader's understanding of these women and their increasingly difficult lives." —*Time*

"A book that you want to share with everyone you know and one that you are desperate to keep in your own possession . . . a new and thrilling voice for readers across the globe." —Sarah Jessica Parker

"Kelli Jo Ford has penned an extraordinary debut set in 1974 in the Cherokee Nation of Oklahoma that is focused on mothers and daughters, the strength and sacrifices of women and the journey that growth requires." —*Ms. Magazine*

"Strife between saints and sinners simmers in this richly drawn, atmospheric debut by a citizen of the Cherokee Nation of Oklahoma." —*Oprah Magazine*

"Engrossing and well-paced, this is a compelling story about women, mothers and daughters, the land, and family." —*Literary Hub*

"A magnificent #OwnVoices debut . . . Ford adroitly, affectingly weaves indigenous history into her spellbinding narrative, exposing displacement, unacknowledged violence, cultural erasure, relentless racism and socioeconomic disparity." —*Shelf Awareness*

"Electrifying . . . A riveting and important read." —*Booklist* (starred review)

"Ford's storytelling is urgent, her characters achingly human and complex, and her language glittering and rugged. This is a stunner." —*Publishers Weekly* (starred review)

"Ford's *Crooked Hallelujah* is more than just a really great title; it's the book that's going to be taught in creative writing programs for decades to come . . . What else can you say about a writer who won the prestigious Plimpton Prize and was published in the *Paris Review* right out of the gate? Nothing beyond 'Take my money.'" —*Buzzfeed*

"A tender and ambitious praise-song of a novel about a family's fight for survival, love, and home." —*Kirkus Reviews*

"At once critical and empathetic, Ford paints strikingly candid portraits of four generations of Cherokee women in all their human complexity, rather than reducing them to figures in a political allegory. The result is a book that is—to borrow Ford's own deceptively poetic turn of phrase—'One hell of a testimony.'" —*High Country News*

"Kelli Jo Ford's first book, composed of interlocking stories set in Oklahoma and North Texas, is like a wildfire that slowly approaches a home and then whips through an entire region . . . Ford's voice rises above the tumult." —*BookPage*

"[A] masterpiece . . . Even through its harsh circumstances and looming disappointments, *Crooked Hallelujah* maintains a sense of hope, centering the women as sources of light in the tiny communities where they land. Its closing scenes are overt in their biblical tie-ins, but also so consistent with what precedes them that they force rear-gazing considerations: was the divine present in every event of the women's lives after all? Or was it their fierce, life-giving love for one another that most warranted emulation and awe? . . . Its events like psalms for mother-daughter bonds, Kelli Jo Ford's novel celebrates bold, everyday acts of enduring love." —*Foreword Reviews*

"In an explosive and deeply emotional debut novel, Kelli Jo Ford keeps a tight rein on the prose and lures the reader into the world of these women, held together by the threads of blood, anger, and the complex duty to self and to each other . . . Ford captures the tension and grace of these relationships, crafting an exceptional story that places the reader firmly in the midst of these lives, feeling the heartache and hope across the pages." —*Lone Star Literary Life*

"[An] engaging, composite debut." —*Arts Fuse*

"Kelli Jo Ford's *Crooked Hallelujah* masterfully evokes loss and displacement, steeped in Native American culture, rife with compassion and deep understanding. Kelli Jo Ford is a powerful new Native American writer who writes beautifully with stunning prose! She is brilliant, and I can't wait for people to read her amazing book."
—Brandon Hobson, author of *The Removed*

"*Crooked Hallelujah* is an intricate, soulful look at three generations of Cherokee women pushed (in Philip Larkin's phrase) to the side of their own lives. At turns gripping and moving, Kelli Jo Ford's characters and the Oklahoma and Texas landscape take center stage in a truly modern drama. Ford sidesteps the easy tropes of spirituality and connection to nature and has created a modern masterpiece peopled with complex, fully-realized characters. A huge achievement."
—David Treuer, author of *The Heartbeat of Wounded Knee*

"Startling close-ups of the sticky relationship between mothers and daughters, between body and nature, between childhood certainties and adult skepticism. Kelli Jo Ford's writing is heartfelt and brimming with talent. This is a stunning, awe-inspiring debut."
—Leila Aboulela, author of *Bird Summons*

CROOKED HALLELUJAH

CROOKED HALLELUJAH

KELLI JO FORD

Grove Press
New York

Some chapters in this book have appeared in the following
publications in slightly different form: "Book of the Generations,"
The Missouri Review; "The Year 2003 Minus 20," *Virginia Quarterly
Review*; "Terra Firma" *The SFWP Quarterly*; "Hybrid Vigor,"
The Paris Review; "You'll Be Honest, You'll Be Brave," *Electric
Literature*; "You Will Miss Me When I Burn," *Virginia Quarterly
Review*; "Bonita," *New Delta Review*; "What Good Is an Ark to
a Fish?" *Forty Stories: New Writing from Harper Perennial*.

Published simultaneously in Canada
Printed in the United States of America

First Grove Atlantic hardcover edition: July 2020
First Grove Atlantic paperback edition: July 2021

This book was set in 11-pt. Scala by
Alpha Design & Composition of Pittsfield, NH.

Library of Congress Cataloging-in-Publication data is available
for this title.

ISBN 978-0-8021-4913-8
eISBN 978-0-8021-4914-5

Grove Press
an imprint of Grove Atlantic
154 West 14th Street
New York, NY 10011

Distributed by Publishers Group West

groveatlantic.com

21 22 23 24   10 9 8 7 6 5 4 3 2 1

Contents

CONTENTS

*For my grandmothers, my mom, my aunties and cousins,
and, now, Cypress Ann*

It was really the world that was one's brutal mother, the one that nursed and neglected you, and your own mother was only your sibling in that world.

—Lorrie Moore, "Which Is More Than I Can Say About Some People"

CROOKED HALLELUJAH

PART I

Beulah Springs,
Cherokee Nation of Oklahoma
1974

Book of
the Generations

1.

When Lula stepped into the yard, the stray cat Justine held took off so fast it scratched her and sent the porch swing sideways. Justine had been feeding the stray, hoping to find its litter of kittens in spite of her mother's disdain for extra mouths or creatures prone to parasites. She tried to smooth cat hair from her lap. She'd wanted everything to be perfect when she told her mom that she'd tracked down her father in Texas and used the neighbor's phone to call him.

"That thing's going to give you worms." Lula dropped her purse onto the porch. She hadn't been able to catch a ride from work. With a deep sigh, she untucked her blouse and undid the long green polyester skirt she'd started sewing as soon as she'd seen the HELP WANTED sign at the insurance office. She was a secretary now, and as she liked to tell Justine, people called her Mrs. and complimented her handwriting.

"I'll wash up," Justine said. She'd already decided today wasn't the day. Like yesterday. And the day before that.

"At least let me say hi." Lula kicked off dusty pumps and let her weight drop into the swing beside Justine. The swing skittered haywire as Lula pulled bobby pins from her bun, scratching her scalp. Her long salt-and-pepper braid fell past her shoulder and curled under her breast. "Bless us, Lord," she said, the words nearly a song. She closed her eyes, and as she whispered an impromptu prayer, she touched the end of her braid to the mole on her lip that she still called her beauty mark.

As a girl, Justine had pored over the pictures from Lula's time at Chilocco Indian School, trying to see her mother in the stone-cold fox who stared out from the old photographs. Lula's clothes hung loosely, even more faded than the other girls' in the pictures, but something about her gaze—framed by short black curls, of all things—made it seem as if she were the only one in the photo. If Marilyn Monroe had come of age in an Indian boarding school and had fierce brown eyes instead of scared blue ones, that would have been young Lula. Justine kept the old pictures in a box hidden in the top of the closet where she kept her *Rolling Stones* and a mood ring, other forbidden things. She hadn't thought of the pictures in ages, but she did so now as she watched her mom in prayer.

4

Lula whispered amen, caught Justine staring at her.

"Granny's out gathering wild onions with Aunt Celia," Justine said quickly.

"Late in the year for it," Lula said. She unrolled her nylon stockings and wiggled her toes in the air. In the way of Cherokee women, Lula could still make you feel that she held down the Earth around her one moment and then seem almost like a girl the next. "Did you do your homework?"

"I swept and did the rugs too."

"My Teeny," Lula said, calling her the nickname that had stuck when Justine's middle sister, Josie, hadn't been able to say her name. Together they pushed the swing back and let it fall forward.

Justine closed her eyes. In the cool air that had come with the night's rain, her mother's warmth felt nice, which made the words she'd been practicing feel all the worse.

"Evenings like this make me wonder how a body would want to set their bones anywhere other than these hills," Lula said.

Justine opened her eyes. The two-bedroom house they rented with her granny sat on the edge of Beulah Springs, the outer walls almost as much tar paper as asphalt shingle. She had her own room now that her sisters, Dee and Josie, had married themselves out of state, but her mother and Granny still split a room barely big enough for one. Hand-sewn curtains strung on a clothesline separated their beds. The low green hills beyond the train tracks seemed like folds in a crumpled blanket after Dee sent her pictures of Tennessee mountains. Justine had a good idea why a body might light out for other hills, other lands.

"I talked to Daddy." Her nerves blurted it out for her.

Lula put her feet down to stop the swing. Justine couldn't read her mother's face, but she wished she could put the words back in her mouth, swallow them for good.

Justine's father had dropped the family off for a Saturday night service at Beulah Springs Holiness Church almost seven years back. As far as anyone could tell, he'd then been swallowed up by the Oklahoma sky. He'd never sent an ounce of child support or a forwarding address, never even called.

Lula held herself together with a religion so stifling and frightening that Justine, the youngest and always the most bullheaded, never knew if she was fighting against her mother or God himself, or if there was even a difference. Still, her father was a betrayal of the knife-in-the-heart variety— something far beyond all their fighting—and here he was on a cool spring evening, right between them.

"He's in Texas. Near Fort Worth," Justine said. She bit her lip. "He asked me to go to Six Flags with him. Just for the weekend. He has a little boy now, I guess."

She almost hoped Lula would hit her, but Lula stared into the hills. It wasn't clear she had heard, so Justine's mouth kept moving.

"Six Flags is an amusement park. With roller coasters. I know you might think it's too worldly, but I can wear a long skirt on the rides and all. It's sort of like a big old playground!"

Justine forced a smile. She pushed a strand of hair back into her bun and waited. "I'm sorry, Mama."

Lula remained quiet, focused on the horizon.

"I guess I pestered Mr. Bean at the plant so much he helped put me in touch." She didn't say that she'd gotten the information from her dad's old foreman almost two years ago and then been so ashamed that she tore the paper into bits she spread over Little Locust Creek. A few weeks back, her treacherous mind had begun to play the numbers across her thoughts, a musical sequence that interrupted her over dinner or during tests.

"I'm real excited about Six Flags," she said, and despite everything, she realized it was true.

"I'll talk to Pastor about it," Lula said, finally. She pushed herself out of the swing and walked inside.

At first Justine was surprised at how well it had gone. Then she saw Lula's purse kicked over on the porch, her comb and Bible in a puff of cat hair. Justine scrambled to retrieve them and ran her hand over the textured leather cover of the heavy book.

She pushed past the screen door and went to her mother's room, where she could hear Lula already in prayer. One of Lula's drawings of a Plains Indian's teepee was tacked to the closed door. Justine knew that on the other side of the teepee, her mother knelt, as she did in church. Instead of a wooden pew or an altar, Lula's face was buried in her twin bed, if she had made it that far. Justine ran her finger over the smooth indentations of her mother's ink. She wanted to take Lula the purse and Bible, decided that if Lula stopped praying, she would make herself push through the door. She would go into the small, dark room, where maybe she would lay her head on her mother's shoulder. If she did, Justine knew that her mouth would open back up. Instead of telling Lula about Six Flags and a new half brother, Justine would tell her about what Russell Gibson did to her.

She wouldn't be able to omit the details of the night she'd snuck out and met him down their dirt road, how he looked back over his shoulder then let her steer the car while he pushed from the open driver-side door, only cranking the engine once they were well out of Lula's earshot. How her stomach flip-flopped over the way he had looked at her as he drove, shaking his head, saying, "Fif-teen," and how her insides had frozen when she noticed a blanket folded neatly in the back seat. She would say how very sorry she was that she had pretended to be asleep that night when Lula stuck her head into the dark room and said, "Good night, my Teeny. Love you." She would tell her how she'd thought his abrupt movements must have been what first dates were made of. She would tell Lula that she said no quietly at first.

But Lula's prayer rose and dipped into a moan. Then great, body-shaking sobs vibrated through the door into Justine's hand, along her arm, and into her chest. She dropped the purse and Bible on the kitchen table and locked herself in the bathroom.

"Shit. Shit. Shit," she muttered. Feeling as if her bones were shaking, she took a can of Aqua Net, covered her eyes, and sprayed it all around her head. She waved hairspray from the air and then scrubbed her face red with scalding water. Her father's blue eyes reflected back at her, not Lula's brown eyes or eyes that seemed her own. Mostly she didn't think about him anymore. She didn't think she wanted to see him, but what was done was done. She decided then that she would go to Six Flags with her father and never think of Russell Gibson again. It was as if her young heart could only hold the two emotions: one, a guilt so deep for betraying her mother that it left her feeling like a human rattle, empty save for a few disconnected bones; and two, a joy so sudden and surprising at the thought of riding Big Bend, the fastest roller coaster in the world, that she felt she might pass out.

2.

"We'd love to have you, babe," her father had said. "We'll go to Six Flags. It'll be a blast." Through the crackly long-distance line, his baritone sounded familiar but busy, his words fireflies that flitted between them without illuminating a thing. She cradled the telephone on her shoulder and counted France, Spain, Mexico, Confederacy, United States on her fingers, trying to think of the sixth flag. "Roller coasters big as mountains," he'd said. "Hold on." She heard muffled talking, then he came back. "Justine, is everything okay?"

"Just dandy," she said, and he was off again, filling the distance between them with empty words. It was a presumptuous question after all these years: *Is everything okay?* Where to begin? She knew he'd meant: *Why now?* Just like she knew that if he'd really wanted her to visit, she wouldn't have had to go to such lengths to find him. She should have called her oldest sister, who was spending the summer on the Holiness Camp Meeting circuit with her new preacher husband.

Six Flags, like the basketball team she'd wanted to join last year, was "of the world." Justine could hear Lula already: "The world passeth away, and the lust thereof: but he that doeth the will of God abideth for ever." Justine was only fifteen, but she held no illusions—nor intentions—of abiding forever. Maybe Six Flags would be less hurtful than the truth that she needed to get away from *here.* And that her father was the *there.*

She had imagined the night for weeks after Russell Gibson had first spoken to her on her class trip to Sequoyah's Cabin. When she'd seen him working on a water leak outside the stone house covering the cabin that day, she recognized him. Her cousin John Joseph played music with him. She knew he was twentysomething, Choctaw, already back from the war. He had his shirt off and a rolled red bandana holding walnut-colored hair out of his eyes. When he saw her looking, he grinned and dropped his shovel for a pick mattock that he buried in the red earth.

She slipped away and let him write a phone number on her wrist, not telling him they didn't have a phone. She liked that he wasn't much taller than her but had wisps of a mustache. She thought the homemade outline of the Hulk tattooed on his forearm was cool and pictured them going to a drive-in movie in Fort Smith. Or maybe he would lean on the hood of his car and sing her a song: sinful, surely, but nothing she couldn't pray her way out of. Every bit of that had been the work of a girl's imagination, nothing else. They hadn't gone to a movie, and he didn't even bring a guitar.

She had her first moment of regret when she looked back at their little house, porch light glowing on the hill, but then he let her start the car. She revved the engine and laughed. Freedom had been waiting just on the other side of her bedroom window! He used his thigh to push her to the middle of the seat and took the wheel. He passed her his cigarette and rubbed her leg when he wasn't shifting gears. Time and place swirled together as he turned onto a two-track road that disappeared into Little Locust Creek. He pushed the emergency brake, and before he cut the lights, she could see where the two-track, broken by the black water, picked back up on the other side of the creek.

She thought she should have fought him, thought maybe she'd unknowingly agreed to what happened. Her mind kept mixing up the jumble of memories from that night, but it returned again and again to Proverbs 5, a favorite of church deacons. She suspected she caused the whole thing.

She told herself that if she could forget the terrible night ever happened, it would be so. She didn't sleep for days. Numbers replaced her thoughts. She found her father.

When her body grew too tired to keep up her mind's tormented vigil, she dreamed of roller coasters.

3.

Lula came red-eyed out of the bedroom. Her voice nearly a whisper, she said that if Justine wanted to see her father, it was her choice. "It seems you're old enough, Justine, that your salvation is your own burden." Then, her voice sharper: "And if you want to ride a roller coaster in your first act as a spiritual adult, so be it." All Justine had to do was make it out of Wednesday night service.

People in town called them Holy Rollers, but the congregation of Beulah Springs Holiness Church referred to themselves as the Saints, the hardy few called to travel Isaiah's Holiness Highway. They set themselves apart from the world with their Spirit-filled meetings, faith healing, prophetic visions, and modest dress. Though even wedding rings were forbidden as outward adornment, they believed once married, always married: Lula's solitude was a sentence of belief and circumstance. They believed Stomp Dances were of the devil, that God healed what was meant to be healed, and children obeyed. Justine learned early that life was made up of occasional threads of joy woven through a tapestry of unceasing trials and tribulations. Life was spiritual warfare, and Six Flags would be no exception.

Justine sat where she always sat, in the back pew with her cousin John Joseph. His father was Lula's brother,

Justine's Uncle Thorpe, but first and foremost he was their pastor. John Joseph's black hair was stuck behind one ear in a greasy clump. He had his father's square jaw and his mom's gray eyes, which made him a hit with girls in town, girls who didn't go to a Holiness church or wear slicked-back buns and skirts down to their ankles. Like Justine, he was old enough to be an adult in the eyes of God and their church, and like Justine he hadn't prayed through, no matter what terrors his soul faced in this world and after. "Jesus wept" had been their favorite Bible verse for as long as she could remember. She always thought it was because it was the shortest and easiest to recite on demand, but lately she'd found herself wondering why the words were so sudden and set apart.

Justine's eyes welled up, so she kept them on her lap while Uncle Thorpe finished his sermon with a story about a teenager who had died in a car wreck on his way home from a concert. The teenager had been raised Holiness and knew better. Uncle Thorpe walked around the simple wooden pulpit, rested an elbow on it, and looked at Justine. He wiped his eyes with his handkerchief. One brylcreemed strand of hair had fallen onto his forehead, like some kind of Native Superman. Justine imagined herself melting to nothing on the floor and sliding away.

Up there in front of the whole ragtag congregation filled mostly with poor whites, mixed-bloods—nearly half of whom were Uncle Thorpe's kids—and a few full-bloods like her granny, Uncle Thorpe spoke to *her*: "The pleasures of this world may seem great. They are supposed to, for if we are not tested, like Jesus in the wilderness," he shouted, raising his voice until it cracked, "how can we find our salvation?" Tears fell down his face. "Justine, God's talking to my heart. You could die on that roller coaster."

Not just a roller coaster, she thought. *Big Bend.*

The Saints began to whisper to God to intercede in her sinful plans. Uncle Thorpe took a long time wiping his eyes. He blew his nose and opened his arms wide, palms to the sky, and said, "Saints, we're going to start up altar call." From a raised platform behind the pulpit, the four-piece band lurched into "Consider the Lilies."

"If you hear the Lord talking to you today," Uncle Thorpe shouted over the music, "even if the voice is small, Saints"—his own voice grew quiet—"maybe it's doubt nagging from the back of your mind. Maybe it's sorrow or quiet longing tucked away in your heart. Maybe it's fear for your children. Maybe it's been too long since you've prayed through. Or maybe you never have." He held his eyes on John Joseph, who never stopped digging dirt from his fingernails with his pocketknife. Then Uncle Thorpe turned his eyes back to Justine. "Come, children. Jesus is waiting. The only way to him is to bow your head and ask him into your heart. It doesn't matter how you got here or what you've done. You will know a new day, children. I love you, but only God can turn this car around."

Lula moved toward the altar first, and then other Saints streamed to the front. Some knelt before the altar in prayer, waving wadded-up handkerchiefs to the sky. Some stood, placing their hands on the shoulders or backs of the others.

Their murmuring and crying pushed at Justine, but she stayed firmly planted in her seat, rubbing the scar between her left thumb and pointer finger.

After a time, three deacons started down the aisle toward her. She'd been weepy since she sat down, but she quickly wiped her eyes. Uncle Thorpe pushed himself up off the altar and started down the aisle. The band kicked into high gear, banging out the rhythm of Justine's dormant salvation. Justine swore she could feel the little wooden church shake as Uncle Thorpe strode toward her.

"Playing you their war song," John Joseph nearly yelled into Justine's ear. His three brothers made up three-quarters of the band, the piano player the only woman of the bunch. The most gifted musician in the family, John Joseph refused to play in church. Instead, he sat in the back with Justine, who didn't find his joke funny.

The Saints banged their callused hands on leather-skinned tambourines, working themselves into a hallelujah frenzy that only stopped when Uncle Thorpe set his jaw and said a prayer over a bottle of olive oil. He poured some into each deacon's upturned hand.

In the hush, Uncle Thorpe hitched his polyester pants high enough to show the green stripe of his tube socks and knelt before Justine. She could have stared a hole through Lula, who now stood dabbing her eyes with a handkerchief in a small group of women behind the deacons.

Justine wasn't going to bow her head. Couldn't. Not if she wanted Six Flags. She knew that the minute she started to pray, she would lose her nerve. Who knew what she might say if she let herself go. Brother Eldon, the deacon with the bushy eyebrows angled into a permanent scowl, was already beginning to speak in tongues and squeeze her shoulder too hard.

"I pray you'll save this young woman, Lord, who is old enough now to know you, Great God, and therefore to deny you," Uncle Thorpe began in his down-low prayer cadence that always went straight to Justine's insides. She hoped he'd finished, but then he shouted, "Show her your glory, Lord!" The band took off again, vamped into "I Come to the Garden Alone," her granny's favorite song.

Playing that song right now was a dirty trick, and they knew it. Her granny sat up front in the perpendicular pews reserved for deacons and elders. Justine could see her face, could see her arthritic brown hands curled on her knees. Granny sometimes kept her hearing aids turned down during services, and Justine wondered if they were on now. She wondered if Lula had told her about Six Flags.

"Keep Justine from this world and the sins within, Lord," Uncle Thorpe shouted. The band picked up the pace until her granny's slow, mournful hymn sounded more like the Stones. People were beginning to convulse and shout, as the Holy Spirit took charge of their mouths and bodies. "Help her to make choices with her body and mind, Lord, that lead her closer to you."

Justine kept her eyes on Lula, but tears began to roll down her cheeks. She wiped her face, angry that they would

16

think they were getting to her, ashamed of the night that had led her to this moment, maybe even more ashamed that Granny would think Justine chose an amusement park—or worse, her father—over her own mother. Her mother—who'd had to quit art school when he left, who had to stand in line for the government commodities she'd always wanted to feel above, whose artist's fingers ballooned with blisters from the first job she'd found at a shoestring potato factory.

She thought about trying to pray. Maybe God would be there and would show her a way. The thought had hardly formed when Brother Eldon pressed her head downward, as if by putting her head in the right position he could force words into her heart and out of her mouth. Furious, she cut her eyes at John Joseph, who chomped his gum, unmoved by his father and the deacons.

Justine felt her lip quivering, but then John Joseph blew a big pink bubble and smirked—for her, she knew. He was her cousin, but she could have kissed him.

4.

When Justine heard two honks from the big horn, she looked around the empty house and felt a sorrow she couldn't explain. She brushed off the hungry cat and climbed into a running Lincoln with whitewall tires, her father a stranger in a car full of strangers. She couldn't think of a time she'd felt more affection for her mother.

There was a minute—the boy was asleep, and she'd thought that his mom was—when Justine caught a flash of what it had been like before her father left. She remembered how special it had been for one of the girls to be chosen to run an errand with him, to stand in middle of the seat next to him and have him put the flat of his hand against her chest as he came to a stop. In the steady hum of the wheels and road, she quit worrying about how Lula would feel when she got home from work and saw that Justine had gone through with the trip. From her place in the passenger-side back seat, she watched her dad adjusting his fingers on the steering wheel, tensing his jaw. She saw the razor burn on the back of his neck and remembered rubbing her fingers along the stubble when he held her in the rocking chair. She'd spent years pretending that dream of him away, and now here he was driving her down the interstate in a new car, a blonde wife sleeping at his side. Before she could catch the words falling from her mouth, she said, "You didn't even call." He didn't understand what she'd said, so he looked back over his shoulder with raised eyebrows. Now she'd have to repeat herself. "Why didn't you at least help us?" she said, a little louder.

At that, her stepmother raised her head, yawned, and blinked around the car. "Oh, honey, you know your mama is plumb crazy." Justine closed her eyes and pressed her forehead to the window glass, praying as she never had before for God to keep her from putting her hands on another person's body, lest she kill her stepmother where she sat.

The trip was downhill from there, no fiery redemption. Justine hardly said another word the rest of the drive to Texas, certain that Uncle Thorpe's premonition was right and that no matter her motives she would die a wretched soul on a roller coaster. Her father's boy was sticky and kept pulling her hair; her father was awkward and overly polite. The stepmother (if the woman who had disappeared your father, the car, and the bank account could be considered a mother of any sort) wore gold rings and a crop top that showed her freckled chest. She made a big show of feeling sorry for Justine in her long dress.

By the time they got there, Justine felt so nauseous and frightened of dying and going to hell that Six Flags was one of the worst days of her life. She threw up on her father's shoes while waiting in line for Big Bend, and one of the ticket takers told her she was not allowed to ride because "vomit at these speeds ain't pretty." Her stepmother took Justine's place in line, and Justine held her half brother's hand as she watched her father and stepmother click up the near-vertical roller coaster track and disappear in joyful screams. She thought her nausea was from fear.

5.

Though she was fifteen and a bonerack, she started showing late. So when it came time to start school that fall, all she knew was that she hadn't felt right since the day she first talked to her father on the phone. She didn't let herself think of any reasons beyond that. She started sitting next to Lula in church, leaving John Joseph in the back to trim his nails with his pocketknife and break wind without an audience.

She'd avoided Russell Gibson since the night she snuck out with him. He'd asked John Joseph to have her call him, as if they were merely two star-crossed lovers, but she cut John Joseph off before he could get the words out. She wanted to forget, and she'd almost been successful with the summer so full of Six Flags and penance.

But then for two days straight she couldn't eat lunch or make it through Ms. Peterson's fifth-period Algebra 2 class without running to the bathroom to vomit. On the third day, Nurse Sixkiller waited outside the bathroom. Justine was still wiping her face with a rough brown paper towel she'd wet in the sink when the nurse put her wide palm to Justine's forehead.

"You're not warm," she said. "Clammy, maybe."

Justine tried to push past Nurse Sixkiller and return to class, but the woman had that way of holding down the Earth. She would not budge. Justine acted like she didn't care about her place at the top of the class, but that was the only thing that kept Lula from putting her in the church school, which she would surely graduate from in no time and be ready . . . for what? Marriage? Justine was no longer interested in a man or boy of any sort. "Ms. Peterson's going to be upset," she said.

"Have you eaten?"

Justine shook her head. Nurse Sixkiller took her in with her warm, brown eyes, head to toe and back to belly, before leading her into her office and closing the door. "When was your last period?"

Justine shrugged.

"You don't keep track?"

Dee and Josie, who'd been getting ready to marry or graduate around the time Justine needed to learn about such things, probably thought Lula had talked to her like she'd talked to them. But Justine's Lula wasn't their Lula. She hadn't told Justine anything.

Nurse Sixkiller handed her a small pocket calendar with a ridiculous yellow smiley face on it. "I want you to mark the day you start from here on out." She didn't let go of the calendar until Justine looked up at her. "Let me know?" She seemed finished but then: "Your family is Holiness, right?"

Justine held up the hem of her long skirt and sighed.

"Well, you need to go to the clinic anyway. If you need me to talk to your mom with you . . . or if need be, I can take you to the Indian Hospital. Do you know what you want to do?"

Justine grew hollow. She felt as if all of her insides were spilling out, and she cupped her tight belly to check. Around her, the white-and-green tile floor shifted. She wondered if she might fall, but Nurse Sixkiller placed a hand against the small of her back and kept talking.

"I want you to know there's a doctor in Tulsa. He will take what money you can pay."

Justine was out the door before she heard the rest. She understood what the nurse was getting at. She kept going down the hallway and out the big metal doors, leaving her open algebra book on the desk in the back row of Ms. Peterson's class for good.

6.

When Justine walked in the door and smelled frying wild onions and salt pork, she felt as if she hadn't eaten in a year. Granny turned from her work over the propane stove and smiled. "Always know when it's ready, an'it? Rinse this," Granny said, flapping two old bread bags at Justine. "And get plates."

Justine washed the bags that had held frozen spring onions and hung them inside out. Then she got hot sauce from the cabinets and a bottle of Dr Pepper, Granny's favorite indulgence, from the icebox.

"Think there's beans left in there," Granny said. "No school?" She handed Justine the plate of pork and began breaking eggs into the cast-iron skillet on top of the long, skinny onions.

"I didn't feel good."

"You call Lula's work?"

"Not yet."

"Eat. Then better call." Granny sat down with the wild onions and scrambled eggs, but she didn't begin to eat. Justine felt the silence between them more than she heard it.

She put her fork down on the table and took a deep breath. Granny tilted the hot sauce toward her. When Justine waved it off, Granny asked, "Sick a lot?"

Justine's heart sank. Had someone stuck a sign to her back? Why had her body chosen today to reveal her secrets to the world? Or maybe it had been blabbing for some time to anybody who cared to listen.

"You okay?"

Justine shook her head.

"Been a long time?"

Justine shrugged.

Granny adjusted her hearing aid, seemed to be thinking. Finally she said, "There's medicine, but maybe it's too long already." She paused again. "I don't remember where to find it anymore. Celia knows maybe."

"Before summer," Justine said. Granny spooned food onto her plate and opened the hot sauce.

"Too long, I think," she said. "Somebody hurt you?"

Justine couldn't lie to her, so she said nothing. She hoped Granny would go on eating, but the room grew quiet. Granny covered her mouth with her hand. Grease had made the deep ridges of her nails and swollen knuckles shiny. She took off her glasses and began to wipe her eyes with a dish towel.

Justine could not see Granny cry. She pushed herself away from the table, walked out the door, and began to run in the hot sun. At the road, she turned west and kept going. She did not stop until she came to Little Locust Creek. She took off her shoes and sat on the edge of the bank, crying until her body stopped making tears and the sound of her dry-socket wails made her lonely. Then she wiped her eyes on her blouse and hugged her knees into her chest, seeing where she was for the first time. It had been dark, but this was where he had stopped the car.

On the far side of the creek, seven buzzards filled a tree whose dead, gray branches spidered into the sky. The great black birds eyed her and ruffled themselves from time to time but were mostly content opening their lazy wings to the sun. She put her feet in the cool water and flipped rocks with her toes, watching red crawdads skitter away into the deep. She felt like a crawdad today. She'd run from Nurse Sixkiller, a kind woman only trying to help, and now she'd run from Granny, who Justine loved as if she were an extension of her own heart. A fat, nearly black cottonmouth S'ed across from the buzzard's side of the creek, holding its bully head high above the water. Justine grabbed a stick and stood, waving it over her head, stomping and screaming at the snake to leave her be. It drew near and opened its white maw until it saw that she was a crazy creature not worth fooling with. Then it turned and went back through the pool and disappeared into the weeds along the bank.

Justine sat back down. She made sure that the snake was gone and checked in on the buzzards before she bowed her head and started at the beginning. Not her first birth, but her second, when her father left and they lost their car and their house and Lula had her first nervous breakdown, all at once like that, leaving eight-year-old Justine and her two big sisters to pack their piddly boxes and figure out a way to get them to Granny's house on their own. It wasn't fair that her mom had to drop out of college, that they had to eat powdered commodity eggs and fight over the cheese, that they hadn't had bacon since he left, or that Granny had to share her room with Lula. It wasn't fair that Justine was one of the best athletes in her class but couldn't join the basketball team because men would see her legs. It wasn't fair that Justine had caused one of Lula's nervous breakdowns herself or that in the midst of it, Lula, out of her mind, had whipped Justine so badly that she couldn't sleep under a sheet. It wasn't fair that Justine was made to fear for her soul over a Beatles album or a stupid roller coaster she didn't even get to ride. It wasn't fair that she was so angry over it all when every little thought she had would probably require forgiveness. She was just a girl, and she told God so. She didn't know what to do next, so she kept talking. Sometimes she yelled.

She went on so long that when she heard a big engine rumbling and opened her eyes, the world went white for a minute. When she could focus, she saw an ancient Chevy truck easing into the creek from the two-track on the far bank. The engine cut off, and two little kids stripped out of their clothes and clambered out of the truck bed. A woman and a man, both laughing about something he said, stepped out of the truck too. As the woman tied up her skirt, she grinned at Justine and waved, "Siyo!" Then she called for the man, who was already splashing the kids, to get back over there. The

Justine watched the family while the sun worked its way over the buzzard tree. Soap bubbles floated past her on brown water headed through town to Lake Tenkiller. She almost offered to tie up her skirt and help, but the family seemed to work together so perfectly, voices sometimes serious or sharp but mostly full of joy or humor, that she felt happy to watch them, same as the buzzards in the tree and the crawdads in the pools and the snake from wherever. Finally, she stood and waved to them. The kids, wrapped in towels on the hood of the truck eating watermelon, grinned.

Justine told the crawdads she was sorry for wrecking their homes, nodded a solemn goodbye to the buzzards, and spit at the snake. She looked back toward the road she'd come from but decided to try the dirt trail that lined the creek. Though she'd never been down it, great sycamores and cottonwoods shaded the way. She started in the direction of town, unsure if the trail went all the way or if she'd have to cut across somebody's pasture to get back to a road. Even in the shade, her clothes dripped with sweat, the air heavy with the water it absorbed from the tea-colored creek with its sedges and lizard tails. Soon the trail gave way to weeds and briars, and she could hardly see her feet. She kept going, though her heart pounded in fear of stepping on a snake. She was beginning to wonder if she'd ever get back to town when she came upon a frazzled rope swing over shallow water that told her where she was. This was where the church gathered for baptisms. She and John Joseph used to come down here when they were kids and could get away with sneaking off during camp meeting. She knelt before the creek and rinsed her face in the cool water. Big yellow grasshoppers thunked against her legs as she followed a side trail up the hill to the row of trees that surrounded the church.

She stood behind a shagbark hickory watching people file in for Wednesday night service. After nearly everyone had arrived, John Joseph pulled up with Granny and Lula in his old Ford Falcon. When Lula got out, she approached the few people remaining outside. Justine could tell by the way men clasped both hands around Lula's and how women hugged her that she was asking them if they'd seen her. Justine should have gone back home or gone on into the service, filthy though she was, but she felt as if a powerful force kept her there watching. After everyone else had gone inside, Lula stood before the open church doorway, scanning the field before her, as if that weren't the last place Justine would go if she had run away. Except here she was, and unbeknownst to Lula, the only earthly things between them were the fireflies beginning to flash before a row of oak trees and one lone shagbark hickory. Finally, Lula turned and went into the bright doorway and closed the door.

7.

Justine waded through the fireflies and weeds to a yellow-lit church window where a fan rattled and shielded her peeping. Inside, people hurried to shake hands or pass sticks of gum. Little children squirmed, and mothers fanned them or unfolded quilts beneath the pews so they could rest when the service stretched into the night. As the piano player tried to cut off the guitar player's noodling with the opening chords of a song, a little cousin ran from her mom and jumped onto Granny's lap. Justine felt a fondness for it all that she'd never been free to feel.

Uncle Thorpe shook hands with a traveling preacher, a man Justine remembered from years back who'd preached a good sermon that had spoken to her in a not-frightening way. Brother Eldon left his spot at the head of the deacon pew and greeted them solemnly. Justine could see Brother Eldon shift his great eyebrows at the other deacons, and instead of returning to his seat, he headed down the aisle toward the church office. The other deacons rose one by one and walked in a line of earth-toned polyester pants and plain long-sleeved button-ups after him. Brother Shane, the young, kind-faced deacon, whispered in Lula's ear, and Lula, after checking the back door again, got up. She slowly draped her purse over her shoulder, tucked her Bible under her arm, and followed him.

"Busted, cousin," John Joseph whispered. Justine nearly jumped through the window. He leaned next to her, digging into his front pants pocket for a pack of cigarettes, grinning. He pulled one out, stepped downwind from the window, and lit it. "Why'd you bug out?"

"It's crazy," Justine said.

"Reckon so." He swiped his black hair out of his eyes and offered her the cigarettes. She waved them off. He raised his eyebrows and slid the pack back into his pocket.

"You're getting brave. Or stupid. Uncle Thorpe's going to beat you up one side and down the other."

"Wouldn't be the first time." He cupped his hand around the cigarette, took a drag. "Might be the last."

"What's going on with Brother Eldon and them? Why'd they come get Mama?"

"Can't be good." John Joseph shrugged. "You need to talk to her. She's going to lose it again."

Justine couldn't believe she'd come to church of all places. For months, she'd been drifting along as her insides turned decisive and took charge, driving every decision that would follow. Then she'd let her feet carry her here because that's what they'd been trained to do. She thought about running again. Once she got home, she could pack a bag and go. Somewhere. To her dad's? He might not want her there but probably wouldn't be able to turn her away. She wasn't afraid to hitch. She wasn't afraid of work, either, would sooner break her own bones than admit she couldn't do something. Then what? Her bones no longer felt like hers to break. But she had time to save up for a place, maybe, if she could get someone to hire her. The thought of asking her bronzed stepmother for help sent a fire through her chest.

Up front, the service was starting. Justine squatted down again and peered inside, wondering if she should go on in. Maybe she'd get something out of it, some direction or at least a chance to rest her blistered feet. Uncle Thorpe introduced the traveling preacher and then walked down the same aisle as the deacons and Lula. Granny sat in her pew watching him go. She whispered to an old woman next to her, and the woman shook her head. Granny waited a minute; then she took the little cousin to her mom and headed down the aisle as the service started up around her.

"I've got to go check on Mama," Justine said, nearly running over John Joseph as she started around the side of the church. She pushed into the glass door and stopped still before Uncle Thorpe's office. She'd never been inside before. She took a deep breath, turned the knob, and went in.

Uncle Thorpe sat behind his wooden desk, the deacons standing in a half circle behind him. Lula sat in the lone chair across from them. Granny pressed a hand on Lula's shoulder, a mountain. Lula's skirt had somehow become caught in the top of one of her knee-high stockings and flopped over, showing a small V of her knee. Justine was so startled at the sight of her mother's knee that she almost turned and walked out. Nobody else seemed to have noticed. Lula's face grew pale as she studied Justine. Justine knew then that Lula must have been the only one who hadn't seen what was happening until now.

"Has the devil had his way with you, Justine?" Brother Eldon said. He looked like a mean old eagle.

Justine put her hand to her belly, and Lula reached out and called, "My sweet baby." Justine took a step away from Lula. She didn't have to go to her dad's. She could just go.

"It's not right having a Sunday school teacher with an unwed pregnant daughter," Brother Eldon said. "What does that say to the congregation and other churches?" His face grew red as he spoke. "I don't think it speaks well of us to have a pregnant girl in the church at all."

"Brother Eldon." Uncle Thorpe put his thumb on his temple and began to pinch his forehead. He took a deep breath. "The deacons are excused."

"We've discussed this," Brother Eldon said.

"Give us some time, Brother," Uncle Thorpe said. "Mama, we'll be okay. You can go on, too."

Granny stood her ground until the last deacon was out the door. Then she leaned down and kissed Lula's head before she squeezed Justine's hand. "I'll be outside, u-we-tsi," she said to Uncle Thorpe. Her voice was sharp and left no room for discussion.

Lula didn't seem to register Granny closing the door. She began to smooth her skirt, oddly focused on the folds of the fabric.

"Do you know who the father is, Justine?" Uncle Thorpe asked.

Justine didn't answer, didn't have time to feel angry or embarrassed at the insinuation. She was watching Lula, who had begun to rock her shoulders from side to side and hum.

This church was all she had. People respected her testimony, her voice, the songs she wrote, the murals she'd painted in the nursery. She could elaborate on any Bible verse as well as a deacon, maybe as well as Uncle Thorpe. People admired her resilience, which to Justine seemed the funny thing about faith. The bigger your obstacle, the greater your heavenly blessing. Lula would be truly blessed.

The night Lula learned Justine's father was not dead in an accident, just gone, neighbors found her at 3:00 a.m. wandering around in her nightgown. She couldn't talk for days afterward, never quite got her pieces put back together right. She'd married him right out of Chilocco, and the church considered him Lula's husband in God's eyes until he died, no matter how many other women he married or how far he roamed. Her house—when she had a house—used to be full of girls and a husband. One by one, they had left.

Justine had fought her at every turn. It might as well have been written. Justine wasn't her sisters, wasn't wired to go along with things for the sake of comfort. In that way, she was as religious as Lula. When she stopped fighting her mother long enough, Justine understood her. And now, because of Justine, Lula might lose the church too.

"It's okay, Mama," she said. She moved to Lula and put her arm around her. "It's going to be okay."

"Who's the baby's father?" Uncle Thorpe asked again.

Justine ignored him. She put her hands around Lula's cheeks and pulled her face to hers. "I'll get my GED and get a job. I'll get two. We'll be fine, Mama."

"How?"

"I don't have an answer for that, Mama. But there is a baby in here. It's true. I've felt it moving." Justine smiled, but her tears were starting up too. "This baby is coming, Mama.

It doesn't matter what the deacons say. I've been praying, and God knows what he needs to know. That's all I'm going to say, except I'm sorry for the trouble it's causing you."

She couldn't have told herself why she wouldn't say his name. Maybe she still thought this was all her fault for sneaking out and for every little bad thing God had tallied over the course of her life. She hadn't asked for what happened, but if there was one thing she'd taken from the nights she'd spent in the pews of Beulah Springs Holiness Church, it was that the Lord worked in mysterious ways. Regardless, the deacons might pressure her to marry him. After all, it was she who had opened her window that night and run down the hill to his waiting car. They might do an okay job of pressuring him too. And then she'd be married to a son of a bitch who made her sick to her stomach, a man who'd already shown her he was stronger than she was. She wouldn't let it happen again.

Things would be simpler if she kept the focus on this baby. Maybe that was as far as her young mind could stretch, as much as it could handle. As far as she was concerned at that moment, the father didn't exist, nor did that night. She was simply a girl, or had been, and now there was a baby, immaculate as could be.

Uncle Thorpe poured olive oil into his hands, put them over each of their heads, and prayed over them. Justine didn't mind for once that her hair would be oily. She let her mind settle into Uncle Thorpe's words. She figured she needed all the help she could get. When he finished, Uncle Thorpe wiped his eyes and hugged them.

"Maybe you two should spend the evening sorting things out at home. I'll bring Mama home. You can take John Joseph's car."

Justine was gathering Lula's purse when Lula hugged it back into her belly.

"We won't go," she said.

"Won't go where?" Uncle Thorpe asked.

"We won't go home. The Lord's house is home, where we need to be."

"I thought you would want to sort things out, Sister Lu."

"Justine is having a baby. It is sorted." She stood and picked up her Bible from his desk. "I won't have us thrown out of here like trash by Brother Eldon."

"He's worried about factions in the church, Sister. You know how he gets."

"I know how he talked to my daughter like trash, and I won't have it. From anyone." She turned to Justine. "It's going to be alright, Justine. You're right about that. God holds us in his hands even when we feel the farthest from him. We can do whatever we have to do. If you want to go back to the service, let's go. Only God can make our way. If you want to go home, I think that will be fine. God will be with us where we are."

"Let's just go, Mama. I don't want to cause any more mess."

"Your decision."

When they walked into the hallway, Granny was sitting in a chair she'd pulled up from one of the classrooms. Lula leaned down and yelled into her ear.

"We're leaving, Mama. You can stay if you want."

Granny shook her head, and Justine helped her stand. Uncle Thorpe walked the three of them to the door and said, "I'll go get John Joseph's keys."

"I think he left them in his car," Justine said, maybe a little too quickly.

Uncle Thorpe studied her for a moment, then squeezed her shoulder and said, "I'll be praying for you."

When the three of them got to the other side of the church, John Joseph was still leaning by the window. Now he was listening to the traveling preacher's sermon. Justine was glad to see he didn't have a cigarette because she didn't want to get into a-whole-nother thing with Lula.

"Where's the party?" John Joseph grinned. Lula tried to scowl, but even she couldn't pull it off. Granny shook her head. He had always been her favorite, Justine knew. It was okay. He was Justine's favorite too.

"Can you please take us home, young man?" Lula asked. She smoothed her hair, and Justine noticed that her fingers shook ever so slightly as she tucked a handkerchief into her bag.

"At your service," John Joseph said. He opened the primer-colored door and pushed the front seat forward so Lula and Justine could squeeze into the back. Then he helped Granny down into the frayed passenger seat.

Uncle Thorpe walked out the back door as John Joseph was backing out. He raised his hand, trying to get John Joseph to stop, but he hit the gas around the corner out of the gravel parking lot. When he did, the car skidded sideways, and Justine slid into the middle of the seat, pressed against Lula.

"John Joseph!" Lula shouted, and Justine laughed. Granny held tightly to the roof outside the rolled-down window and muttered something in Cherokee that Justine couldn't understand. Lula's shouting only goaded John Joseph. He pressed the car faster up the big hill into town. The wind whipped in the windows, and Justine forgot for a minute what would happen when they got home and the real questions and shouting and crying began. She couldn't know how in a few months she'd be flooded with a crippling love for another human being that would wound her for the rest of her days, how her insides would be wiped clean, burdened, and saved by a kid who'd come kicking into this world with Justine's own blue eyes, a full head of black hair, and lips Justine would swear looked just like a rosebud. For now, that little car filled with three—almost four—generations flew. And when they dropped over the top of the hill, Justine threw her hands up, her mouth agape in wonder.

PART II

The Care and
Feeding of Goldfish

My mom, Justine, brags on how I set my own alarm and
have since kindergarten. She was usually working the night
shift, so I got up, dressed, and brushed my own teeth. Then
I'd sneak into her and Kenny's room and sit on the edge of
the bed where she'd brush through the rats in my hair and
pull it back in barrettes. I knew not to wake up Kenny. He
didn't exactly work, not like she did, but he was on a night
shift of some kind.

If I whined about her pulling my hair, Mom shushed
me with a brush upside the head or a good hard yank. Sometimes she'd rub the spot and kiss it real quick. I knew she
was just tired and worried about Kenny getting mad, but on
weekends when we had time to just be, she'd want to say
sorry. It was usually when we were watching cartoons and

eating cereal, two things she never got to do when she was a kid because they were too religious for TV and too poor for cereal. She might say something like: "Mama used to jerk me bald when I was little. It's a wonder I had any hair left to pigtail." Then she'd get lost in stories about being raised so strict and the switches and belts Lula took to her. My mom told those old stories like she talks about a lot of stuff, like it's a little bit of a favorite joke she loves to tell and a little bit of a sorry memory she wishes she could forget.

She'd say, "Lord and Mama forgive me," if she went on too long. Then she'd close her eyes real tight and whisper, "Bless her, Jesus."

They found a tumor in Lula's brain when I was just a baby. The doctors call the terrible spells she gets grand mal seizures, but Lula doesn't believe in doctors. She believes in God. I think Lula breaks my mom's heart in more ways than she could ever count.

"I love you more than anything, my Teeny Reney Bean," Mom would say after she fixed my hair, and then she'd pull me into her arms and squeeze. Just when it felt like she wasn't ever going to let me go, she'd kiss me and point me toward the door. Then she'd stretch her never-ending arms and fingers to the ceiling, take a sip of water from a glass on the dresser, and fan her long, black hair over her pillow.

I'd drop a few flakes of fish food into the bowl for Blinky, grab the lunch Mom packed before bed, and catch the bus at the little pond out front of the apartment managers' office. I didn't feel special using an alarm clock or locking a door with the key that hung from a string around my neck or walking myself down the sidewalk to wait with other kids for a school bus, but I think it makes Mom proud to say I am—and always have been—perfect.

After I heard somewhere that goldfish grow as big as their container, I kept after Mom to let me put Blinky in the pond. She always told me the same thing, that 1) he'd freeze to death out there and 2) I was too tenderhearted. "You'll be bawling for him as soon as you dump him, Reney," she'd say and push her hair behind her ears. "And I'm not getting you another fish if you let this one go."

We got him at the carnival when Kenny, who was high on life and the Wild Turkey he'd snuck in his boot, got to feeling happy and calling us a family. He said, "I love you like my own, Teeny Reney," and forked over enough money for me to play all the games I wanted. Then he rubbed my hair so hard that one of my barrettes pulled out and my hair fell into my eyes.

Why Mom married him, I do not know. She was still half Holy Roller. Couldn't help it, I guess. She only wore a bun to keep her hair back at work, but she still wouldn't cut it. She parted it down the middle—like a hippie, she said— or pulled it back in two barrettes just like mine. She didn't wear makeup and hadn't even started drinking in those days.

I was used to Kenny and how he got, though. I even missed him sometimes when he took off with his buddies and didn't show up for a while. I came home from the carnival with an armload of junk, a little bowl of Blinky, and a mad hornet for a mom because Kenny got mouthy and jealous after his happy bubbles popped.

I couldn't get off the idea of setting Blinky free once I got on it. Maybe letting him out of his sad little bowl felt kind of like a good or right thing that God calls a person to do sometimes. Or maybe setting Blinky free to see if he got huge was just some kind of science experiment to me, because I don't know if anybody can really love a fish.

He was a really good fish, though. He swam happy zigzags at the top of the bowl when I came into the room. He even let me feed him by hand when the apartment was quiet. I kept him for longer than I'd ever kept anything alive. The carnival came and left and came back again, and I still had little Blinky swimming circles in our living room, watching us live our lives like a TV show he couldn't turn off.

My mom and Kenny argued. Sometimes they fought. I won't say I ever got used to it, but I did get used to laying awake in the dark after the sounds faded, feeling nervous they were going to pick back up again. The night of their big knock-down-drag-out—their last fight—I lay in bed with my pillow over my head for what seemed like half the night when it started getting real rough. That's when I busted through my bedroom door and saw Kenny holding my mom up against the wall by her jaw. He had her pushed up there so her neck looked long and skinny, like the rooster I saw my cousin slaughter with a knife he'd just sharpened. Mom was calm as the rooster that day. She looked as mean as him, too, her eyes staring at Kenny, daring him.

When she saw me, she started trying to tell me everything was going to be okay, trying to get me to go back to my room. Kenny kept his eyes on her and wouldn't let her down, so I kicked him. Then, on accident, I called him a sorry-ass pissant motherfucker.

Mom and Kenny froze in place. It shouldn't have been such a shock. What I hadn't heard from Kenny I'd picked up from the apartment kids when we were hunting ghosts or making potions out of junk we pulled from the dumpsters.

I wondered for a second if we all might laugh, but Kenny kind of shook his head, then turned his red eyes back to Mom and started yelling. The way spit was flying off his lips, I could tell she wasn't going to take it much longer. I took off to the kitchen, grabbed a butcher knife, and ran at him screaming.

His black mustache crinkled up like he couldn't believe I'd do such a thing. He dropped my mom, who slid to the floor and wrapped her arms around me. I held on to my knife and kept it aimed at Kenny. He started backing up, blubbering about loving me like his own blood, patting behind him on the door until he found the handle. Once he got the door open, he stepped through it and didn't come back to say goodbye.

I sat on the couch watching Mom cry while she packed up boxes and trash bags full of our stuff. Little Blinky swam on the table next to the TV, watching. We were going across town to Granny and Lula's, the only place we should have ever been as far as I was concerned. I knew Lula didn't like animals in the house, so I asked one more time to set Blinky free. Mom said, "Reney, do what you want with your fucking fish." Then she threw a roll of duct tape across the room. I was out the door before she could gather herself to say sorry.

For a while, we stopped by the apartments to say hi to Miss Bee and Bones, the old couple who ran the place and lived in an apartment behind the office. Mom called Miss Bee more wisp than a woman. She had to pull around an oxygen tank, but her voice carried all the way across the parking lot to our apartment when she wanted it to. Bones towered above her, worrying over every little step she took. He had a dagger tattoo on his forearm that all us kids were sure meant he'd killed somebody in prison. Not that he gave us any reason to think that. They'd always kept an eye on us when we waited for the bus and sometimes even watched out for me after I got off the bus.

When we came back, I always went straight to the pond and plopped down on my belly to look for Blinky. Sometimes I got so close that the tip of my nose dipped in the water and a goldfish came up and took a nibble. Every now and then, Blinky would come up to the top of the water and take a piece of bread from my fingers.

Miss Bee would shuffle outside, dragging her tank. She'd stand there and smoke above me, talking about how I'd grown and complaining about the parties people were throwing. After catching up on the apartment gossip, Mom would disappear to have it out with Kenny. Miss Bee would hand over a big plastic jar of fish food she kept in her desk drawer and gripe about all the fish that got dumped when people up and moved. Sometimes while my mom was gone, I felt bad for what I'd done to Kenny or what I'd done to Kenny and her.

There were more goldfish in the little pond each time we stopped, until I wasn't so sure that we'd set Blinky free at all. The fish stayed on the surface looking for handouts and took on a sick yellow color. Miss Bee got wheezier and wheezier, and Bones stopped coming out to pass me butterscotch and tell me jokes. Mom stopped staying gone so long and coming back with red, been-crying eyes. Blinky stopped coming to the top. He got bigger and bigger until I wasn't even sure which fish he was. Then Miss Bee died, and my mom said Bones got so sad he started drinking again and lost the place.

A boy on the bus said the new apartment manager yelled at some kids for throwing candy in the pond and said he was going to fill that stinking mosquito trap in with concrete. The boy said he guessed it was true because the pond was marked off with construction tape by evening and had a bunch of sacks of Quikrete stacked around it. I had to keep wiping my eyes with the sleeve of my shirt the rest of the ride home. I couldn't stop thinking about Blinky and all those little apartment fish flopping around on the sidewalk suffocating.

Mom's old Pinto and a couple of other cars were sitting out front when the bus dropped me off at Granny and Lula's. I ran into the house and slung my backpack in a chair without catching the screen door behind me.

Mom jumped. She'd been sitting at the kitchen table staring, rubbing the scar on her hand. She shushed me, thumped me hard on the arm, and whispered, "Lula's been having spells. Saints have been in there with Granny praying."

"Is she going to be okay?" I asked.

"She's stubborn," Mom said, and her eyes started filling with tears. "Been resting for a while now."

"We have to go get Blinky," I said, and she looked at me like I was crazy. I told her that the new apartment manager was going to fill in the pond and all those fish were going to die.

She looked at the clock and chewed her pinkie nail. Instead of saying no, she said, "You don't have your bowl anymore."

"It ain't big enough anyway," I said. "We have to take them to the lake. All of them. We have to set them free."

For some reason, that was all it took. Mom stuffed some trash bags in her purse and rummaged beneath the kitchen sink for a metal bucket. Then we were out the door.

It took us an hour to scoop up all those fish with the mop bucket. The manager kept trying to talk Mom into going on a date with him but stayed out of our way. We splashed around in that mossy little pond with our pants rolled up, bumping heads and knocking elbows and butts. We didn't stop until we got the last fish caught. Mom didn't even complain when I splashed her, so I splashed her some more. Once we got all the fish in the trash bag, Mom tied it off and lugged it into the back of the car. She spun gravel taking off for Lake Tenkiller.

Some of the fish were small, and some of them must have weighed two or three pounds. I got to thinking on the car ride that I wasn't sure I'd seen Blinky at all.

"What's up, Bean?" Mom asked.

"I don't even know if Blinky was still in there," I said.

"Think I saw him," she said. "Pretty sure I did."

I leaned my head against the window, watching the trees go by, and smiled.

We pulled up to a public boat ramp and wrestled the big green trash bag onto the dock. We could only carry it a couple of steps before setting it down to rest. When we got to the end of the dock, Mom pulled at the knot in the bag with her teeth and helped me pour the water and fish into Tenkiller.

Those fish shot off in every direction like fireworks. A few did great, leaping belly flops. A couple stayed close by the dock, coming to the top every few seconds. Mom and I sat there tossing them cracker crumbs, dangling our feet off the dock, and watching the sun gathering itself for bed.

When we got back to Granny and Lula's, the house was quiet. Granny stuck her head out the door to make sure we were okay and tell us Lula was finally sleeping. Me and Mom ate bologna sandwiches on the porch swing. Then we shared the sink while I got ready for bed and she got ready for work. I couldn't sleep with Granny when Lula was sick, so before my mom left, she tucked me into her bed and checked my alarm clock.

"You're too tenderhearted, Reney Bean," she said. Then she kissed my forehead and whispered, "Wish I was more like you," before she turned off the light.

That night I dreamed me and Mom were splashing around the banks of Tenkiller calling for Blinky. Granny and Lula were there. They were watching us from two lawn chairs they had sitting just in the edge of the water, and there was a glowing lantern between them. We waded all over the lake but couldn't find Blinky anywhere. I wanted to swim deeper, but Mom grabbed hold of me and wouldn't let go. She kept saying that the water was full of cottonmouths. And then I realized that it was, and I started crying. That's when Blinky appeared, and all the snakes scattered. Me and Mom started hugging and laughing at the sight of him. That fish was golden as the evening sky and big as a blue whale.

He nudged me onto his back, and I put out my hand for Mom. We waved goodbye to Granny and Lula. Then I hung on to his top fin, and Mom held on to me. Blinky dove all the way to the deepest part of the lake, chasing catfish and nosing great turtles, showing us all the treasures he'd found down there. My mom's long black hair trailed behind us, and we didn't have any trouble breathing at all. We held on when he leapt for the sun, shimmying high up through the clouds until we splashed back down into the lake.

I woke up just before my alarm went off. Mom was curled around me, sound asleep, so I eased out of her arms and turned off the alarm. She mumbled something and turned over onto her other side. I pulled the covers around her and laid down next to her for a long time, remembering how it felt to be moving through water and clouds, both of us together.

Annie Mae

July 23, 1982—*I never can forget. I got the news my poor lost grandson John Joseph passed when I was braiding my hair, fixing to walk to Dandy Dalton's to pay on my grocery bill. I already had my purse under my arm when Thorpe Rogers called on the telephone. I couldn't put any of the sounds he was making into words, but right off I knew.*

Thorpe Rogers preached on faith power in a special service the night before—Saints got to be sanctified, he said, got to live good and right so little lost ones can see light. He said it in his language and then he tried to make it right in Cherokee for me and the other old ones. Thorpe Rogers raised up his arms like a picture of Good Lord's love—In Heaven, he said, we shall reap our rewards. Then his face kind of broke in two and he said—But we got to get there, Saints.

We had a good, long service, like the ones that used to set my soul to burn. But going home I did not feel good. The Sequoyah Hills, always sweet to me, looked down like cold mountains. Even the moonshine on my arm felt like a stranger. Dear babies Reney and Sheila by me in the back seat did not make me better. Maybe I knew, but only in my heart first. John Joseph was going cold right then.

The boy never could stay out of trouble, even when he was a little one. Cracked his head diving in Bluff Hole, July 3, 1972. He could hear a song one time and play it all the way through, humming it out as he go. Didn't matter—he sold the electric guitar Thorpe Rogers gave him for five dollars so he could buy up Dandy Dalton's candy, January 12, 1969.

I used to back then put down things that happen in this nice notebook Lula gave me. Always put my thoughts in there as best I could, just for me. John Joseph passed the day before his own birthday, the day before this country would ever call him a man. After I put that down, I could not write another thing in here for a long time. The nice leather book was just ledger. I added up my charges for the month—

39 cents, shortcakes
89 cents, hairnet
3 lbs. Crisco, 2.10
25 cents, pop
66 cents of Liver loaf
1 dollar cash

I stay on my knees after altar call ends now. But I don't hardly pray. I look for pictures in the altar wood. Try to make out long-gone faces when I know I should lean hard on myself to get up and go back to my seat. I stay there so long the church goes still. I hear little ones rustling on pallets and sweet sister Saints praying—Thank you, Jesus. Thorpe Rogers and Lula start up again. They weep and moan with Good Lord's love. My children, so strong in their chests. That muscle can only be from Good Lord. Cannot be me or their cowboy daddy, with his drinking and Good Lord knows what else.

I feel hands on me. Skirts dance by, fan me cool. I know they pray this old Indian is finally meeting Holy Ghost, praying good like I should, with fire. Truth is, all I pray is to be able to pray. Maybe pray to be strong when I need to be.

One night right before he passed, I woke to a broke front door and John Joseph asleep on the living room floor. He had 12 stitches sewed up over his eye. Drunk running around in Sequoyah County and an argument over a girl got him hit with a tire iron. He opened his eyes to me standing over him. He looked scared for minute but not of me. Then he came back to me. He stretched and poked his finger on the end of the thread holding him together. He said—She's so pretty, Granny. He could not pray either.

I shushed him. Lula was still asleep with one of her spells. She would be in a bad way with John Joseph there smelling like beer joints and the screen door broke. Thorpe Rogers wouldn't let him come home from drinking no more already.

I should have got on my knees and prayed. Drag him by his hair and tell him—You pray! And tell my own self too that Good Lord was listening and believe it down in my pitiful heart. But I thought to myself—I will fix it. I put bologna on to fry and called my sister Celia in Hominy.

Celia married an Indian like she should. A big Osage who spoke his language and went to college. A man who kept his hands where he should. He would have work for John Joseph.

I blackened the edges like John Joseph liked and handed him the phone. Celia said—Nephew, you come stay with us, but don't you come home drinking. He hung up and tried to argue, but Lord Lord, that boy listened to somebody finally.

He went to Hominy and didn't come home to Celia's one night after he got up there. He took up with some running wild cousins and didn't come back ever. Demons know fire too. Maybe demons chased him so hard that he could not slow down until he stopped for good on the side of the road where he came to such terrible awful rest after 18 years. Nearly 18 years.

He told me before I sent him up to Hominy to die—Granny, them old boys and their tire iron ain't got nothing on me.

You should have seen them! And then he laughed, squinched up his busted eye, and doubled over. Black hair sticking all everywhere, needing a haircut.

John Joseph tried to fix the broke door with masking tape and a screwdriver before he left. That boy fiddled all morning with the flapping door, singing Elvis Presley songs to me. Never fixed it right. It's still stuck together with tape. Needs a new screen. I told him so that morning. I told him so and I sent him off to that highway in Hominy. I should have locked the door and never let him leave. Should have tried to scare him with the love of Good Lord. John Joseph probably would know better. That boy has a way right to my insides. He tapped the screen with the screwdriver and winked with his good eye. He grinned, said—I'll take care of it, Granny.

I give nickels to pay on dollars I charge. I add up, take away. Nothing evens out, and I don't think it will get fixed ever. I just as soon it stay that way. I see the tape and remember John Joseph holding a screwdriver and eating fried bologna I fed him, grinning up at me, good eye and bad eye trying to hide behind that greasy hair. I remember him like that. Try to. Bent over but looking up. Just a warm boy still, saying he's sorry for the trouble, but he'll make it all right. And this old lady don't say nothing to him. Don't drag him down to pray, don't pick up the telephone to conspire him away to death. I take that sweet, running boy in my arms. I press my face in his wild hair and hold on.

The Year 2003
Minus 20

Reney's bones can feel a fight long before the rest of her wakes to the rising voices and clattering bottles. She is eight, almost nine. Granny and Lula live in a new rent house across the tracks and down a long hill, not so very far. Over there—standing on a chair rolling up balls of dough as Granny's hearing aids whistle or lying curled into Granny's great body napping—is Reney's best place. But Reney knows that *her place* is with her mom.

Tonight, Reney is leaning against the bathroom door-jamb with her arms crossed, watching Justine and Christy, a junior in high school with permed black hair and thighs that bulge around her cutoffs. The young women dig into a pink suitcase of makeup samples that just arrived in the mail.

"Emerald Noir, fancy!" Christy says, opening a plastic eye shadow tray. "I can't believe you signed up."

"Wrote a check, so it won't cost anybody anything," says Justine.

"An'it," Christy says, and they laugh like bouncing a check is the funniest thing in the world. Reney doesn't laugh.

"Just kidding," Justine says, tossing a cotton ball at her. "Besides, if I get good at this, we'll be in our own place before you know it. We'll probably get a pink Cadillac and drive to Dallas and dine with Mary Kay herself."

"I'm definitely skipping school for that," Christy says, bumping Reney with her butt. "I've never seen a vampire."

Reney and Justine rent the two upstairs bedrooms of this big, old rickety house from Christy's mom, who Justine worked with on the line before switching to days. Reney likes it here okay. Christy lets her come into her room and listen to albums sometimes. She lets her watch television with her and her friends after school. Justine isn't quiet like she was at Granny and Lula's, isn't so mad.

Justine makes a V with her fingers. She puts them over Christy's cheeks and tells her to hold still and quit grinning. She colors in dark rouge, first on Christy's cheekbones and then her own, just the way the lady had shown her. She pulls out a deep maroon lipstick to match the rouge and turns to Reney.

"Sure you don't want to get dolled up, Bean?"

Reney shakes her head. The lipstick is so dark it looks almost black in the fluorescent light of the bathroom mirror.

"Doesn't matter. You're the prettiest little Indian I ever did see." Justine rolls her lips together, smoothing the lipstick, and then kisses a piece of toilet paper and hands it to Reney.

Makeup, Justine had said, was just one reason they couldn't live with Granny and Lula, who quoted Timothy so much that Reney could mouth the entire Scripture along with her: "In like manner also, that women adorn themselves in modest apparel, with shamefacedness and sobriety . . ." and so on. Reney could count on Justine to follow with a crack about Timothy's next verse: women staying in silence and subjugation. Then there would be stretches of hard quiet, and they were just better off here, so said Justine.

Reney takes the toilet paper and presses her own lips to it, rolls them into the color. She stands on her tiptoes in front of Justine and looks in the mirror, then wipes her lips with the back of her arm.

A good-time crew from the factory drifts in and out of the house. Cigarette butts transform ashtrays into morning-after volcanoes. Reney turns the ash-dusted tabletops into canvases, tracing hearts in her path when she creeps to the kitchen in the morning quiet. Men, some with union money to spare, bring occasional gifts (a bone-handled jackknife, a book of knots, the licks of a bobtailed dog). They fill the house with noise and a sweet-smelling smoke that Reney has come to know. They leave behind safety glasses, a stray sock here or there. One leaves the *Waylon and Willie* record that Reney keeps stashed beneath her bed.

"If being with my ex taught me anything," Justine says, "it's take not one ounce of shit from a man." Justine, who won't call Kenny by name anymore, holds her eyeliner to the flame of a match to soften it before touching it to her eyelid.

Reney leans in the doorway, waiting for the familiar sermon.

"You can't trust a man to take care of you. Remember that, Reney. You can't trust them at all for that matter. They'll lie to get what they want. And they always want something."

Justine steps over Reney and disappears into the kitchen. She is going to work tonight at the second job she's picked up, waiting tables at a cowboy bar. Justine walks back in with a shot glass of tequila.

"I wish you wouldn't go to that job," Reney says. The low-cut blouse Justine has to wear makes Reney feel equal parts angry and embarrassed.

"I wish Granny and Lula didn't have to walk to the laundromat. Wishing won't get that washing machine out of layaway." Justine does a little shake with her hips, holds up her tequila, and winks at Reney.

Reney digs through Justine's purse and finds the lemon-shaped squeeze bottle and disposable saltshaker. She passes the salt and squeezes a bit of lemon into her own mouth before handing it up to Justine, who has already licked the back of her hand.

"I go and prepare a place for you," Justine says before giving the salt a shake and drinking the tequila down. She cackles, then gets mock serious—maybe, Reney is not sure—and says, "Father, forgive me."

Kenny seemed good-natured enough until he didn't. After him, men ran together in Reney's mind. There could have been one or ten. There was the one who traveled around sharpening barbers' razors and scissors and prided himself on keeping the kitchen knives sharp. There was a rodeo clown with the sweet dog and his own bag of makeup. Then there was the one whose friend owned the bar where Justine worked. This one wore a .38 Special in a holster he clipped to the inside of his cowboy boot. He had a long red ponytail and plenty of money but no job. After Justine ended it the first time, he stood at the bottom of her bedroom window crying and strumming a guitar. The second time, he snuck into her locker at the plant and filled her purse with poison ivy.

Reney doesn't know what her mom is looking for in the men or nonstop working. She doesn't know what makes her squeeze Reney so hard and so long sometimes that it seems like all the air might leave Reney's chest for good, what makes her sit up all night watching Reney sleep some nights and stay up making noise with the good-time gang others. Reney doesn't understand what makes it so hard for her mom to keep still. As far as Reney can tell, they don't need much at all, and between the one job and Granny and Lula, they have all they might ever need in the world.

Like a cowboy from *Waylon and Willie* come to life, in saunters the jockey from Texas. A towhead with blue eyes and skin like orange leather, Pitch stands a whole head shorter than Justine. Despite his size, he fills the house with bellowing laughter and a Texas jangle, tight as a new barbed wire fence. He doesn't drink much. When he's around, whatever it is that keeps Justine wound so tight seems to ease up. He buys Reney a Zebco reel one visit, then shows back up to take her and Granny fishing. He lets her braid racehorse mane and stand in winner's circle pictures. Reney beams when he remembers to leave her eggs runny and fry her bologna black on the edges.

One Friday morning before school, Justine's flurry of getting-to-work-on-time chaos comes to a stop in the kitchen doorway. She stands there, tying her hair up in a bun, watching as Pitch flips a pancake shaped more or less like Texas. It grazes the ceiling, and Reney doubles over giggling as Pitch stretches himself as far as he can to catch the pancake before it slaps the floor. When Reney straightens, she notices Justine's eyes are not on Pitch, but on the sink piled with dishes.

"Go comb your hair, Bean," Justine says. She sticks her safety glasses in her shirt pocket. "I have to go, and you don't have time to be playing."

"But we made God's country for breakfast," Pitch says, offering her a plate.

"You better be out there when the bus comes, Reney," Justine says.

Pitch and Reney listen to her bang down the hallway. When the front door closes, Pitch makes a scary face that gets Reney laughing all over again, but as she lies in bed that night, worry washes over her. She knows the beats of their old apartment by heart. Two doors slammed, one after another, meant guaranteed trouble. The sound of skin hitting skin had been rare, but Reney's bones zapped like a mosquito trap before it happened. She remembers the grunts and knocks of two people falling together in a room, still stupidly—lovingly—trying not to wake a child. She knew when she would be herded from her room before she had half of what she wanted and driven across town where she would wake up at Granny and Lula's. If only one door was slammed, Justine might sneak into Reney's room. Crying, she would curl into the bed beside Reney and stroke her hair until the night hummed quiet.

Reney loves her mother more than anything. She feels thankful for this old house and for goofy Pitch, but she can't shake her uneasiness. She squeezes her eyes shut and whispers a prayer for all of it, all of them.

"He didn't invent the pancake, you know," Justine says, as they pull into Granny and Lula's driveway. "Or tap a damn maple tree."

Justine had to pick up a Saturday shift, and Reney knows she is annoyed that Pitch left to gallop horses before the sun came up. He'd said he was going to take her fishing. The ride over was quiet, and now Justine's words seem to come from the middle of a conversation, an argument.

"I'm glad I get to see Granny today," Reney says. She opens the door and pulls on her backpack. "It's okay."

Justine takes a deep breath before leaning over for a hug. "Pitch isn't ever going to leave Texas, Reney. Plus, he's got girlfriends in every town from here to Santa Anita. Don't get attached."

"He wouldn't if you told him not to," Reney says. "And he doesn't have another me."

Justine begins to make excuses when they go fishing. She tries to stay out of photos, but Reney pulls her back into the frames. When he goes back to his beloved Texas or packs up his gear for another track town, the good-time crew returns, and to Reney its edges feel sharper than before.

Reney gets up for a drink of water but stops at the foot of the stairs. The ponytail guy is kicked back on the couch. His feet rest on the coffee table, and he's hugged up on Justine, whispering in her ear.

"What's that sorry sack of snakes doing here?" Reney says. She can't believe how calm she sounds. "Did he bring you some calamine lotion?" She had been nearly sleepwalking before, but now she is wide awake.

"Reney, you need to mind your business," Justine says. "Get back to bed." Her mascara is smeared.

Reney stomps up the stairs, thirsty.

Two nights later, Reney hears his voice downstairs again. Justine's been picking up more shifts at the bar. Nobody wants to buy the Mary Kay, and Justine and Christy have gone through most of it themselves. Justine won't let anybody answer the phone because of bill collectors.

Ponytail guy laughs. His low voice rumbles through the walls, up the banister, and under her bedroom door, where it rattles her bones.

When they begin to yell, Reney's feet hardly touch the stairs before she's in the living room and sees that they have already passed through the fight into something else.

"Go to bed, sweet girl," Justine says. She pulls away from his embrace and glances at the coffee table full of party stuff. In the middle of it all, a leather holster with a metal clip swaddles the .38.

Reney's about to say something else, something that will probably get her into big trouble, when she feels a hand on her neck. It's Christy.

"Come on, Beenie Weenie," Christy says. "Let's go upstairs."

Reney goes, but she cannot get her mother's eyes out of her mind. There was something wild about them, something sad. She waits until she hears her mother's bedroom door close. Then she waits some more, watching the flames of the gas heater dance on her walls. When she knows they won't be awake for a very long time, she creeps back down the stairs.

The gun is heavier than she expected, the handle a hundred sharp, tiny teeth in her hands. When she turns back toward the stairs, she accidentally kicks over his cowboy boots. They are expensive, with lizard toe boxes and garish stitching up and down the shaft. She grinds the heel of her foot into one boot's counter and the other one's toe box. Then she carries the gun upstairs to her room. She sits on her bed, holds the gun in her lap.

Reney thinks about what she might do next. She could walk to Granny and Lula's for good and bury the gun on the side of the road, far away from anybody who might do any harm with it. Once she got to Granny and Lula's, she would wash her hands and face and maybe get something sweet out of the fridge. Then she'd go get in bed with Granny, where everything would be alright as alright could be.

She could put on a mask and hold up the store on the corner where the man behind the counter always made her feel like she was stealing anyway. She'd take the money and all the Reese's Pieces in the place. She'd leave a trail of them to her Cookson Hills hideout and send her mom a letter telling her all their troubles were over, telling her she could follow the Reese's trail, but only if she came alone and ate the evidence.

Reney cocks the gun, then holds the hammer and gently releases the trigger. She doesn't know how she knows to do this, but she does. She does it again and again. Then she gets on her knees and puts the gun deep under her bed, next to *Waylon and Willie.*

The next morning, when Reney goes downstairs, pony-tail guy is pacing the living room, wearing nothing but jeans and an unbuckled belt. He has long red hairs spilling off his big toes that make Reney sick. Justine is sitting on the couch chewing a thumbnail. The party stuff is still strewn on the coffee table before her.

"Where is it?" he says to Reney. It doesn't really seem like a question.

She settles onto the couch next to her mom and tucks her legs into her sleep shirt, rests her chin on her knees.

"Where's my fucking gun?" he says again.

Justine stands but doesn't go after him like Reney expects her to. "I told you—you probably left it at the bar. Reney wouldn't dare touch your gun."

"I don't leave it anywhere," he says, starting to yell. "That's the fucking point, Justine. It was right here, and somebody stole it."

He stomps down the hall. When he starts banging on Christy's door, Reney runs up the stairs. She gets on her hands and knees and inches under the bed for the gun. When she gets ahold of it now, it no longer feels like power and possibilities. It feels just like the danger she always knew it was, and she wants it far away from all of them.

When Reney gets to the hallway, Justine is stepping between him and a messy-haired, cursing Christy. "Here," Reney says, shoving the gun at her mom.

He yanks the gun from Justine before she can react and takes one hard step toward Reney. Justine slaps both of her hands against his chest, pushing him back back back into the living room and out the front door.

Reney hears him shout "about like a bunch of Indians" and runs over to the window in time to see him yanking open the door to his truck. Justine bursts back through the door and grabs his boots. She throws them from the porch all the way to the driveway, and Reney smiles.

"I don't know what I'm going to do with you," Justine says.

Reney's been getting in trouble at school. She leaves her lunch sack on the kitchen counter and won't eat all day long. She feigns a stomachache if Justine works overtime and talks back to Lula. Granny gives Reney her own key and says it doesn't matter if nobody's home. She can always come inside; she can always stay. Even stern Lula nods her head and says, "Always." But as soon as Justine drops her off, Reney starts walking home. The belt doesn't work.

When Justine catches her trying to light a roach left in an ashtray, that's it. She ties her hair up in a bun and spends an entire Sunday cleaning house. Then she gets on the phone. The next weekend Pitch makes the drive across the Red River and into Oklahoma even though he didn't have a race. Reney crouches at the top of the stairs listening to the two of them talk deep into the night. Pitch stays for three weeks before Reney suspects that the good-time crew might be gone for good.

They take her to Padlock Pizza to tell her they are getting married. The three of them are moving to Texas, and she'll get a horse. Reney's eyes well with tears. Though she is no farther from Granny than she had been a minute before, she thinks her heart might burst from the way she suddenly misses Granny, dear Granny who speaks Cherokee best and wraps her up in arms that smell like Shower to Shower and something good cooked over the stove. A single gray braid curling to the middle of her back, she crushes Reney's bones the good way, like only love can.

Justine sits across the table from Reney and Pitch, and Reney can feel her waiting for a response. Not knowing today would be special, Reney has brought along her book of knots and one of Pitch's lead ropes. Parmesan cheese and red pepper jars balance on either side of her open book, holding open the page for bowline knots. Reney sets the jars off the book and lets the book slap shut.

She feels the long skeleton key that hangs from a piece of twine to the middle of her chest. Granny and Lula's back door is still held together by a cast-iron rim lock with a heavy doorknob that feels like a small heart in Reney's hand.

Reney looks at her mom there waiting. Reney had never had a dad. She didn't think she was missing anything. She thought about ponytail guy and Kenny. She thought about her mom, beautiful, unable to let herself come to a rest, no matter how hard she worked. And then there was Pitch, sitting next to her, loudly finishing his Dr Pepper with a straw.

"Is it going to be a Paint Horse?" Reney asks.

"We can get you an Indian pony if that's what you want," Pitch says. He grins and hugs her against his side. Then he props Justine's elbow on the table, takes the rope, and flips it around Justine's arm. "This is the rabbit," he says, holding up one end. "This here is Mr. Rabbit's home," he says as he makes a loop. He shakes Justine's arm. "And this is the tree."

Justine sighs and rolls her eyes but plays along as he runs the rope up through the rabbit hole, around the tree, and back home. Reney reaches across the table to try it.

"What about your job at the plant?" Reney asks, rounding Justine's arm with the rope.

Justine shrugs. With her free hand, she pulls a string of cheese from the slice she'd put on Reney's plate and drops it into her mouth. She smiles a little, and Reney cannot tell if it is forced. "I was looking for a job when I found that one. I'm sure I can find something." And with that, it's decided.

When her bones buzz her awake that night, all she hears is the gas heater's low hiss. There had been a party, but it was across the street. She had fallen asleep to the muffled thumping of country music and occasional bursts of laughter. Now everything is quiet.

Confused, she chalks it up to nerves. Still she is too unsettled to sleep. She flips one of her granny's tied quilts to the bottom of the bed and walks across the hallway. She puts her ear against her mom's door but hears nothing that would set her bones so abuzz.

When she pushes into the room, she finds Justine and Pitch crouched on the floor before the window, a wool Pendleton blanket over their shoulders. "New neighbors are fighting," Justine whispers.

Relief moves through Reney's limbs. Whatever it was that had woken her is outside. She and her mom are safe inside this house. In Texas, there would be a whole house and a Paint. Maybe the nights would be punctuated with barking dogs and stamping horses. Maybe Texas would be quiet.

From the darkness, the three of them kneel before the window, looking down across the street. Bare oak limbs spider their view. Pitch pounds the frame twice with the palm of his hand to break the paint seal. When the window pops up, cold air blows across them, and the branches rattle. Reney shivers in her sleep shirt. She reaches up and slides her fingers across the fogged glass, drawing a heart that drips down her arm. Justine opens up the blanket that Granny had saved money to buy for Justine when she graduated eighth grade. Justine pulls Reney close, kisses the top of her head.

A yellow bulb from the porch lights the man from behind as he stands over the neighbor lady. The man's hair seems to glow, but his face is a shadow. Reney hasn't seen him before, but she can imagine just what he looks like in

71

the light. From up above, Reney, Justine, and Pitch have just watched the woman run down the cement steps, her long brown hair streaming behind her. They heard the smack when she slapped him. When he pushed her away, the woman fell onto her back in the dry yellow grass and kicked at him.

The man bellows, her name lost in his throat, and grabs at her foot.

"She needs help," Reney says. Pitch is already reaching for his wadded-up jeans, and Justine has started for the phone. They are too late; from down the street comes the sound of the sirens. Reney presses her forehead against the cold metal screen.

Two cops, one Indian and one white, jump out of the car, and it seems to Reney that everybody across the street starts yelling at once. The man is on his stomach now, the white cop's knee in his back. The woman cries out and flashes up the steps inside.

When she runs back outside and down the steps, one of the cops shouts, "Gun, gun, gun." And it is so. Three quick shots.

Pitch covers his head with his hands and ducks before wedging himself between Reney and the window. Justine, too, reaches for Reney, tries to cover her eyes.

The white cop is on the ground now, and so is the woman. The man with the glowing hair struggles to his knees and cries out in a voice so wild, so full of despair and love that it shakes Reney from the inside out.

Pitch tries to pull the window shut, but now it's stuck open. He puts all of his weight behind it, but it will not close. Instead, he grabs the pull-down vinyl shade, but he fumbles it, and it springs up inside its roller. "Real nice setup you got here," Pitch says. "Nice town."

"There's work," Justine hisses, straining to pick Reney up.

Pitch doesn't answer. He takes a deep breath and drapes the blanket over the rolled-up blind. Then he slides down the wall to the floor.

Reney wraps her legs around Justine's waist, locks them at her ankles. Everyone is quiet as Justine carries Reney over to the bed. Pitch, looking smaller than before, stays put.

Justine pulls Reney's head to her chest. Reney can tell her mom is quiet crying, so she is relieved to hear Justine's heart pound steady and regular, if a little too fast, a little too loud. Reney thinks she is too old to stay in her mom's lap, but she doesn't care. Reney settles her head onto Justine's shoulder and closes her eyes. Even after the flashing lights spin out of the room and the sound of sirens deepens before growing faint, Justine and Pitch stay fixed to their places, as if they are on a stage waiting for curtains that will not come.

Terra Firma

When Reney's adventures through the pumpjack pulse of the oil fields grew old, she'd climb the fence, wrestle the saddle off the Paint, and place the pad upside down to dry like Pitch had shown her. She might sneak an extra handful of sweet feed to a colt or let the dog, a blue heeler pup named Hesdi, chase her across rows of round hay bales. When she fell between the giant bales, he'd come bounding after her, and they'd both come up scratching and spitting hay before taking off again. From the top of the bales, it was easy to see across the Red River to the scrubby ocher ridge that was Oklahoma.

She'd look upon the low ridge wondering how her granny was doing. She thought about her old friends back in Indian Country, getting ready to start fifth grade too. She'd won the fourth-grade regional Ready Writing Contest after they moved. Then she hit a lanky phase, and because her new school was so small, she was asked to try out for the junior high basketball team. Her friends, she figured, were probably still running around playing freeze tag after lunch.

Nearly every afternoon that summer, storm clouds popped and played on the ridge before dissipating into a burst of color along the eastern horizon. Reney and Hesdi kept a close eye on the storms, anxious until they passed. Sometimes she waved or cupped her hands to her mouth and shouted, imagining somebody might be on the Oklahoma side looking back at her, but she never heard anything in return other than a distant roll of thunder.

When she got tired of animal company or bored with her jump shot, she'd pick the hay from her long brown hair and head toward the old farmhouse where Pitch's mama and daddy, Nina and Ferrell, lived. If the house was quiet and dark other than the sparkle dust coming through the blinds, she'd tiptoe to the back bedroom. There she would crawl into bed beside Nina, click the three-way lamp to the lowest setting, and tap a finger along a row of serial killer biographies and Stephen Kings. Snuggled against her new grandmother's back, she squinted herself into worlds far scarier than any she knew.

She might shuffle to the far side of the room and select one of the Westerns that Nina taped when she was in good spirits and obsessively poring over the *TV Guide* from her lady-size recliner, twirling her gray curls, timing the pauses for commercials perfectly. Nina had captured every John Wayne movie ever made and labeled each one in her perfect cursive. Reney did her best to watch them all that summer. She cheered for the Indians, though she knew John Wayne would always end up the hero.

Eventually her mom would come home from work and bang twice on the front door before coming in to tell Reney the catfish or crappie were biting and that if they hurried, they could be back in time to fry fish. Reney never failed to believe in these short evenings: Justine's long black hair absorbing the sun, the beer only making her happy; Pitch rubbing the small of Justine's back, showing her again to let the crappie take all of the minnow before she set the hook; everybody laughing when her mom's hook came up bare. Reney remembered her mom's words before they left Oklahoma: "We'll be a family."

This was something like the family Reney always wanted, the one living out these evenings when the beer brought happy and nobody was talking about finding work or trying to coerce anybody to be something they weren't. These evenings, her mom seemed ready to throw out the flattened boxes stored in the barn and stay. But when the happy spilled over and voices grew sharp, Reney would tuck her tied patch quilt under her arm and write Justine and Pitch a note that she was going to watch movies with Nina. During the summer, she didn't even have to ask to sleep over. She'd shuffle out the door where Hesdi would meet her on the trailer steps and bite at her legs all the way across the drive.

Nina was the opposite of Reney's granny in almost every way. A tiny lady—loud and prone to delightfully creative cursing—she colored and permed her hair at home, snipped the curls herself with orange-handled sewing scissors. When her slipped disk acted up, she stayed woozy in the back bedroom surrounded by pill bottles and ashtrays, smoking and reading, tugging at the tiny gold pendant that hung from a chain around her neck.

Just when it seemed Nina might not ever leave her bedroom again, Reney would wake to find her in the kitchen flipping bacon, a cigarette pinched between her lips, ash curling over the skillet. "Garden seed, papoose," she'd say, the pitch of her voice registering high among the ceiling tiles. "Rats been congregating in your hair?"

Reney would rub the sleep from her eyes and grin. She was browner than she'd ever been now that she lived in the country and passed her days outside. Her hair, long and nearly black, was uneven at the ends.

On these days, Nina set about fixing up the rattletrap farmhouse where Pitch and his daddy were born as if she might never have another chance to set things right. That summer she covered the whole place in wood-grained contact paper. Wood-grained counters. A wood-grained deep freeze and fridge. She even put contact paper on the already wooden kitchen chairs and the lid of the toilet seat.

It was on one of these bacon days that Reney followed Nina out the back door and down its sagging steps to the cellar. Reney raised the heavy concrete door enough for an odd rusty piece of iron to counter the door's heft.

"Hey, it's got those teeth just like your necklace," Reney said.

"It's a drill bit. It chews up earth and spits it out so they can ramrod a pipe into the mud and pull up money," Nina said. "Goddamned useless now. Like most of this Shinola."

Reney kept quiet. She knew better than to get Nina talking about how drillers were pulling up and stacking oil rigs all over the state, much less Ferrell's mineral rights.

Nina pushed past Reney into the dark cement room. You could hardly find a spot on the floor that wasn't cluttered with hardened race bridles, jangly bits, or boxes of filthy, broken china. Nina opened the vent, lit a cigarette, and twirled a piece of hair around her finger as she surveyed the mess. Reney started by sorting through a box of curled victory pictures but soon stopped at a magazine with a front cover picturing a tremendous cloud of black that spouted a tornado with three dancing vortices. *Terrible Tuesday* was written in white horror font in the middle of the main cloud.

"What's this?" Reney asked. Nina reached for the magazine.

"It was a storm. A terrible storm. Fifty people or more died. Wiped out half the town."

"Were you there?"

"Ferrell was. Or I thought he was. Thought it killed him."

Nina flipped the magazine closed and put it in the trash pile.

"But he was okay?" Reney asked.

"Turned out he'd gone over to Ross Downs to see Pitch ride. Fingers too by-God busted up to call home, but yes, you could say he was okay. Go get us some trash bags."

When they were finished, the cellar looked like a perfect little jail cell. Coal-oil lamps separated two springy cots covered with quilts, and they'd maneuvered a bookshelf down the steps where Nina stored jars of potatoes and green beans put up in a previous fit of activity. They bought a case of tuna fish and a big tub of Jif, so much more festive than the black-and-white commodities from her granny's that Reney imagined the disasters that would lead her to unscrew the lid and break the smooth surface with her fingers.

Before she hauled out the trash, Reney snaked *Terrible Tuesday* out of the bag and hid it between the cot springs and mattress. After much thought, Reney put *Huck Finn* on the shelf, leaving *The Stand* and the John Wayne whoevers for life aboveground. She didn't question their preparations.

Cleaning out the cellar left Nina bed-bound for weeks. She groaned and grasped at pill bottles when Reney crawled into the bed beside her. She threw an arm over her eyes if Reney turned on the light. When Reney wasn't on the Paint

Horse or shooting basketball, she stayed in the cool of the cellar, leaving the door open, reading, reading, reading. She worked on her clove hitch and began to keep her eye out for driftwood. She squirreled away rope from round bales and stashed cans of tuna here and there. She saw warnings on the horizon, kept careful count of the seconds between lightning and thunder.

By July, the storm clouds stopped passing them by. It seemed every afternoon brought a storm. When the trailer began to strain against the tie-downs or the shutters of the farmhouse began to bang, Reney was the first and usually the only one to go to the cellar. She'd light a lamp and spread herself facedown across a cot, readying her bones for the freight train sound of a tornado. She whispered pained prayers for her patchwork family, who stayed inside doing dishes, banging on the television, playing cards, loving, fighting. She wouldn't creep up the narrow stairway and lean her shoulder into the door until she was certain the storm had calmed.

There wasn't any notice, of course. Pitch, laughing at something her mom said, had hardly stepped onto the farmhouse's front porch to check the clouds when the storm door slammed against the outside wall. The hinges wrenched and moaned terribly against the frame, and Reney swore she felt the house wobble under her feet, like the hull of the V-bottom boat when she stood up too fast. Then, just as quickly, the wind reversed course and sucked the door shut.

For a moment, Nina, Reney, and her mom stared dumbly at one another, clutching canasta hands, mouths agape in the glow of Coors Light cans and Nina's special apricot brandy.

It was Nina who reclaimed time, shouting, "My God!" and throwing herself out the door. Reney moved to the doorway, afraid to run to the cellar, afraid to stay inside. The metal double-seater rocking chair hung in the splintered limbs of an oak tree. The tire swing had wrapped itself around the naked trunk before coming to a slapping rest, straining against the rope, and blowing back the other way. There was nothing at all on the porch, which before the storm had been cluttered with oil field detritus, muddy boots, horseshoes, and all manner of collected crap dragged in by Pitch and his daddy. Most especially, there was no Pitch. All that was left was a fading roar and the black-orange glow of the evening sky.

Reney's mom was suddenly dragging Reney past rattling windowpanes and out the door. Nina bowed in the wind on the last step, shouting Pitch's name. Reney grasped her cuff as they bounded past. Heavy drops of rain pelted them, sparsely at first. By the time they reached the cellar door, the rain beat their bodies so violently that Reney could not hear what her mom was shouting, could barely see her mouth O-ing words into the storm. Reney strained toward the sky looking for some sign of Pitch's boots, hoping to catch the flash of his grin or the sound of his voice as he passed over, imagining him huddled over, going to the bat, riding the cloud to victory.

Then, she was clinging to her mother, crashing into the hole. Their wet bodies mashed together, pulling and grunting into the cramped, cool stairwell. It took both of them to hold on to the concrete door so Nina could latch it. Reney could hear Nina sobbing once the storm was muffled, could hear her fumble open the cellophane of a new pack of Merits.

A lighter clicked. Nina's face glowed, then darkened.

"Give me one," Justine said. The thin, yellow light led them down the steps. The lighter clicked again, and Justine was briefly illuminated.

Reney sat on one of the cots and felt for the lamp, her fingers lifting the glass bulb and rolling the wick by habit. When the light settled on the room, there was Pitch, huddled in the far corner. He held his knees tight to his chest, and when he looked up at them, he took a deep breath and spit between his legs.

"The wind," he said. "It took a pumpjack weight right off the porch. Spiraled up like a piece of paper."

Justine took a drag of her cigarette. Her ember deepened, and for a moment it seemed to Reney that everything might be fine. Justine must have felt relief, too, for a few seconds. Pitch was okay. They were all okay! Nina rushed to Pitch and took his head to her tiny hip, crying, "My boy, my baby."

Pitch almost let her continue, but then he looked at Justine and pulled away.

"We thought you were gone," Justine said. "Thought the wind took you." An accusation. She tapped the cigarette with her index finger three times and reached to open the vent. Lightning flashed through the slats, and Reney waited for the thunder.

"Thought I was goddamn going to die," Pitch said.

"So you left your family to get blown away?"

Nina put a hand on the small of her back and shuffled over to the other cot and lay down. She twirled a curl and hung her cigarette hand off the cot. Justine didn't say anything else, which to Reney was the weirdest thing she could have done. Instead she clicked on the radio and started spinning the knob across the static.

Pitch stood and dusted off his backside. Reney thought he might say sorry. She knew Pitch wasn't good at sorry, but if he at least tried, maybe her mom would let it go and they could go on with their night.

Outside, the sky still popped and shook the window with thunder bumpers, as Pitch called great, booming thunderclaps, but the roar of the wind was already letting up. Reney still hadn't heard the freight train. She reached beneath the thin mattress and pulled out the *Terrible Tuesday* magazine.

"Did you see the funnels, Pitch?" she asked, hoping they could all just talk about the weather.

"Just that weight. It was more the sound and the force of the thing. Felt like my eardrums was going to burst."

"If you had your lariat rope, you could have lassoed it."

Pitch poked her in the ribs. "Shoot, I'd be flying to kingdom come."

"You think Hesdi and the horses are okay?"

"Animals know what to do," he said, taking the magazine and flipping its pages.

"Two kids," Justine said, her eyes still on the radio that wasn't picking anything up.

The way Pitch looked up from the magazine made Reney's heart lurch. She didn't exactly understand what her mom was so upset about, but it felt old and worn, not like something that just happened. Not like this accident of Pitch leaving them inside while he ran to the cellar.

"I said I didn't know I was getting two kids out of this deal. But I should have."

In an instant, Pitch had flung the magazine against the wall and kicked the bookshelf, knocking a low shelf loose. Cans of tuna scattered across the floor, and the Jif jar busted. His quick violence still surprised Reney. She'd only seen it on occasions when her mom wouldn't stop nagging and once when the stud kicked him bad in the thigh. Pitch looked at the mess on the floor and shook his head, like he was trying to decipher something just beyond reach.

"You made it clear my pockets ain't big enough." Pitch's face seemed distorted to Reney, hardly his face at all. "Now I ain't man enough to by-God fight off a tornado, so I imagine you ought to start taping together boxes like you've been threatening to do since you got here. If you want to get back across that Red River, I ain't stopping you."

Reney wondered what her granny was doing. She thought of the soft one-dollar bills Granny had sent for her birthday, the sweet, looping letters pressed deep into the paper. She remembered the last time they'd talked on the phone and how she'd told Granny she had to go because she wanted to help Pitch wash the stud, how she'd cried that night in bed feeling bad about it. Each night since, she had dreamed her granny's soft, brown skin into being, feeling the bend of her arthritic fingers in her own. They'd take their cane poles to Little Locust Creek and catch perch for supper, and Granny would wipe cornmeal on her big, aproned belly. Then together they'd sing the sun up. Always too early, Reney would wake in Texas. Even as she wiped her granny from her eyes, the sound of the stud blowing snot and stamping outside her window always made Reney smile.

A loud bang startled Reney back to the cellar. Pitch was leaving. Outside, the wind had blown the heavy cellar door from his grasp and slammed it against the ground. Reney started after him, but her mom caught her. As she pulled Reney into her body, Reney tried not to cry. She tried to banish the pictures of twirling vortices carrying Pitch away.

"He promised me it wouldn't be like this," Justine said, stroking Reney's hair. "When I quit my job to come down here, he promised me. Hell, Nina, we're barely bringing in enough money to keep the place you gave us lit. They're supposed to be putting in a Walmart in Sunset, but I can't get him over there to apply. He's not lazy. What's wrong with him?"

"Just like his daddy," Nina said. "Don't want to be tied down." She set aside the crumpled magazine she was smoothing, tapped another cigarette out, lit it, and sat up. She was so tiny her toes only brushed the concrete floor.

Ferrell was hardly ever around. Tonight he was on a trip to Kansas looking at a mare nobody could afford. He was big fun when he was there, always trying to get Reney to do the circle game and making her look, then giving her a thump on her arm when she did. Nina cackled at his foolery when people were around. Other times, she mostly shook her head, if she responded at all.

"It's never going to change," Nina said. "He'll love you, but he'll be looking for a runner or running that river until the day he dies. There's a lot to love about them. More to hate, so I'll tell you like I told the last one. If you can't take it, you might as well leave now."

Justine kissed Reney's head and sniffed. Reney considered her life back home: her granny, growing older, Reney knew, by the day. Her mom's double shifts. The second job at the track bar. First Kenny, then the shared houses. The boyfriends with big buckles and talk who promised microscopes, telescopes, puppies, and all manner of things a Cherokee girl with no father and a mother who loved her fiercely but worked herself ragged might dream of. You had to work hard to find Pitch's mad streak. Reney figured the walls or bookshelves could take it. She'd seen worse.

"Leave if you want," Reney said. "I'm staying." Then she ran up the stairs and into the storm.

The rain was just an idea now. Overhead, she could hear big boughs sway and settle, hear the tiny limbs click. The thunder no longer felt like something exploding from her skull outward. She pulled her T-shirt over her head and ran to the driveway where she watched Pitch's taillights bounce over the cattle guard and seemingly float into the sky.

She picked up the soggy basketball that somehow still rested where she left it at the base of the light pole. When they had first moved to Texas, Pitch salvaged a door to the ancient barn's loft and got an old hoop from the school maintenance yard. He spent a whole day sawing, sanding, and nailing it all together before he stuck it, just cockeyed, to the light pole in the driveway. He'd never straightened it like he said he would, but it worked.

Reney tried to dribble, but the heavy ball landed with a thud. She picked it back up and bent her knees low for a free throw the way Pitch had taught her, but her shot still fell a foot short of the goal.

She saw Justine walking up but got her rebound instead of saying anything and set herself for another free throw. Before she could loose the ball, Justine took her by the arm and held tight.

"I'm so sorry, Reney Bean."

The taillights, tiny now, disappeared at the highway turn. They watched the white glow of headlights push through the night on an even plane toward town. Hesdi came trotting up, shivering and soaked.

"We were supposed to be a family." Reney pulled her hand away so Hesdi could lick it.

"You deserve better."

"I wish you'd quit making him run off."

"Reney, life don't run on shits and giggles. I've worked two jobs since I was sixteen to make sure you weren't raggedy. I had a good job back home. You were in school. We had Lula and Granny." Her voice dwindled as she looked over at the trailer house. The porch light was flickering with a short that Reney knew she'd been after Pitch to fix. "He couldn't bear to part with his horses and the Red River."

"Everything wasn't great there, either, so don't act like it was," Reney said. She kissed for Hesdi and was halfway up the trailer house steps and through the door before she heard her mom call her name.

Reney spread a towel on her quilt and patted it for Hesdi to join her. She wrapped herself around him and rested her forehead on his nose. The broken bookshelf was bothering Reney. It made her think of Kenny and their old apartment. She remembered the quiet crying after he left, how her mom would harden when Reney walked in, then smile and say it would all be okay. When he came weeping to the door of their next house, Reney sometimes wanted to let him in, though she couldn't remember, now, why.

Reney heard the front door close. When her mom sat on the edge of the bed, Reney squeezed her eyes shut. She wanted to sit up and let her mom hug her and tell her how she was the most important thing in the world, in that way Justine had of looking deep into Reney so that Reney knew her words were true no matter what had happened to the contrary. As her mom smoothed her hair, Reney's heart began to fill with love the way it did when it felt like it might burst. She wanted to sit up and say: *You are my family, Mama. No matter where we are, you are my family.* But then she thought of Pitch and the tornado and how he must have been scared. And how maybe her mom didn't know the first thing about being scared because all she knew was love and mad and love and mad all over again. So Reney kicked her leg, feigned sleep, and rolled toward the wall.

Justine shooed the dog. She outlined Reney's bent legs with her own, pulled Reney into her, and clasped the top of Reney's hand. Reney could hear from her mom's breathing that she was crying. They lay like that, Reney thinking to herself, *I'm going to turn over now, I'm going to turn over now and say sorry, I'm going to turn over now* until her mom sniffed one last time, in the way she had of turning off sad, like it was a radio and you could just stop the sounds and all the feelings would go away.

"I know you can hear me, and I know you love me," her mom said. "It's okay that you aren't going to talk right now. Mama's got to go to town, baby. I'll make it all right. You wake up scared, you go get Nina. Go on over there now if you want. Mama and Pitch will both be back soon. We'll be okay. Don't let that dog back up here. He has fleas, and he stinks."

Her mom got up and moved to the door. Reney could feel her, knew she hadn't left.

"I know you love Pitch, Reney. I love Pitch too. I guess he's just Pitch, is all. But I love you more than anything in the whole wide world."

Reney stayed put. They couldn't know it, but the storm had only meandered that night. Even as her mom's truck roared to life, powered by the grace of dead dinosaurs and desperation, the system was wrapping back around itself where it would settle on top of the old farmhouse and trailer. There it would stay, intent on letting out all of its howling fight on the five-acre sticker patch sucked dry of oil and useless for growing anything but the horses a certain breed of man's dreams are made of. Heartbreakers. All Reney knew as she lay there listening to her mom's truck rattle over the cattle guard was that outside the horses were sleeping upright and anywhere they could be heard, her mom's words were true.

Greater the Mass, Stronger the Pull

We had to sneak to turn on the window unit Mom brought from my bedroom in Texas. Lula was so happy to see us she followed Mom and me from room to room, worrying about the electric bill, worrying somebody might trip over the cord, and—our favorite—worrying we'd catch cold. It had to be 100 degrees in there, but she insisted I wear a jacket because exposed skin was a sin. Or led to sin. I was never exactly clear on the reasoning behind Holiness doctrine. At any rate, Mom and I had hardly unpacked our room, and already Oklahoma July and Lula were bringing out our crazy.

"Justine and Reney, don't you just love these?" Lula said. She dabbed sweat with a handkerchief and spread two ankle-length skirts on the bed for Mom and me.

"We'll go to a motel, Mama," Mom said. It was a threat. "We're not wearing those skirts. Not taking our earrings out either." A dare.

We'd come up to Lula's to stay awhile. Or to stay. We did that sometimes—left Pitch in Texas and headed back to Indian Country. Once we packed up all our stuff and drove all the way to Tennessee where Mom's two sisters lived. I was hardly enrolled in my new school before Mom and Pitch decided they couldn't live without each other after all.

Lula pursed her lips and got after a fly with a rolled-up magazine. I mouthed "be nice" at Mom, but she shrugged and passed a note that said: *me and u + 10killer sunset 2night = cool deal?*

She turned to Lula and said, "Let's make a grocery list, Mama." Then she motioned me out the door. When she came outside waving her list and grinning, I was sitting in the driver's seat of her new used Mustang with the engine running. "You must be crazy too," she said and jerked her thumb toward the passenger seat.

We ran by the truck stop for a six-pack of baby beers and a Dr Pepper, and then we were flying through town with the T-tops off and windows down. I pushed *I Do Not Want What I Haven't Got* into the tape deck, but before Sinéad could finish the serenity prayer, Mom popped it out and put in *1999*.

We'd done a version of this the whole five-hour drive from Texas. I'd put in some of my music and feel for a minute like I wasn't in a car sagging with the weight of half our lives, headed to Lula's where there was no TV and the only records were Mahalia Jackson and Gospel Elvis. Mom gave everything a chance, but the Prince tape she'd bought at our first fill-up always went back in. She'd go right to "Little Red Corvette" and sing like the car was her shower and I wasn't sitting there so sick of Prince I could puke.

Her whole life she'd wanted a Corvette, but she was married to Pitch. Or used to be. Who could say? She'd taken over payments on the Mustang before we left. The thing sounded like it'd been run into the ground, but I think it had her thinking about possibilities again, the future maybe.

"Please can I drive when we get to the highway?" I asked. I had my hips hovering over the seat, trying to zip the cutoffs I didn't dare wear at Lula's.

Mom whipped her head around and downshifted. Before I knew what was happening, we were mid-U-turn, pulling into the Fill'Er Up parking lot.

"Reney—" She killed the car and took a big breath. "Don't look, but there's your daddy." We bugged our eyes at each other. Then we started laughing.

My father wasn't a wound or even a scar, not a black hole or a dry desert. He just wasn't. Not for me anyway. Mom was my sun and my moon. I was her all, too, and that was us. Her: equal parts beautiful optical illusion and fiery hot star. And me: an imperfect planet she kept as close as she could. So when she pointed her lips at a man getting gas and said, "Don't look, but there's your daddy," it was Arsenio, not the *Nightly News*. I got all tingly. I said, "Better late than never."

Mom was still nervous laughing when she yanked the parking brake, but everything shifted in the evening swelter. A truck passed by with a one-two country bass pumping. Then the only sound was an occasional tapping coming from the tire shop across the street.

I tried to smooth my hair and did my best to pull my shorts from my butt, wishing I was still wearing my jeans. A drop of sweat ran down my stomach into my belly button. Straining to see without looking, Mom and I found each other's hands as we crossed the parking lot.

Even from the opposite side of the gas pumps, I could see why I was so much shorter than Mom and why people in Texas mistook me for Mexican more than they did her. The guy wasn't much taller than the pumps, and beneath his cut-off denim shirt, his shoulders and arms were a deep, reddish brown. He had a white cowboy hat with a big turkey feather sticking out of the band pulled low over his eyes. I nearly stopped in the middle of the parking lot trying to see his face. But then Mom was pulling me through the jangly glass door and dragging me down an aisle with a clear view of the register.

We stood there long enough for the lady at the counter to get to thinking we were stealing, which seemed pretty close to the truth of the matter: Mom thumbing through Slim Jims way too nonchalantly, me pretending to care about the ingredient list on a can of Pringles. "Can I help y'all?" the lady finally said and started moving around the counter to check on us, but before she made it, she yelped "Hey!" and ran for the door.

Mom took off after her. I grabbed the Slim Jim she dropped and followed just in time to see that the man in the cowboy hat was now a man in a truck, pulling away. A redheaded kid about my age with britches tucked into stupid pointy-toed boots met the lady at the door.

"Seven twenty-eight on pump two, ma'am," he said, all breezy, like it wasn't 200 degrees outside and my alleged father hadn't just skinned the fuck out before I could get a good look at him. Suspicious, the lady looked from the wad of ones to the kid's face.

"Feller told me if I paid for his gas I could keep the change. Important business, I reckon," he said with a smirk. I was sure all that kid was going to do with the change was buy something he could huff into his blank brain.

"That son of a bitch," Mom said. She pushed into the parking lot and shouted—at the sky I guess because the man was down the road—"FUCK YOU!"

I shoved the Slim Jim into my shorts and went after her.

"Motherfucking bastard," she shouted, which I only later understood to be irony.

Mom pushed the engine hard and shifted. She hit the speed limit quick once we were on the highway, then pulled a tiny Coors Light from the sack behind the seat.

"Told you not to look." She forced a grin, then steadied the wheel with her knee and twisted the beer open. "Shit. I'm sorry, Reney."

"Doesn't matter," I said, turning toward the window.

"I never would have said anything—"

"How'd he know it was us?"

The question was dumb. Her oldest friends called her Teeny and me Tiny Teeny. I had her thick, straight black hair, before I permed the shit out of it on skinny rods, introducing my Disco Diana Ross moment. Our blue eyes were the same, our round noses, and don't even get me started about our teeth.

Before she got me braces, she'd say, "Let me feel," and run her finger over my one slightly bucked tooth when she lay down to say good night. Then she'd feel hers and say, "You're just like me, Reney." She'd shake her head in wonder, like our matching half-buck teeth were the craziest things in the world. It wasn't crazy to me. Being her daughter was all I'd ever known.

Now that I was in high school, she worked harder than ever to make sure I wouldn't have to get a job that would interfere with studying or basketball practice. She made sure I understood that I could call her no matter what time it was or what I'd gotten myself into. I'd hardly started seventh grade when she started telling me how important it was to "wrap that rascal" and that the pill was only a phone call away.

Before she got around to saying good night, she'd run rough hands over my face and kiss my head. Factory grease lined her nails, all moons and ridges of pink chewed into perfect half-circles. By the time she was sixteen, I was a baby in her lap. When I started pulling away that summer—doing what kids do—she'd lived exactly half her life doing all she could to make sure my life was better than hers. After taking stock of all the ways we matched and saying, "Good night my Tiny Teeny Reney," she'd hold me close and whisper, "Don't be like me. Don't ever be like me."

Sunday morning I woke up to the sound of a hammer and knew Lula was standing over Mom, worrying a handkerchief in her hand, pointing out broken shit. That's what they did. Mom tried to jam everything right with sweat and force of will and Lula pointed out what didn't work and prayed. I'd been trying to stay out of their way more than usual since the daddy incident.

The night before, I'd gone to Tulsa with my cousin Sheila, who'd been bound and determined to see some skeezeball called Ned the Head. She was almost twenty and separated from her Holy Roller husband, running wild in the way that only backslid Holiness kids can be.

In Tulsa, we'd smoked dope in a boarded-up house that Ned said belonged to his friend's aunt. Everything in there was in place but covered in a thick layer of dust, like the people had just walked out one day and never come back. There was a saucer with a coffee ring but no cup on the kitchen table next to an open newspaper and some reading glasses. One plate in the sink. Solidified milk and other god-awful things filled the fridge, which I didn't dare open a second time. A can of hairspray, a comb, and a still clock sat on a bedside table next to an unmade bed.

We huddled on the far side of the kitchen table from the paper and the saucer, out of respect or fear or something like both, and burned candles for light. I tried to roll joints from the bag of leaf Ned had sold us. Nobody was getting high, but for a while we pretended. We pulled beers from a twelve-pack of Budweiser and planned the wild times Sheila and I would have now that I was sort of back home and she was backslid and sort of single. But before long, the weirdness of it all—the creepy house, Sheila being single, me being back in Oklahoma—settled over us. The room got quiet except for the sound of Ned fiddling with a candle.

"Maybe whoever lived here got raptured," I said, licking another pregnant banana joint.

"Don't." Sheila shot me a look. "You'll get me paranoid." Her eyes were heavy with shimmering green eye shadow and thick, black mascara, making up for all the years makeup had been a sin. The truth was, I'd *been* paranoid. I couldn't get over the feeling that we were all on the verge of something terrible and somebody or *something* was watching it all happen.

I guess Sheila and I were getting a little too heavy because Ned jumped up with the flashlight and started waving it under his chin making ghost sounds. Sheila must have found it charming because when he said, "Come on, girl, let me show you the *other* bedroom," she let him take her hand and lead her down the hallway.

I worked up my nerve to open the stiff *Tulsa World*, straining my eyes over old news and obituaries until I came to a review of *The Outsiders*. There was Tom Cruise from before *Top Gun* made all the guys in school want to play volleyball and be fighter pilots, Patrick Swayze before *Dirty Dancing* made him every girl's dream, and a scared-looking Ralph Macchio. I loved the book but felt wronged somehow that they'd put movie star faces on those kids from the book. It seemed everywhere I looked there was something else taking me completely by fucking surprise. Like as soon as I figured out walking, someone threw me into a lake and said: *Here, baby, learn how to swim.*

I put the paper back in place, tidied up our ashes and cans, and wandered out to the dark porch. Tulsa was filled with noise—music from three different directions, people laughing, kids squealing, crotch rockets racing down the neighborhood streets, what I hoped were fireworks in the distance. I gulped my beer and stayed in the shadows until it was gone. When I tapped on the bedroom door and said Mom was expecting me, I think Sheila was relieved.

Mom was sitting on the porch steps talking to Pitch on the cordless phone when we pulled up to Lula's. I figured I was done for—she once smelled a baby rattler that got inside the house with a closed door and a whole set of stairs separating them. She'd probably smelled the weed and beer on us when we turned the corner. I pushed my hair out of my eyes and tried to close Sheila's car door and wave goodbye like I would any other time. Suddenly I wasn't sure how that looked or felt, so I chewed hard on my gum as I opened the gate and got indignant about Ralph fucking Macchio lying in Johnny's hospital bed.

"Be to bed in a minute, Tiny," she said. She tried to smile. "Have fun?" She was bouncing her foot on a loose board that squeaked each time she let up.

I nodded, kept going.

"Love you." She half turned toward the door, and I thought she might want to hug, but Pitch must have said something that drew her back into herself.

I showered and got into the football jersey I slept in and brushed my teeth. I couldn't find mouthwash, so I swallowed as much toothpaste as I could stomach. Then I crawled into the same bed I used to share with Granny. She died not long after we moved to Texas, but I still felt like she should be here. A part of my heart broke every time we came back and I walked into the house without her. A children's choir had sung "I'll Fly Away" in Cherokee at her funeral, and I kissed her on the forehead, not understanding how cold she would be. Mama'd had to carry me out after that when I cried so hard I couldn't catch my breath and threw up in her hand. It hadn't taken many run-ins with boys for me to realize that I'd met my soul mate as a girl, and she was my great-grandmother. Some people wait their whole lives.

I was lying there feeling guilty for coming into Granny's room half-wasted when Mom came in. I turned over, pretended to be asleep.

She sat on the bed a long time before she said, "You better not be drunk."

I waited her out.

"Listen," she said. "I'm pretty sure I can go back to my job."

She wanted me to say something, but what was I supposed to say? Nothing felt okay. Not Lula and her religion, not boarded-up houses, not creepy dudes and beer buzzes, not Texas and all-day arguments about bills or somebody's whereabouts or who drank how much, not the weird in-between we seemed to exist within. Not fathers and not not-fathers.

"We're going home Sunday afternoon, tomorrow I mean. Back to Texas, okay?"

I was so tired of the back-and-forth I thought about just staying put no matter what Mom decided. When we'd left for Tennessee, I wrote a goodbye note to my sixth-grade teacher and made a big show of crying and hugging my best friend. When I showed back up in class two weeks later, I couldn't look at either one of them. This time, I'd barely brought any of my stuff.

By the time I traipsed onto the porch and collapsed onto the porch swing the next morning, the step was fixed. Mom was in the yard raking the red dirt, leaving dry grass hanging by the roots. She straightened her back and blew her nose with a bandana. "You hungry, Tiny?"

"Would you like to take a ride to Tenkiller, Reney?" Lula said before I could say "starving."

"I told you there's too much to do here," Mom answered. She rolled her eyes but then softened. "Maybe we can go later, Mama."

"Reney could ride with me now," Lula said.

"Reney's not riding with you anywhere."

Lula's seizures had started right after Mom had me. They were terrifying. She wouldn't take anything for them because the spells were the Lord's will. The reinstatement of her driver's license, which had been a surprise to Mom, was the Lord's will too. Mom and her sisters were mad as hell.

"If you want to kill yourself on the roads, so be it, but you're not about to take Reney."

I picked dried hairspray from my bangs, imagining myself from any family except this one. When Lula got into her fear-of-God voice, I walked inside, picked up the phone, and called Sheila at her mom's house. She already had her mind on getting back to Ned the Head. I was pretty sure he had his mind on any piece of ass he could get, so I didn't feel bad when I said, "Can you come get me first? There's something I want to do."

When I got into her dented-up Caprice, Sheila pointed to the glove box where she had the bag of leaf.

"Not me," I said and offered to light her one of the joints I'd rolled the night before.

"Uh-uh," she said. She sounded different from our phone conversation, quieter.

"Can we just ride around a little while?" I put the bag back in the glove box. I wasn't feeling so gung ho either.

"Last night was weird," she said.

"What do you think happened in that house?"

"Ned said they were just there one day and gone the next. He said his friend's mom didn't even know." She turned toward the lake. "Witness protection?"

"Maybe it was aliens." She didn't laugh, and I wasn't positive I was joking.

"Daddy always preached against the rapture. Trials and tribulations and all, but we are all here together until the end."

I could still hear my great-uncle Thorpe's voice, big and booming over all of us at the peak of his sermons or even more scary: soft when he cried and pleaded with somebody to get their soul right or risk eternal damnation. It was no wonder Mom couldn't pray at all anymore.

"I wish he was still here," she said.

Mom always said he reminded her of Indian Superman before he got sick and withered away. People used to ask him before they took vacations and all kinds of stuff. Mom said they went out and bought a coffeemaker after he decided caffeine was okay.

"You thinking about going back to church?" I asked.

"All I do is try not to think about it."

"You don't think you're going to hell for cutting your hair and wearing jeans, do you?" I knew from Mom that shit could really mess you up.

"It's what the Bible says. And, hello!" she said, waving a hand in the air. "Adultery."

"You're a good person." I thought we agreed about the bullshit restrictions now that she'd left the church, even if in spirit she was still a believer.

"Was I a good person last night?" She shook her head, kept driving.

"Well, maybe you are a good person with shitty judgment sometimes. Besides, you didn't do anything."

"I cried all the way home. Then I woke up thinking about that nasty Ned all over again, like some kind of addict. Mama came into my room after you called this morning. Said she had a dream there was a cloud over me, and she could see two angels and a devil fighting for my soul. She tried to get me to pray through."

She started really crying, and I just sat there, dumb. I didn't like thinking about a soul in terms of right or wrong, heaven or hell. I was starting to think maybe she *should* go back to her husband, but what did I know.

"I got so tired of the same thing every day. Washing Samuel's clothes, starching and ironing his pants stiff, cooking breakfast, making lunch, cooking dinner, washing dishes. Making love. Every night!"

"Girl!" I said, and we fell into a laughing fit. I'd gotten close two different times with different guys, neither of which bothered to pay me any mind afterward. Sheila and I were three years apart, but it might as well have been ten. Because she had grown up in the church, though, there were ways I was the older one. We started down a hill, and I caught my first glimpse of the lake between the trees as she started up again.

"Eventually I didn't feel nothing at all, not even during altar call. I kept going up when I was called to sing, until I just turned around and walked out the doors. Didn't feel right to pretend."

At the Snake Creek Marina sign, she slowed and put her back into turning the big steering wheel. "Reney, thank you for coming to get me last night." She wiped away the last of her tears and took a deep breath as she put the car in park. Lake Tenkiller opened up before us, emerald green as big as the sky. "I don't want that pot. I don't even want it in here anymore, unless you want to keep it."

I couldn't take it. Mom and her nose would be all over it from a mile away. Besides, despite trying to play it cool the night before, I'd never had weed of my own. I was scared to death to have it on me. And if I did end up going back to Texas, the coaches were threatening to start drug testing us after summer. We walked out onto the dock and let it all go into the wind. Then we tore the baggie up into a thousand little pieces and let those fly too.

"Hey," I said. "Do you know my father? Like my real father?"

"You mean Russell Gibson?"

"Yeah, that's his name." I'd never talked to any of my Oklahoma family about him. Never asked, never told.

"Sort of," she said. Then she turned around and walked down the dock toward the car.

"What do you mean 'sort of'?" I yelled, nudging a piece of plastic that had blown back onto the dock into the water. By the time I caught up, she was already starting the car.

"So?" I slammed the heavy door.

"It's a small town." Our tailpipe scraped rock as we started up the hill.

"What do you know about him?"

"Just hearsay," she said and turned back toward town. "He moved back to his homeplace after he got out of the army."

"And?"

"Well, he put roofing nails on his neighbor's drive, and he cuts people's fences. The Littledeers say he poisoned their dogs."

"Fuuuuuck."

"Sorry, Reney."

"We saw him getting gas the other day. He took off before I could get a good look."

"About right."

"But, like, I never did anything to him. Mom never asked him for a dime."

"You're better off," she said.

"Do you know where he works?"

"He might get a crazy check. Think he had a crazy uncle too."

"Great," I said. If my outside was all Mom, I was starting to worry what my insides might be made of.

"We see him every time we go to the donut shop," she said. "I mean *I* do now."

"Let's go," I said. She shook her head, but I guess she was still used to doing what other people said she ought to.

This is what I knew about Russell Gibson before that day: Mom was fifteen. She said no. He was closer to thirty than fifteen. He waited down the road until she could sneak out that night. She didn't want to wear her long Holy Roller dress, so she'd stashed a change of regular-person clothes in the bushes. They pushed the car down the hill, coasted until they could start it away from Lula's earshot. He wore a white cowboy hat with a turkey feather. And drove a green Ford truck. His mom was Choctaw, full-blood. She brought over fifty dollars and a coat when I was a baby. When I asked what it looked like, Mom said, "I don't know. It was just a coat."

DoRight Donuts was in a lopsided old house that needed painting, just three blocks from Lula's. Sure enough, the green Ford sat cockeyed in the gravel lot. All that time, he'd been right around the corner and down the road.

"You sure you want to go in there?" Sheila said.

I was already stepping out of the car.

107

When we pushed in, the sweet, yeasty smell of donuts turned my stomach. I stopped in the doorway, and Sheila had to nudge me forward to get through the door.

There he was at a back booth, napkins wadded up all around him, a newspaper spread out on the orange Formica table. He was wearing the same cutoff shirt. I could see now that his black hair was buzzed close to his scalp. The cowboy hat sat on the table beside him. His nose was long and straight.

He glanced in our direction but didn't seem to recognize me this time. Or maybe I only imagined that he glanced at us. Sheila pulled me to the glass counter where a dark-skinned guy with a big white Frank Zappa mustache rested on his elbows next to a little kid who had his legs dangling down.

"Can I help you?"

"A half dozen éclairs and a skim milk, please," Sheila said. "Want anything?"

"You're getting six éclairs."

"Day-olds are good heated up. I ain't been cooking."

"Just a Dr Pepper," I said.

As we sat down at a clean table, the little kid came from behind the counter with a coloring book and a box of crayons. The Zappa guy followed behind him with a glazed donut on a paper plate and a carton of chocolate milk. The guy tucked a napkin in the boy's shirt, then opened the milk.

"I do straw myself!" the kid shouted, and the guy guided the kid's little hand so he could tap the straw on the table to push it out of the paper without breaking it.

"Grammy'll be back in a minute," the Zappa guy said. He glanced toward the back where Russell Gibson was huddled over the paper with an ink pen. "Be good." He tousled the kid's hair, went behind the counter, and started running water.

Sheila pushed the box of éclairs at me, but I was shaking all over. I didn't know why I was there, what I expected to happen next. This all felt so stupid and pointless all the sudden. And most of all, wrong. What did I care what this guy looked like or who he was?

"Let's go," I said and stood up. Sheila was shoving éclair into her mouth and tucking the donut box closed when the little kid dropped a crayon. It rolled down the aisle—real slow like we were in a movie and the crayon rolling was the last thing to happen before the place got shot up. It stopped right in front of Russell Gibson.

The little boy jumped down from his chair but pulled up when he saw where it landed. Russell Gibson leaned down for the crayon. He didn't smile or hand it to the kid. Instead, he set it there on his own table next to his paper. Then he saw me. Or he saw my mom in me because he jumped up and took off out the door, leaving all of his stuff.

I wish I'd told him to give the motherfucking crayon back or gone over there and taken it myself and told him what a piece of shit he was for keeping a kid's crayon and for running from the Fill'Er Up and for being a sorry piece of shit probably every day of his life. I should have said all of that. I should have stood on one of those tables and shouted: *She was only fifteen.*

Instead I stood there like a dumb statue while he brushed past me without a word. I was pretty sure I smelled his B.O. even after he was in his truck throwing gravel. The little kid ran down the aisle and grabbed his crayon. Then he looked at me and spun his finger around his ear, saying "cuckoo, cuckoo" and giggling. I grabbed the hat and hooked Sheila's elbow and together we took off out the door to her car.

"What now?" she said, but I didn't answer. She started to drive, I guess, so we didn't sit there like donut-thieving maniacs. I didn't have any idea where we were going, no real sense that we were moving at all, when we turned onto Lula's street. I didn't even realize we'd stopped in the middle of the road until Sheila squealed her tires and pulled over.

When I looked up, Mom was huddled on Lula's front steps, her back to us. Sheila had jumped out of the car and was running through the yard before I could grab my backpack and get the door open.

Lula was lying on the porch having a seizure. Mom knelt over her, rocking back and forth and talking in a strange, sweet voice.

"Sure is a pretty day," she said. "Hear them birdies peeping, Mama?"

Mom was trying to hold Lula's hands, but they were clamped into tight little balls. Sheila took Mom's hands into her own and made her let go of Lula. One of Mom's hands was bleeding.

"We used to keep wooden spoons all over the house," Mom whispered. "What if she's biting her tongue?" Wild-eyed, Mom pushed the flat of her hand into her belly, her face breaking in two. "I didn't have a spoon."

Sheila took her by the wrist and held her hand in the air. Blood tendrilled down Mom's arm. I'd made it up on the porch by then, so Sheila put Mom's wrist in my hand and pressed a handkerchief she picked up off the porch to a gash in Lula's head.

"Put pressure on it," she said. I leaned over Lula, still holding Mom's wrist up with one hand.

Lula was calming, starting to blow spit bubbles and make the sounds she makes when she's coming back to us. One of her pink house shoes had fallen off. I could see the stocking seam crooked over her big toe. I wanted to fix it for her, but I was stuck between her and Mom.

Sheila palmed the top of Lula's head. She closed her eyes and started whispering "dear Jesuses" and "thank you, Lords." Before long, Sheila's voice grew loud and forceful. Then she got quiet again and began to speak in tongues.

I didn't want to hear it. I focused on Lula's stockinged foot, still slowly twitching, and pressed the handkerchief as steady as I could. Mom hung her head and cried so hard she hardly made a sound. After what felt like an eternity but was probably only a minute or so, Lula opened her bewildered eyes and looked at each of us, searching, searching, searching.

"It's okay, Mama," Mom whispered. She smoothed Lula's hair with her good hand. I handed Mom the handkerchief and scooted down to straighten Lula's stocking along her toes. Then I leaned against the house, wishing I could zap myself away from all of it. I thought about the rapture house again and wondered where the people went. I wondered if things were better for them. I hoped they'd won the lottery one morning and said to hell with all of you people and all of this shit, but I knew those chances.

Lula finally settled her eyes on Sheila and seemed to focus some. Sheila's voice slowed down, grew quieter until all I could hear were whispers and sniffles. Mom took Lula's arms and pulled her upright. Lula sat there awhile, the heavy gray braid from her bun falling across her breast like a rope. Mom got ice to press to Lula's forehead and mouth.

When she could stand, we helped Lula to her bed to lie down. After a phone call, Sheila's mom and a few lady Saints arrived and joined Sheila in prayer around the bed. While they prayed, Mom paced the kitchen with the phone pressed to her ear, arguing with her sisters about what to do. They thought she should force Lula to the hospital.

"They ought to fly here and do it themselves, if they're so damn sure about it," Mom said. We were sitting on the front steps staring at the loaded-down Mustang. She'd gotten us ready to go that morning, before any of this happened.

Before I had time to answer, she got back up and went inside to hover in Lula's doorway again. She couldn't stand to be too close to the rising and falling of their voices—that kind of praying gave her a little bit of a wild animal look.

When she sat back down, she picked at her bandage a little while, then chewed on the side of her thumb. "She's going to be sleeping for a while," she said, finally. "I guess she's as fine as she was before it happened, but I still hate to leave. Sheila said they're going to take turns sitting with her and praying through the night."

"Maybe we should just stay here," I said. I wasn't sure how I meant it, or if I meant it at all.

"I guess we could force her to go back to the clinic," Mom said, talking to herself it seemed. "Again! Damn sure can't make her take their drugs any more than we could last time." She put her face into her palms and kept talking. "What are we supposed to do? Be here when she falls. A lot of good I by-God did." She let loose a long, agonized scream, muffled by her hands. Then she wiped her face and took a big breath and put an arm around me. "We're a hell of a team. I can shove my hand down her throat, and you can fix her pantyhose."

"Look," I said. The shadow of the house stretched into the road. The light had turned, making everything a richer, deeper color, giving things a sort of purple glow or turning everything more the color it already was, maybe. In front of us, an orange moon was rising, huge and full.

"To hell with it," she said. "Let's fly out to the lake before the sun goes down." She went inside to check on Lula one more time. I stayed on the porch waiting for her. I heard the screen door slam shut when she came back out, but when she didn't come down the steps and pull me along to the car, I looked back to see what was going on. She stood one foot on the first step, blinking back tears. I was about to ask her if Lula was okay when I caught sight of the cowboy hat lying in the corner where the steps met the porch. I'd had it in my hand when I ran up. I jumped over and fumbled it into my backpack, but of course it was too late.

"It's okay, you know," she said. "If you want to get to know him, whatever. I guess I understand. I mean, my daddy's an asshole who wasn't ever around, but I've heard his voice."

"I ran into him today is all," I said.

"And?"

"Nothing," I said. "It turns out he's an asshole."

"Yeah," she said, shaking her head.

"Or still an asshole."

Mom handed me the keys and walked to the Mustang that wasn't ever going to be a Corvette. She didn't say one word about leaving myself an out or staying four car lengths behind. I stayed right at fifty-five until the speed limit slowed at Snake Creek.

By the time we got out of the car, the sun was just a sliver above the hills over the lake. We'd missed it. I took my backpack onto the dock anyway, and Mom followed. When I pulled the hat out and dropped it into the lake, she rolled her eyes.

"Don't do that for me," she said. "I'm fine."

She leaned over, fished the hat from the water, and tossed it into my lap. I flung it like a Frisbee as far as I could.

"He ran again," I said. "That's why I have the hat. He took off so fast, he'd have left his ass if it wasn't stuck to him."

"And?"

"Fuck him," I said.

"Feed him fish heads," she finished.

"I got the better end of the deal, you know."

"Yeah, no shit," she said.

"No. I mean I'm glad I don't know him at all. You had a person to miss when your dad left. I'm glad you never let him into our lives."

"All I've ever done is screw up and react, Reney."

"All you've ever done is take care of me."

The hat was washing in and out, inching closer to us with each wave. Mom picked at her bandage. "What do you want to do, Reney? What do you really want to do? Go or stay?"

"I guess I'd like to get someplace and stay there," I said.

"But where?"

"I want to go home," I said. "I miss Pitch." It struck me that despite how I'd mourned leaving Oklahoma as a kid, Texas *was* my home now. I didn't want any more Tulsa rapture houses or speaking in tongues or—bad as it sounds—front porch seizures. I damn sure didn't want to run into Russell Gibson again. I already had a dad.

"Pitch has been tore up since we left. He thinks of you as his own."

"Don't tell him about the Russell Gibson thing, okay?"

"Don't worry."

We sat there on the dock watching the waves pull in and push out, our legs dangling over Lake Tenkiller. The hat worked its way ashore but sank just before it got back to us.

"It's okay, Reney," Mom said as she stood to go. "I can take most anything."

We left the next evening as the moon was rising. I didn't try to play my music. I popped in "1999," a song about a future that people must have felt would never come but was now upon us. Mom didn't sing along or dance this time, but before the song ended she reached across the console and took my hand. By the time we got off I-40 at Lake Eufaula, the moon still hung in the sky like a big, glowing orange. I knew its light was only a reflection, but I watched it grow smaller and brighter all the way to Texas.

Hybrid Vigor

By the glow of the headlights, Reney counted again. A calf was gone. A bawling cow trotting ruts into the fence line confirmed Reney's count. She shoved her work gloves into the back pocket of a pair of Wes's greasy coveralls. She'd slipped them on over her underwear and a Dairy Queen polo, and now static electricity popped as she climbed into the idling diesel to get the shotgun.

With new babies dropping by the day, neither the feral hogs nor the coyotes would be far off. The hogs had pretty much planted a flag and declared the rooted-up land around the river their own, and the coyotes had grown brazen in the drought, killing two neighbor dogs and countless goats down the road. Still, she didn't think it was hogs or coyotes. Her mule, Rosalee, was gone too.

Shotgun cradled in the crook of her arm, Reney whistled, squinting toward the pale sliver of sunrise, hoping to see her mule's big ears come bobbing over the hill. Wes's sweet but useless stock dog, Rowdy Rotty, munched on a dried piece of cow shit.

Even Wes held a small appreciation for the mule, now that he'd heard stories of mules protecting cattle from predators and seen for himself how Rosalee kicked the shit out of a neighbor dog that had gotten too close to his calves. The calves, he'd said time and again, were the only thing keeping them off the dole. Reney had been working toward a degree for years, but it didn't take a degree to see that Wes was full of shit. She did the paperwork in the evenings and wrote the checks to the feed store and the vet. The cattle did little more than break even. But the money left in a steady trickle and came in chunks, and Wes, for all his tenderness, had become a man fond of a big chunk of money, or at least the appearance of such.

When Rosalee didn't come after a few sharp whistles, Reney killed the truck's chugging idle and left the shotgun barrel to the floorboard. She took out the cattle prod and lead shank and started walking the fence. "Where are they, girl?" Reney said to the dog, who gave her a quick lick. Reney hung wide around the mama cow in her manic vigil, all swinging udder and mournful cries, and nearly lost her boots in the mud suck crossing what was supposed to be the creek.

Most every spring the river devoured huge chunks of sandy loam. Scrub oaks crashed into the water like imploded high-rises. One good thing to come of the drought—they wouldn't lose any more worthless land to the river. But less rain meant more feed bills—their leased thirty acres were grazed to the root—and that meant more beery moping out of Wes.

Reney balanced on the second row of barbed wire and whistled again. Nothing. Their part-time neighbors from the metroplex had forty acres of bramble and bluestem that sat empty except for a couple of deer feeders and the dirt-bike trails Wes had bladed into the land for free. A whole day's work, wear and tear on their sputtering Farmall, not to mention the cost of fuel, for two cases of beer and some good old-fashioned Dallas backslapping. She scanned the empty field and climbed over.

The first time Rosalee took a calf, Reney had been scrubbing green scum from a water trough when the mule's slow, purposeful movement caught her eye. Reney stopped what she was doing and smiled at the silly creature, who made her way over to a baby calf napping in the sun. Suddenly, Rosalee snorted two times in the direction of the grazing mama cow. Before the cow could get over there, head lowered and bellowing, Rosalee took the calf into her mouth by the nape of the neck. Then Rosalee turned and ran across the pasture, baby calf a clenched ball. Reney never would have believed it if she hadn't seen it.

Rosalee jumped the creek, calf swinging like an off-kilter metronome and beginning to low. By the time Reney got across, Rosalee had reached the northeast corner of the pasture, calf tucked against the barbed wire fence. Rosalee's ears sagged. She made strange whimpering sounds and licked curlicues into the calf, starting at the head and slowly working her way down its small body. She kicked her hind legs at anything dumb enough to close in, even Reney.

It took Reney all morning to coax Rosalee away from the calf. She had to call in to work and sweet-talk Jack to keep him from cutting her shift. Luckily, Wes had been on his two-week hitch, and she'd mentioned the story only in passing when he got home, laughing about the calf accepting its fate as half donkey and trying to nurse. Wes didn't see the humor. Though he'd not even been able to bring himself to dock his rottweiler's tail, he promised that if the mule ever tried the stunt again he'd shoot her himself and sell her for dog food. Reney had hoped it was, like so many other things with Wes, bluster.

It struck her this morning that she'd rather lose a calf to the petty violence of coyotes than deal with Wes. She wiped her face with a rough sleeve.

"Fuck," she muttered. She checked her watch again and saw that if she was going to make it to work at all, she had to go. "A mule," she said, cutting into the morning chorus of whip-poor-wills. "My glorious goddamn kingdom for a mule."

Behind her, the mama cow cried billows of steam into the air. The poor beast had quit running the fence and was instead staring after Reney with dumb, worried eyes. "I know,"

Reney said. "I'm sorry." She hurried toward the back of the property, where a few scrub oaks crowded a rocky outcropping. With each step, the bluestem crackled beneath her. Wes's sagging coveralls, dampened from what little dew the March morning left, tripped her up. In her front pocket, she still had an apple she'd taken from the bowl on the counter for Rosalee's morning treat. She took another look at her watch. After one last whistle, she threw the apple as far as she could and headed back home.

"I'm late, Wes." Reney opened the mini blinds and hit the alarm clock, silencing two idiot disc jockeys midguffaw. She remembered their catchphrase—"Big bucks, no whammies!"—from a game show she had watched with Nina after her mom had first married Pitch and moved them to Texas. As a girl, she'd kept one eye on Oklahoma—the wooded hills and late-night church services she'd left behind, her great-grandmother. As she got older, with the help of MTV and books, she kept her mind on anywhere but Bonita, never for a minute imagining she'd stay and, like her mom, be responsible for holding together a household that most days she'd just as soon burn.

She looked one more time out the trailer window before dropping the coveralls and sliding into her work pants. She sat in the crook of Wes's body and pushed his hair back. He was still as handsome as he had been when they met at a party, her in Dr. Martens and flannel, trying too hard to not fit in, and him in standard-issue Wranglers. How quick he'd been to fling the snuff from his lip when she made a crack about it. Now, a can of Copenhagen and a spit cup sat on the bedside table, and she was late for work at the Dairy Queen, worried about a mule. She jostled him.

Wes rolled onto his back and stretched his arms and legs as long and stiff as they'd go. Turning back into her, he wrapped her up and pulled her toward him. He untucked her shirt, buried his face in her back, and rubbed his chin against her. His goatee was long and he'd not shaved around it in a week, making him look like a billy goat with his big brown eyes. He made gnawing sounds up her ribs, across to her breasts, said, "Big bust, no whammies."

"Get up. Unless you want to be without the truck," she said, pulling away. "I've got to go to work."

"Morning to you too."

Wes didn't notice the mama cow's bawls when he stomped down the metal stairs. He bent to scratch Rowdy's ears and kiss her head. Then he licked his thumb and wiped at a spot on the truck's door before climbing in. Reney was already sitting in the passenger seat.

"Why didn't you leave it running?" he asked. "Told you it's hard on the engine."

Reney waited until they'd turned onto the highway. "Are you going to fix the back fence today? Something's going to get cut up out there."

"Got to go over some stuff with Sammy at the Iron."

The Branding Iron cost twice as much as the DQ, though its food came in twice weekly on the same Sysco truck. Reney had graduated with Sammy Boyd, and she wasn't a fan. Wes never had been either.

But since he'd lost his job, Wes had taken to putting on his good boots and sitting at Sammy's table as weekday mornings stretched into afternoons. Sammy's grandpa's grandpa, or whoever, had made a fortune in oil way back, and, like his father, Sammy had been set up with cattle and hundreds of acres of his own as a teenager. He carried himself accordingly.

She'd made the mistake of walking over one day when she got off early, and there was Wes, kicked back in his chair picking his teeth, hoping some of Sammy's cowman shine would rub off on him. Reney endured Sammy's ribbing when she ordered her tea unsweetened and felt her face burn at Wes's talk about his "ranch," how he was planning to double the herd in the next year. Sammy egged him on, inviting Wes to talk smart. Wes, who'd never felt comfortable on a horse, even mentioned getting a couple of cutting horses before Reney excused herself to study in the truck.

On the ride to work, she counted one dead possum, two coyotes, and a hog wearing a blue scarf hung, by hunters or ranchers or drunk kids, over barbed wire. The land beyond the fences turned colors as they passed winter wheat and geometric coastal patches dotted with cattle. The drought hadn't passed over the wealthy or the spoiled, though the

Sammy Boyds of the world never seemed thirsty regardless. If you had enough land to rotate your cattle instead of overgrazing a scrub thirty acres to China, you could feed less, and beef prices go up in a drought, so everybody who doesn't need a dime makes three. Wes had grown up with less than nothing and somehow thought there must be magic in cattle. She'd never wanted to know a thing about cattle but soon saw that, like Pitch's horses, the cow business was more gamble than business.

When Wes came home after whatever happened on his last Wyoming hitch, he took his garbage bag of greasers from the back of the truck and put them in the fire barrel. Reney stopped short when she came onto the porch to greet him. "We can't afford new clothes, Wes."

"They can take their 'oil field trash' and stick it up their asses," he said. From then on, it was all cows. He wouldn't hear of trying to get on with another outfit. The picture was clear for him. He just needed a few more cows and a little more land and a woman with a better uterus.

"Rosalee's gone," she said.

"She take a calf?"

Reney stared out the window.

Wes shifted his cap, pulled the brim lower.

"I told you I'd shoot her."

"I know."

"I don't know why you want a goddamn mule in the first place."

"We've been over it, Wes."

"She's taking food from our mouths when she fucks with my calves." As they approached the stoplight, he shifted down, softened. "Shit. It ain't always going to be like this, Reney."

A glass gallon jar at Reney's feet knocked into the door. The day before, she'd bought half a tank of fuel for Wes's truck with the tips she'd been saving. It didn't matter how many shifts Reney picked up or how often she emptied her jar—he acted as if it were his calves that kept the bank at bay.

Wes turned into the Dairy Queen and pulled up to the side door. Reney took her backpack and stepped down. She paused before she turned toward work.

"Don't kill my mule."

"I know, Jack. I'm sorry," Reney said.

Her boss raised a palm toward the clock.

"Hi, Liza Blue," she hollered across the room. An old lady facing away from Reney in a red booth raised her hand without turning. "Morning, Ferrell," she said to Pitch's daddy. The old cowboy came over and made a big show of taking a red bandana out of his back pocket and wiping the tobacco juice off his lips before he kissed her cheek. Then he winked at the cigar-store Indian and went back to his talking.

"I think Rosalee took a calf," Reney said, tying an apron around her waist.

"Again?" Jack asked.

Reney was already banging old grounds into the trash, licking her fingers for a new filter, popping open a fresh bag of coffee.

"Listen," Jack whispered. He looked around at the bored-looking teens working the counter, high school–age kids who for one reason or another weren't in school. He folded his flap of hair over his bald spot and pushed up his brown plastic glasses. "I know you've got things going on, but you're the manager now. Can't Wes help out in the mornings?"

Reney stopped her wiping and turned to him.

"I've got class tonight, but I'll come in early tomorrow if it helps."

"The kids. They talk, you know."

She'd heard them whispering about how much she made, which wasn't much more than them, she'd be happy to tell them if they asked. She didn't think Jack encouraged the talk exactly, but she figured he probably didn't discourage it either.

"I appreciate you being flexible," Reney said, her voice sharp. "And I'm sorry, Jack, but I understand you've got to do what you've got to do."

Reney looked over her shoulder to where a kid at the register lolled his head back and yawned. It wasn't many years back that she was one of those bored high schoolers, but it might as well have been a lifetime. She didn't say that she got three times as much done as most of the employees when she was there. She didn't have to.

"Well, when you get things lined out for lunch, come on to the office so we can go over the schedule."

The schedule for the next three weeks was set. And she knew that when she got back there, he'd have an unsweetened ice tea with lemon waiting and he'd ask her about her classes and she would lose track of time talking about her instructors and the reading and she would become embarrassed when she realized how much she was enjoying their talk. Last week he'd given her a nice leather-bound day planner with a matching journal and heavy pen.

"Think the schedule's good until somebody calls in to say it isn't."

Jack frowned. "I was thinking we could look at payroll again, this time in relation to quarterly sales."

Jack's polyester slacks hung off his hips and his short-sleeved dress shirt always had spots of coffee or worse. She wasn't sure why he was so intent on their meetings. She wanted to think he was a little like Pitch—that is to say, a little like a father—if Pitch showed up when he said he would, stammered more, and didn't have brown, leathered skin from days spent on the back of a horse.

"Sounds good, Jack," she said and sniffed a tub of lemons before tossing them into the trash. She swirled tea dregs in the big metal urn, carrying it to the sink to clean.

She'd gotten to work too late to catch Pitch, who flew in sideways most mornings for a bacon biscuit and a Dr Pepper. If he'd been there, he would have ribbed her about Rosalee, saying the mule needed a dentist after all the sugar cubes. Reney figured Pitch was a little proud of how she'd taken to the mule, glad it'd given her something to care for after she and Wes got news another baby was lost and there'd be no more.

That's what she had told them, anyway. In truth, having kids with Wes was the one thing she had decided to have some say on. She might have married him, and she might still love him, but she wasn't going to bring a baby into all of it. She'd let Pitch pass the news to her mom.

She didn't care what anybody said or what they, in their infinite armchair wisdom, decided was the reason for her devotion to Rosalee. Her life after high school had become work and Wes, Wes and work. Her friends had gone to college for good or were busy starting families. Her mom was her mom. Right as Reney was stubborn. The mule was the one thing that was Reney's alone. There wasn't a place in their cramped trailer she could call her own. The cattle were Wes's, though it was she who scattered the cubes and broke the ice on the cold mornings because he figured she was up anyway and never stopped to refigure that now that he was home, he should get up and do it himself. The truck she drove some but was never once made to feel it was part hers. Even her closet was shared, and the coveralls she wore were his. Let them think what they would. She loved Rosalee, and what small joy she got out of harnessing her up and giving kiddie rides during rodeo season was hers to keep as far as she was concerned.

Pitch had been beside himself when his mare came up in foal that year. The only thing male and ungelded on the place had been Reney's mom's donkey, the only animal her mom had ever let herself get attached to. The little bastard must have jumped the fence, Pitch said, had his way with the mare, and jumped back over before anybody but the mare knew the difference. So it was, a hybrid molly was born, a barren beast of burden Pitch pretended he'd as soon spit at as see. He acted upset that his beloved quarter horse had wasted a year of her foal-bearing life on something as ugly, unprofitable, and slant-assed as a mule. In truth, he was a sucker for babies of any sort, but Reney's mom insisted they couldn't take on another mouth to feed. Pitch had probably called Reney the minute her mom's truck got out of the driveway. He usually did.

To Reney, the molly was irresistible from the get-go, all antenna ears and wobbly legs. Frying-pan eyes. She had said she would take her before Wes had time to swallow his coffee and get out a complaint. She loaded the little thing into the truck wrapped in one of Nina's quilts and made Wes stop at the feed store for a forty-pound bag of powdered formula.

"I don't have time to play nursemaid to your mom's mule, Reney. Your mom damn sure wouldn't do it for me," Wes said.

"Nobody's asking you to," Reney said, climbing back into the truck with a rubber-nippled bottle tucked under each arm. The molly's eyelids fluttered as she nursed on Wes's finger. Her ears sagged in an upside-down V until Wes pulled his finger back and wiped the slobber on his pants.

"You know the cost of hay."

"I'm not asking, Wes." She leaned over and changed the radio to an eighties station playing a Prince block.

He put the truck in reverse, and neither of them talked on the way home. When they got there, Wes went into the house, leaving Reney to haul Rosalee and the formula to the barn.

For all his softness, Wes carried a mean right punch. Reney had experienced it only twice. They were kids the first time, kids in the kind of thing that starts in the boozy bench seat of a pickup and proceeds to oversized homecoming mums pinned to a girl who thought she didn't care about such rituals. It should have ended in a screaming match at a riverside blowout, with Reney moving on to UT–Austin in the fall and Wes off to the oil field and a younger girl who would make him a baby that fit, just barely, in the palm of his callused hand and grew to fetch beer from the fridge and follow in his footsteps until, if all went right, the kid took a jagged turn and decided to read some books.

It didn't end there. Wes bloodied her nose that night at the river. She was a senior, and he was three years removed from school. She was able to cover the bruising with makeup. She didn't talk to him for almost a month, certain that they were finished and she was off to school soon anyway. She couldn't remember what happened first—the Pell Grant falling through or her taking him back. He'd sat in the DQ parking lot while she worked, leaving notes under the windshield of her beat-up Ford Ranger, pages upon pages filled with his sweet, crooked letters and misspelled words. She refused to look his way, unlocked her truck, and drove away. He even talked to her mom, coming nearly clean, and getting run off their property with a shotgun in the process. Her mom, whose nonunion factory job bumped her pay just enough to disqualify Reney from the Pell, forbade Reney to see him, swore she'd kill him. If it wasn't the heartfelt letters that brought them back together, her mom's mandate must have. Soon they were hand in hand, more in love than ever, and Reney had plans to work for a year and save money to pay for UT on her own the next fall.

The next time is not important except to know that it came, and she was pregnant again, though they did not know it. Wes did not have anything to do with her losing the babies. It was her own misshapen insides that did that. But after the punch and the second lost baby, one that had lodged herself in the wrong place and nearly took Reney with her, Reney'd had enough.

Wes had just left for Wyoming, full of tears and apologies that he would never touch Wild Turkey again and begging her to go back to school if that was what she wanted but to please, just please not leave, because he couldn't live without her and he was a sorry piece of shit that loved her more than life.

She didn't leave, and this time she couldn't say why not. When she started bleeding, she could have gotten word to Wes, but she didn't. She told old Dr. Mac to take care of it for good, close it all off. "You're young," he said. "There is still a chance that you can carry a healthy baby full term. No guarantees, but no guarantees you won't. Don't you want to wait and talk to Wes or your mother?"

"No. I don't want you to either," she said and turned to stare at the giraffes and elephants on the wallpaper. They'd been busy that day and stuck her in a kid's room. Dr. Mac set his flabby jaw as he scribbled something on his clipboard. He didn't say anything else until she woke after the procedure. She always wondered whether his wife knew, and if she did, who else did, but when she told Wes they'd lost another one and that Mac had said it wasn't likely there would be any more to lose, he'd kissed her head, held her, told her they'd keep trying when she was ready.

Of course Reney had dreams. She still dreamed of her great-grandmother, but more often she dreamed of her mother now. They'd always joked about growing old together, since her mom had been a kid herself when she had Reney. Occasionally her dreams included Wes, a different Wes. A Wes who didn't bite his nails and throw them on the carpet or long for magic cattle. She could talk to this Wes about her literature classes and the jokes the instructor made. She could tell him about the headache of filling out a schedule made up of burnouts and half-wits, and he would do more than say, "Cocksuckers ought to pay you more." They packed picnic baskets and laid their heads on the same blanket under the stars without saying a word. Dream Wes loved her for more than who he thought she was in high school, a pretty possession, a Cherokee princess, a wild girl in the good classes, scary from behind the three-point line and sneaky on defense. Of course he had a job. But he didn't have to be rich. That wasn't what she was after. If it had been, maybe she could have figured out how to bring herself to touch sweet, sad Jack, who probably wasn't rich, either, but didn't have to worry about his light bill or how he would fill his sensible-man's car with gas. In her dreams, Reney donned a backpack and trekked through forests and airports alike. She carried candy in her pocket for the children she came across. There was rain. Her mother spoke to her and didn't have to break her back day after day in a factory that might as well have been an oven. At night, Reney didn't have to close the bedroom door to read over the sound of the television. She hadn't given her heart to a mule.

Reney had already changed shirts to get rid of the grease stench and rebraided her hair, but Wes still hadn't called and asked her to make him a Frisco burger with double meat and extra cheese or a Strawberry Cheesecake Blizzard. She tried to get ahead in her reading but couldn't stop checking the window. She was watching what had to be the tenth black diesel pickup turn into the drive-through when Jack passed by her table carrying a load of towels.

"Do you mind if I use the office phone again?" Reney asked.

"Wes?" Jack said.

"He's probably just running late."

"I have to go to Gainesville anyway," Jack said. "I'd be happy to take you to class and pick you up after I run my errands."

"Would it be too much trouble to take me home instead?" Reney asked. "I've got to check on Rosalee." She thought a minute. "I might be able to make my late class."

"I can go to Gainesville anytime," Jack said.

They passed through town not saying much. When the speed limit increased to seventy-five, Jack kept pulling to the shoulder of the two-lane road to let cars pass. He twice took a deep breath as if he were going to say something.

"There's something I've been meaning to say to you, Reney," he said finally.

"Okay?"

"I'm real proud of you."

Reney kept her eyes on the road, clasped her hands around the tattered brown backpack in her lap.

"I just mean you sticking with your classes all this time. That's really something. You're really something."

"Jack."

"I don't mean that in a bad way. Not that." Jack let a tanker truck pass. The wind nearly blew the LeSabre off the road. "Not that I haven't imagined something else, but Reney, you deserve better. You deserve better than all of this."

"Thank you, Jack." Reney had steeled herself to let him down easy. He was a kind man. He had been good to her. She felt a little embarrassed when she saw she wasn't going to have to let him down at all.

"Please, just . . . I've been putting a little money back here and there. You know I don't have anybody to spend it on, and a man can only sponsor so many baseball teams." Jack sighed. "I want you to know that if you ever might find yourself in a situation where you need some money . . . Maybe you want to get closer to school. Really dedicate time to that. Work less, try to knock this thing out? Well. There wouldn't be any strings attached is what I'm saying. I can help." He smiled at Reney. "I want to help you. As a mentor or maybe a friend. As somebody who might like to know how far your dreams and your mind and your work take you. Somebody who imagines it might be the moon. Somebody who wants the moon for you, Reney."

"Get closer to school?" Reney said, trying to understand. She realized that her next thought, stupidly, was: *What about Rosalee?*

She thought she was long past crying over her place in life. It was a place she had made as a girl, and then as a young woman in a wave of stubbornness, and now in near indifference. She hadn't seen community college as a means to an end. She hadn't stopped long enough to consider the end. Motions upon motions, feed the animals, bang the coffee grounds, read the books, fall into bed. Just as she felt her tears would surely spill over and drown them both where they sat in the leather seats of Jack's beige LeSabre on Highway 52, closer to Oklahoma than Austin, almost to the windy patch of home where she'd breathed in so much cow shit and bone-dry dust that it seemed her insides couldn't be made up of anything else, they passed a faded billboard: BONITA, IT'S NOT TOO LATE TO TURN BACK, Y'ALL! Reney cackled.

"I understand this must seem inappropriate," Jack said.

"No," Reney said. She'd embarrassed him. "It's the stupid sign. I'm sorry. It's been a day." They rode for a while before Reney spoke again. "Why would you do this, Jack?"

"Fair question." He drummed his thumbs on the steering wheel, took a big breath. "All I can say is you're strong and bright and you work hard. Of course you're beautiful." He raised a hand, and Reney thought he might put it on her knee, but he dropped it onto the gearshift. "I just want more for you is all. And it's not too late."

Reney watched as a dust devil moved across a fallow pasture. It crossed the road in front of them and moved over a wheat patch so dry the devil grew darker before sucking itself back up into the sky.

"I've been working in the restaurant since I was twelve, you know. I hated my dad for forcing the business on me, but when his heart quit, I was more than ready to run a business. I'll be retiring before long. I'm going to need a GM, somebody good. I've been thinking about what I could offer you to make it worth your while. I know I wouldn't have to worry about a thing." Jack looked over to her and tried to smile.

She knew she was supposed to feel something, excitement, nervousness, relief. She felt nothing. She wished she could say something, but Jack rescued her.

"This morning, see. I was running the numbers again, and then you came in troubled the way you were. I just . . . it breaks my heart to think of you here. I know the money would tie you to this place. I understand how that works."

"This is my road, Jack."

The blinker was the only sound until the tires bumped over the cattle guard. Reney noticed the rusted-out stock trailer hooked to Wes's truck. Jack eased in next to it and killed the engine.

"I mean it. The offer is good, Reney. Both of them, I suppose. Think about what you want to do."

When Reney saw Wes emerge from the barn, she pushed her backpack tightly to her stomach, as if it could hold her together. He had a Coors Light in his hand, and she could see from his walk he'd had a few. He was limping and filthy. She had probably hated him for some time. Real quick, she leaned over to Jack, pressed her cheek to his, and squeezed.

"Thank you, Jack. I don't know what to say." She pulled him tighter. "You've been good to me."

Reney pushed her shoulder into the door to open it against the wind. She was surprised to see Wes standing over her. When she let go of the door, Wes caught it and leaned into the car.

"Jack."

"Hi, Wes," Jack said. "Some kind of wind out there." He started the engine.

"Why don't you stick around? See the ranch." Wes popped the thin aluminum of his beer can with his thumb. "Give us your businessman's eye?"

Jack managed a laugh, smoothed his tie.

"Won't take long." Wes let the wind slam the car door.

"Wes," Reney said.

"You don't want to share your nice little moment with me?"

Behind them, Jack cracked the car door open and eased a foot onto the gravel.

"He offered me a promotion, Wes. I was thanking him."

"You fix your hair for him? Put on lipstick?"

Jack stood on the other side of the car now, watching.

"Fancy car. Le-Sabre," Wes said. "That French or Spanish?"

"French," Jack said, smiling weakly.

"For what? 'I got a stiffy, but my tie covers it.'" Wes started toward Jack.

"Wes, don't," Reney said.

"I think it means 'the saber,'" Jack said quietly.

"Are you being smart with me?" Wes said.

Reney mouthed "go" over Wes's shoulder, and Jack lurched for his door. Wes sneered but didn't go after him. Once in the car, Jack quickly locked the door.

"Are you okay?" he yelled through the cracked window.

"Just leave!" Reney shouted.

"About time you give her a raise. She runs the fucking place," Wes growled. He kicked in the front fender as Jack fumbled with the gearshift.

As Jack reversed up the drive, Reney grabbed Wes by the arm. He threw her off him, and everything stopped for a moment.

She'd hit the driveway cheek first. She sat up working her jaw. Reney saw Jack stopped at the end of the driveway, squinting into his cellular phone. He pressed it to his ear. She wondered whether she could make it to the car, but Wes started after Jack first. Jack, with one last look at Reney, sped away, spraying gravel on them both. Wes picked up a rock and flung it. He watched it bounce across the highway. Then he saw Reney on the ground.

"You ain't hurt, are you?" he said, not really asking a question. He squatted over her and tried to pick a speck of gravel from her face.

Reney spit grit and blood as she stood up. Wes was waiting. He needed her to tell him it was okay again.

"We had one job between us, Wes. Jack's going to make me GM, but I guess you took care of that."

"One job?" Wes said. He looked hurt. "Your mule's in the barn," he said and limped toward the doorway.

Reney thought about leaving, just taking off without another word. There was the truck. She had her keys. She looked around. Her backpack lay in the dirt nearby. What did she need from the house? Nothing she would miss. She could do this now, this thing her mother had never quite pulled off. But of course Reney couldn't just leave. She'd never been smart or strong or brave enough to just leave.

When she walked into the dark barn, it took a moment to see Rosalee tied up in front of the one good stall. Reney noticed that Rowdy was lying much too close to Rosalee.

"There's my girl," Reney said. The mule raised her nose and tried to make her always strange half-horse, half-donkey bray, but it sounded like wind blowing through a hole in a piece of tin. As Reney's eyes adjusted, she saw that the mule was bleeding from her hocks. She knelt to look closer but recoiled. Wes appeared above her.

"She's chewed through to the bone, Wes. What happened?"

"I went out to work on the fence and look for the calf. When I found them, there was a coyote with its head kicked in lying next to what was left of the calf. Another one was good as dead. Three or four kept circling until I shot one of them."

Reney walked to Rosalee's head. The mule rubbed her halter on Reney's shoulder. Reney gasped when she saw that one of her ears was a bloody stump. Usually the mule kept working the halter until she got it slipped off. This time, she left her head resting on Reney.

"They got her nose and up under her jaw too," Wes said.

"I'm so sorry, girl." Reney leaned into the mule's neck.

"Vet's on his way," Wes said. He pulled a pint bottle from his back pocket and drank. "He said if she's already taken two calves, she won't ever be broke of it. But I don't even care about that."

He tried to stroke Reney's hair, but she jerked away.

"Today after I dropped you off, I went on home, and I thought about you and me the whole way. I went out to fix the fence and find your mule. She kicked me in the thigh trying to keep me away from a dead calf. Took me an hour to drag her off it and get her in the trailer. But I called the vet to get her taken care of. All for you, Reney."

Rosalee began to pull against the rope, and the iron frame of the barn groaned.

"Then I see you hugging on him?" Wes began to cry. "We was going to make better of ourselves. I've about got Sammy talked into leasing me a hundred acres real cheap. He's going to sell me a good bunch of calves. This year was our year, Reney."

He kicked the stall door. The frame rattled the tin from one end of the barn to the other. Rosalee pulled harder against the rope.

"Easy, girl. Come on, now," Reney said. She stroked the mule's shoulder. The wound in Rosalee's neck had started bleeding badly again. Blood streamed down her chest and both legs onto the floor, pooling in the dust.

"Tell me you ain't fucking him, Reney."

"When did you find her, Wes?"

"I don't know."

Reney steadily moved her hands over the mule's bloody flesh, calming her. "How long have you left her here like this?"

"I couldn't do it, Reney. I tried. The vet was tied up, but he'll be here soon." He tossed the bottle aside and started for the door.

Finally, Rosalee filled her belly with air and sighed. Reney rubbed the soft middle of the ear that curled forward at the tip.

"I'll let all this go," Wes said, appearing in the doorway again, a silhouette with a shotgun for an arm. "We'll work it out. I don't want you to serve another man his coffee for the rest of your days."

Reney patted the mule one more time and straightened. She heard nothing except her own footsteps on the hard dirt floor.

"Give me the gun, Wes." She put her hand on the small of his back.

"I'm sorry, Reney." He handed her the gun butt first, crumpling at the waist onto her.

"I know, Wes," she said, and it was true. She believed that he felt bad. He always felt bad, but right then, the smell of his whiskey breath mixed with the blood and hay and shit was choking her.

The sound of the shot moved across the barn in waves, and the frame shook like it might fall in on them. Rosalee's legs folded up under her like she was resting, but her head, held tight to the barn by the rope, pointed toward the roof.

Reney walked out past Wes, whose face had gone slack. She found her backpack and climbed up into the big diesel, placing the shotgun next to the gearshift. She drove away slowly, carefully, checking her mirrors as the trailer rattled over the cattle guard.

At the highway, she passed the vet and, not far behind, a deputy who didn't seem to be in any particular hurry. She checked her watch. Pulling the trailer, she felt the truck's power. She pushed the engine until it howled before shifting up. This is what the truck was made for, to haul a load, to work. She thought about swinging by her mom and Pitch's, but she passed seventy-five with ease, then eighty, eighty-five, and ninety into town as she hit the green light. She drove on past the Branding Iron, where some form of Bonita royalty was surely holding court, and didn't slow at the DQ with its grease stink, blue hairs, and benevolent cowards. On the other side of town, she found the limits of the truck, settled into a steady cruise just shy of flying. When she ran out of gas, she shouldered her backpack and walked.

Then Sings My Soul

Mose Lee's dearly departed mama had been a shut-in and a woman of tremendous size. He'd spent his twenty-six years at her bedside or close by, with little thought beyond a world where the bluestem grew to the swept porch and the sound of yapping coyotes filled the night air. He carried her signed disability checks to the grocery store and delivered their monthly payments, following instructions she wrote in a pocket spiral notepad. When there was something left, he surprised her with crossword puzzles and Baked Lays for her cholesterol.

Each night, she helped him tally their existence in a composition notebook, reminding him when to carry, when to borrow. Preparing him, she said. They read Scriptures in her room on Sundays. She scratched his head as they watched their evening shows. Neighbors might have said she turned him backward, hiding him from the world with her girth. Neighbors might have said he never had a chance for frontward what with a whale for a mother and such a pitiful moron for a likely father. As it was, the old Birdwell place was the only other house on all of Dump Road, and it sat busted and empty-eyed on the little knob that looked down on Mose and his mother. There were no neighbors to talk.

That is until the morning of the funeral when a big Ford pulled an Airstream up to the Birdwell place, bringing with it the smacks of hammers. Mose hardly noticed the commotion when he was dropped at his doorstep by Justine Barnes, a sailor-mouthed Indian lady who lived on the edge of town and never passed him on the side of the road without stopping to offer a ride. He balanced Justine's foil-covered Pyrex dishes on his knee and stumbled inside. A black bobtailed cat ran through his legs out the door. A saw screeched up the hill. Someone laughed.

Grief filled all of the spaces inside the small house that was now his. It found its way between the few shirts hanging in his closet, clattered the wire hangers, and blew lightbulbs he'd just replaced. It hovered over the kitchen sink, wilting the little seedlings he had growing on the windowsill, and crept into his outlets, burning the sockets black. At night, it sucked the breeze out of his room. The blades of his fan sat still or ticked slowly backward.

* * *

A white Jeep Cherokee pulled into the bare patch in front of the house where Mose crouched sweating over a rusted tiller. His inclination was to run and hide, afraid somebody was there to talk about moving on after the death of a loved one or to ask him to sign more papers. The driver put large, expensive-looking sunglasses on top of her curly head and waved. Her hair lit up fiery red in the sunshine. "I'm your new neighbor, Marni," she said. "How you doing?"

"Making it alright," Mose lied. He wiped his hands on the back pocket of his pants, looked back at the empty house, and dabbed his eyes with a bandana. "Planting beets."

Marni looked past him to the sad little sprouts he had lined up in a neat row of school-size red-and-white milk cartons. "Beets?" she asked, stepping out.

"Yes, ma'am. They're supposed to be good for the blood." He thumbed the sharp blades of his hipbones where a thin leather belt gathered his pants.

His mother had been rolled on the count of three by strangers in blue latex gloves. The two men had talked about a softball tournament as they waited for extra hands to help jam a horrible tarp beneath her body. Mose had shrunk into the corner breathing sawdust as they cut through her bedroom wall and backed the ambulance. At night when he let himself, he worried about who would fetch his groceries, who would put on his socks when he couldn't bend to do it himself. Though he was a birdlike man, with one leg visibly shorter than the other, he had taken to doing pushups and jogging to the dump and back before the sun rose.

"I'm afraid your sprouts might be drying out," Marni said. She knelt down in her white capri pants and stuck a finger in the soil. "You're going to need some shade for them, Mose. That's your name, isn't it? Mose Lee?"

Mose gave a slight nod and picked at the side of his thumb.

"Nice to meet you, but honey, I'm afraid beets are a spring plant. That temperature gauge has been stuck on a hundred for a month. Were you thinking to plant anything else?"

He pulled a crinkled store display from his back pocket that trumpeted the wonders of raw beets.

"Well, the first thing to do is get them out of this afternoon sun. Might be too much of a good thing." Marni straightened and looked around, and Mose noticed a bead of sweat and makeup running down her temple. Spotting a spigot on the side of the house, she gathered up all the milk cartons she could carry and motioned for Mose to follow.

With all of the seedlings cooled and watered, Marni surveyed the yard and asked Mose where they were going. He pointed.

"If you want to give them a chance, you better give them some cover. What about over here on the side? They'll be closer to water, and they'll get shade in the hottest part of the day." Marni dusted her hands. "Tiller trouble?"

Mose nodded.

"Well, if it'll help you get them in the ground, you can borrow ours. Beets are good for you, but I'm not sure what they're going to think about this damn clay we got out here, much less August."

"You said you was my neighbor?" Mose asked.

"Look at me. I get to talking and plumb forget what I came over here for in the first place. We bought the old Birdwell place—my partner, Stevie, and I—but that old thing's going to need a lot of work. A whole lot if we're going to be out of that cracker-box travel trailer by the time school starts."

Mose caught himself staring at a spot of red dirt on her thigh. When she repeated herself, he jerked his eyes to meet hers.

"So"—she paused—"we'll be hauling water from town until we get the well redug, and I was wondering if we might come over and use your spigot sometimes. We'd be happy to pay you."

"We got good well water," Mose said. "Don't need to pay for it."

"The other thing I was wondering is if you might want some work? Stevie thinks we can do it all." She leaned in, as if to share a secret with him. "I have my doubts. I thought we might hire you to help with the heavy lifting. Stevie's the new middle school science teacher and girls' coach, and I'm going to be teaching special ed. Coach Gilbert recommended

I talk to you when I told him where I'd be living. Said you were a real good hand."

Mose blushed. "I'd appreciate the work. Especially now that Mama's gone." The bobtailed cat came running up from behind the house and began to curl itself around Mose's spindly legs. "I'm sorry you got your pants dirty."

"Hell, I know better than to wear white pants in the country." She looked toward the hammering sounds coming from up the hill as she slid into the truck. "But it's good to be back."

"Justine Barnes gave me more casserole and brisket than I can eat, if you're hungry." Mose picked up the cat and scratched its chin. "She's the Indian lady in town who gives me rides and lets me use her phone sometimes. Mama always said I'm Indian, too, on my great-grandmother's side."

"I remember her daughter. Good ballplayer," Marni said. "Anyway, it's real sweet of you to offer, Mose, but I better get up there and see what Stevie's got tore up."

After she pulled away with a quick wave and a honk, Mose watched her truck curve over the hillside. Dust lingered in the still heat. He waited until he heard the door slam and the high pitch of her voice float down to him. Then he stomped his feet on the front porch and went inside and pulled a dish out of the refrigerator. The cat meowed and purred against the chair leg.

He pulled the foil off and forked through the melted, re-refrigerated cheese. Congealed grease floated on top of a white, peppered sauce. He took a bite and looked toward his mother's room. For a minute he forgot that she wasn't lying back there ready to scratch his head when his eyes grew heavy.

Her door was shut, as it had been since he'd stolen into the room sobbing to sift through the closet for a good dress, none of which fit her for the funeral, leaving the funeral director to drape two rose-print sheets over her, gathering them around her with safety pins. Mose had felt ashamed that she didn't have a dress, but she looked beautiful and at rest lying there. Now there was the hole cut six feet wide in her wall. Insulation and wiring hung down like entrails.

Mose swallowed a sob, and cold potatoes stuck in his throat. Choking, he grabbed for a drink of water that only made it worse. He knocked the chair back and doubled over, hands on his knees, until his face turned red and his eyes watered. He ran out the open door onto the porch and leaned over the railing gagging. After he had thrown up everything, he sat down on the steps, wiping the spit from his beard with the back of his arm. The sounds of work floated down from the hill while the sun set around him. After a while, the cat slipped through the door, sat on his lap, and licked white gravy off its paws, purring into Mose's beard.

The next day Mose showed up at the travel trailer at 6:00 a.m. The tin door gave under his knuckles when he knocked. "I wanted to see if y'all needed some help," he yelled, running the brim of a stained mesh cap through his hands. "I can come back."

"Open up," Marni yelled. She sat in a white robe at the tiny fold-down table cuddling a mug, her mop of curly hair piled high on her head. She waved him inside, offering coffee.

"I can't believe Coach Gilbert is still at it," she said. "He was coaching the boys when I was playing. Running four corners half the game, screaming his fool head off. Kicked me off the bus once for kissing Lew Johnson in the back seat on the way home from Krum. Of course Lew didn't have to find a ride home. He ran four corners!"

As manager of the boys' basketball team, Mose had sat in the front seat of a Blue Bird bus, his forehead pressed to the rectangular sliding glass window as he watched Orion, the Hunter, stretch above the mesquite and sleeping cattle. He poked his nose into the metroplex as a junior when the team with no better than a 50-50 record had lucked into the regional tournament by way of a putrid district and a half-court miracle lobbed at the buzzer.

He was supposed to keep the stat sheet but didn't have a head for numbers. He had complained to his mother how the figures jumped around on the page and how the players prodded him.

"Don't let them run you off, Mosey of mine," she'd said. "Just listen to Coach and do your best."

In the added pressure of the big game, he kept confusing the assist column with the point column, and it was easier for the lanky, acne-faced boys to focus on Mose's managerial skills instead of the drubbing they took at the hands of a 1A team whose home gym sat in the middle of a wheat field.

When Coach nodded off on the way home, the boys made a game of tossing tape balls at Mose's head, a game at which they surprisingly excelled and therefore did not let up on. Instead of charging down the aisle, fists swinging, Mose sat lower in his seat and leaned his forehead against the vibrating glass. He kept his gaze on the Hunter, closing his eyes to his own weakness as the bus carried him back home. In his senior year he was not asked to return.

"Coach Gilbert was real good to me. I had to quit on account of Mama's health." Mose immediately felt bad for his lie. "Well," he said. "She needed somebody here."

"You sure loved your mama, didn't you."

Mose passed his fingers through his beard and looked at the floor.

"I'm so sorry, Mose."

"Just over a week ago she was talking about us planting a good garden next year," Mose said, his voice low. "She asked me every day how many more milks I had to go to get all my seeds planted."

When she'd lost her appetite, he bought baby carrots instead of Ore-Idas, decided to grow some beets. He began to talk about them taking walks. He knew now that he should have gone for help.

"Her breath wasn't nothing but a whisper," he said. "I couldn't bring myself to leave her. I opened all the windows wide and patted her face with a wet washcloth. I sang the main part of her favorite hymn like a broken record because that's all I could remember. I finally ran for a phone as fast as I could, but she was gone when the fire truck pulled up."

Marni motioned for Mose to sit on the vinyl bench beside her, but he was still talking at the floor.

"Them EMTs handled her like a sick dog didn't nobody want to touch." He shook out his bandana and touched it to his eyes. "They sat her down to catch their breath and let her gown fall open. Said there wasn't room for me to ride to the hospital with them."

"It sounds like she was sick for a long time."

"I could have planted beets last year. I could have spent more time with her instead of down at the tank fishing or pilfering around the stores when I went into town," Mose said. He bit the skin on the side of his thumb. "I should have got them there sooner."

Stevie, a tall woman with a dark bob tied in a green scarf, pushed through a curtain that hid the bedroom at the back of the trailer. Mose felt his face warm. He didn't know these ladies, and here he was blubbering on.

"Mose, this is Stevie."

"It's a pleasure." Stevie said. She dropped onto the bench beside Marni and jerked twice on each lace of her new work boots.

"Mose was just telling me about—" Marni started, but Mose cut her off.

"Y'all aim to sell the old Birdwell place after you fix it up?"

"We're going to live here, Mose," Marni said.

Mose studied his thumb. "You said y'all are *partners*?"

Stevie looked up from her boots and shook her head, giving Marni an I-told-you-so look.

"Yes, honey," Marni began. "We're partners." She sighed and began again. "In the sense that we can't get legally married because the state of Texas is just short of the Dark Ages when it comes to these things? Stevie is my wife. I'm hers. I thought that was clear yesterday."

"I'm sorry," Mose said. "I didn't know ladies could marry like that."

"Ladies can't marry like *that*," Stevie said, walking to the small half fridge and pulling out orange juice. "Not here."

"I'm real sorry," Mose said, stepping toward the door.

"Sorry for what?" Marni said.

"I don't know," Mose said. "I didn't know. I never . . ."

"Met lesbians before?" Stevie asked putting the juice box in the trash.

"I guess not."

"Well, Mose, meet the lesbians. Lesbians," Stevie said, sweeping her hand around the trailer, "meet Mose."

"You still want the work?" Marni asked. Stevie crossed her arms and legs and leaned against the small stove.

Mose didn't know what to say. He'd never had to consider what he thought of it before. It was nice to think of people up here, and he guessed it couldn't hurt to help them with the house. His mama's disabilities wouldn't be coming anymore, and he couldn't live off catfish.

"I reckon so," Mose said, placing his hand on the small latch. It was warm from the sun that was already brutal and peeking over the hill. A fat buzzing fly bounced, trapped in the curtain.

"Can you swing a hammer?" Stevie asked.

Marni snorted into her cup.

Mose cut his eyes at Marni, unsure if he had done something else to make himself look foolish. He hadn't let go of the latch. "Busted my thumbs enough to aim straight, I guess."

"It's not you, Mose. I've never in my life heard Stevie say 'swing a hammer.'"

"I built our garden boxes in Austin and rehung the door that got broken during your 'solstice party,'" Stevie said.

Marni made a big show of winking at Mose.

"Oh, you're funny. So funny I almost forgot we were sitting in a roasting oven in the world's last dead zone, next to a . . . " Stevie searched for the right word as she disappeared into the back of the trailer again. After a cheap drawer snapped shut, she yelled, "Rattrap . . . on *Dump Road!*"

"I told you we can petition the county to change the name. You wanted to move here, too, my dear," Marni yelled.

Mose liked the way Marni's eyes sparkled and the way she seemed to be letting him in on some kind of good time.

155

He let go of the door latch and looked through the curtain at the broken, gray house. The fly looped lazily free, and Mose caught it between his hands, opened the door, and let it go. "The old Birdwell place used to be a mansion," he said. The heat pushed at his legs, almost knocked him over.

"Finest farmhouse on the south side of town when my mama was a girl," Marni said. "Old man Birdwell raised Holsteins. This was when people still had a milk cow if they could afford one, but Birdwell saw the time coming when people would have to work away from the farm. He started shipping his milk around to stores and doorsteps before anybody else thought to."

"Mama said the same thing."

"It's true. And shut that door. You're letting all hell loose in here," Marni said. "Don't worry about Stevie. She doesn't like having to drive into town to get cell service. Some meth heads gave her mess outside the DQ yesterday. Called us names when we wouldn't give them money for 'gas.'" Marni made air quotes.

"Skinny fellas?" Mose asked. "I seen them the last time I walked to town for groceries. They was still asking for gas?"

"I don't think it's gas they are after, Mose," Marni said. She shrugged. "It's changing all over, I guess. Anyway, Stevie's fine. If we get Dish installed before training camp, she'll be right at home. She wanted to move to the country too. Live out some weird redneck fantasies." She pointed to a shotgun leaning in the corner next to a golf club. "She's getting ready for dove season," she said.

Mose and Stevie sweated through gutting the old horsehair plaster without much talk, except when Marni was with them. Things went smoother then. Mose worked through the hottest part of the day, like a mule, pausing only to talk quietly to the black cat that followed him up the hill every morning. Stevie seemed uncomfortable with the chaos of their days, unsure of Mose. She was prone to fits of cursing when she wasn't walking around muttering "measure twice, cut once." She developed a habit of flicking her tape measure and hitting golf balls into the pasture when the work became too tedious. With Marni there, the engine hummed along, her providing humor and patience to Mose's dogged earnestness and Stevie's precision. The three had started a competition to see who could pry the biggest piece of plaster off intact, but it continued to crumble in tiny pieces, exposing the skeleton of the house one lath rib at a time.

After Mose put in twelve hours' work on the first day without a bite, Marni had begun making him lunch and pushing water on him. Now she and Stevie sat side by side trading bites of an apple, tinfoil from their hummus sandwiches wadded up beside them. An ant crawled over Mose's pecked-at turkey sandwich. The cat materialized, as it had every day at lunchtime, to sit politely on its haunches waiting.

"Sure you can't eat just a little, Mose?" Marni asked.

"He doesn't need you mothering him," Stevie said. "He'll eat when he's ready."

Marni's sharp glance at Stevie made Mose think they might have talked about this before. He wasn't sure whether to feel grateful to or hurt by Stevie.

"How about those beets?" Marni said. "They taking ahold?"

"Ain't got them in the ground yet," Mose said. He draped a wet bandana across his neck. He'd become so caught up in their old house that he'd forgotten about his garden. He flicked the ant off the sandwich and wrapped it back up. "They probably died."

"Tell you what let's do," Marni said. She stretched and rested her head on Stevie's shoulder. "We've got to drop my Jeep off in town because the tailpipe rattled loose on this damn road. We'll come back and finish the kitchen, then let's go plant your beets."

"They'll be dead for sure if we're waiting on the kitchen," Stevie said. She swatted a wasp out of the air, and Marni yelped.

"Have you been keeping track of your hours, like we discussed?" Stevie asked.

"Anything is fine," Mose said. He leaned heavily on his shovel to stand.

"We're at fifty-two hours, so five hundred and twenty dollars." Stevie looked at her watch. "Plus the rest of today."

Mose shrugged his shoulders. Again, he didn't know whether to feel grateful or hurt. He wasn't sure he'd ever held that much money at once. But helping these ladies didn't feel too much like work right now. Even when it was just him and Stevie.

"We'll run by the bank and get you cash," Stevie said. "Fair's fair."

"You look a little peaked, Mose," Marni said. "Why don't you go home, drink you some water, and sit in the cool?"

Mose raised his hand over his shoulder as he walked into the doorway of the old house.

"Don't forget your dust mask, then!" Marni shouted. "Who knows what we're unearthing in there."

Marni said she wouldn't hear of leaving Mose to put the plants in the ground alone, no matter how much he protested. Surprisingly, Stevie, too, insisted, saying something about the carbon cycle and what goes around comes around. It didn't take long with their new tiller to put a patch alongside the house big enough for the beet plants and the fall plants that Marni insisted on.

When they finished, the three stood looking down on the milk cartons and their sad contents. The heat hadn't let up, and the beet leaves hung down the side of the cartons, limp and pale. Mose wobbled and then knelt to the ground.

"Are you okay?" Marni asked. "You don't look good."

"I killed them," Mose said, the thought sending a shudder through his heart.

"Just get them in the ground and see what the good Lord has in store," Marni said.

"I can't even keep plants alive," Mose said, holding the leaves of a tiny cluster in his fingers.

"I don't want to hear it, Mose. The weather's not your fault. Now get up, dust yourself off, and help me make them a place in the ground."

Marni stood above Mose, blocking the evening sun where it was beginning to set in a giant fiery ball on the hill. She glowed at the edges, and as Mose squinted and fixed his eyes around her, she lit up in a halo of color.

Stevie appeared beside her, and both of them were enveloped in the light. Mose fell back, dazed. For a minute there was nothing. Summer faded away, and all was cool darkness. Then a glow beyond his eyelids carried him along with it, or after it, like a leaf pulled into the channel of a creek. Mose awoke to Stevie slapping her hands.

"Hello? Would you like to plant your beets now?"

"You okay?" Marni asked.

"I went woozy there for a minute," Mose said.

Marni cupped his cheek in her palm. "You have to eat something, Mose."

"Ain't had an appetite."

"Doesn't matter. In times like these, you've got to eat when you're not hungry. Sleep when you can't. I know the world's upside down."

From the back of the truck came the sound of bagged ice being broken up. Stevie came around with an orange cooler and filled it with water from the hose. Marni went inside for glasses, leaving Stevie and Mose alone.

"Sorry for being trouble," Mose said. "I thought I saw something in the sun, and it shook me is all. Must have got too hot out here."

"Saw something?" Stevie said, settling onto the ground next to him.

"I don't know." Mose pointed toward the sunset. "I saw you and Marni in the sun, and colors kind of ran together. It was dark for a minute; then my eyes lit up like God was waving a sparkler for me to chase after."

Marni came out with three jelly tumblers and she filled one for each of them. Stevie poured hers down Mose's neck, and he leaned forward and hung his head, catching his breath. It felt like heaven to him.

"You know," said Stevie, "when I lost Mom last year, I couldn't eat either. The only thing I could do with myself is shoot free throws. Hundreds of them at a time. For hours one after another, nobody to rebound. Just me. Sometimes I couldn't see the bucket for the tears, but I kept shooting. I shot so many free throws I went blind. I didn't need to see. I heard what I needed, heard where I pushed it too far with my thumb, gave it too much leg. Heard it when I was dead on and the net cried with me. I shot until I was hungry. I shot myself to sleep. I shot until I could talk to Marni again." Stevie rubbed condensation from her glass. "You need to find you your free throws."

Mose blew sweat and water off his lip and rubbed stinging salt from his eyes.

"You want to go inside and lie down, finish this up tomorrow?"

"I want them in the ground," Mose said and motioned toward the sun. "Sure is pretty."

They sat there on the ground listening to the pumping units move oil and watching the sun until it was nothing but a line of fire on the far horizon. Then the three pulled the milk cartons close and put their hands in the dirt, making room for the little plants, and for no good reason, they planted them in a circle, with the biggest, best-looking clump in the center of it. They let the hose run free over each plant, listening to night sounds emerge. The women would leave only when they were sure that Mose had plenty of water and he had promised that he really would eat as soon as he could.

Mose watched them pull up the hill to their home, and he knew they would talk about his spell, but he didn't care. He lay down in the dirt and felt the cool of the soil against his cheek, and he did not close his eyes until the stars became his blanket and even the bullbats and cicadas began to quiet.

He woke to the rattle of a car over the rutted road. The ground was still cool after the soaking Marni had given it, and he had fallen into a deeper sleep than any he'd had since his mama passed. He lay still, listening to the purr of the cat that was curled up in the crook between his shoulder and neck. It took him a minute to know where he was. When he sat up, he was confused by the taillights that bounced their way up the hillside.

The lights made long, red rectangles that didn't belong to Marni's Jeep or Stevie's Ford. It was an old car; that much he could tell. The car got closer to the top of the hill; another second and the brake lights came on. Then the lights were killed, and in the still night, Mose could hear a car door being pressed shut so as to not make any sound.

Mose bolted upright, and before he had time to think what to do or who it might be that was creeping up the hillside in the dark, his feet were dragging him as fast as they could up the road. He heard a scream just as he crested the hill and the Airstream came into view. The door hung open, and a light was flipped on in the bedroom. A beat-up gold-colored car sat out front.

Mose's breath caught in his throat. This wasn't how it was supposed to go, not tonight after the light and the earth they had toiled over. In two leaps, he was on the tiny steps and in the door.

Marni ran into the kitchen. Eyes wide, mouth agape, she wasn't making any sound.

Mose glanced into the corner where the new shotgun was supposed to be. It wasn't there. Just the golf club. In an instant, a man dragged Marni down from behind, and Mose had the club in hand. Then he froze.

"You got no business here," the man said to Mose as he slammed his skinny knees into Marni's arms and hovered over her. Though greasy blond hair covered the man's eyes, Mose recognized him. One of the men asking for gas money.

"My purse is on the counter. There's a checkbook and cash. Take it. Truck keys are in there too." Marni said.

"Saw you and that other one in town," the man said. He leaned his face to hers and swept his hair back with a snap of his head.

Marni bucked and jerked away. Then she seemed to almost relax. She breathed deep and looked hard at Mose. "Go get help," she whispered, the words breaking in two as the man punched her in the mouth.

Mose caught the man's cheekbone with the club. The man stayed down long enough for Marni to roll to her side and push herself halfway up.

There was a quick commotion and a shout from the back, and then another man burst from the bedroom dragging Stevie by the wrist. He had her shotgun in his other hand, but Stevie didn't look afraid so much as angry. The man raised the shotgun but relaxed his grip on Stevie to steady the barrel.

Marni screamed as Mose leapt forward. Mose saw the gun steady just as Stevie took up a claw hammer from the little kitchen bar and swung. He heard the blast only after he was already knocked back, bleeding into the rug. And then everything went away. No lights, nothing.

Mose saw his cat first. Something he couldn't see had him pinned to the floor, and his cat was kneading dough in the cool wet that was his chest. He felt like the cold earth he'd slept on had seeped into him, except he wasn't in the garden anymore. He couldn't move his right arm. When he tried to tell the cat to stop, he couldn't get the words out. He realized without looking that his arm was broken just below the shoulder and his bicep was mangled. He moved his left hand along his chest but didn't feel any big holes. The bulk of the birdshot had hit him in the arm and spattered the wall behind him.

Past his feet, he saw the red tangle of Marni's hair. He blinked, tried to swallow. To his left, the door gaped open in the dark. He tried to push himself upright but could not. As he reached for the golf club as a brace, he heard Stevie's voice.

"Come on, Mose," she said. "Come back to us."

Stevie slouched against the bar cabinets, legs splayed. He hadn't seen her before, but it was her lap that Marni's head rested upon. The shotgun rested next to Stevie. The man who'd had the shotgun lay in a halo of blood, a tea towel over his head. The other man seemed to be gone. Mose wanted to check on Marni.

"Where are you shot, Mose?"

Mose worked hard to steady his breath as he closed his eyes and leaned his good arm into the golf club. He thought he heard a faint moan, but when he looked up, Stevie seemed just the same. He still hadn't seen Marni's face.

"Is Marni okay?" Mose asked. "Stevie, is she going to be okay?"

"We need help, Mose. Can you walk?"

"What's wrong with her?"

"Can you walk?"

"I don't know!" Mose shouted.

"The other guy had a gun, too, Mose. He took off in the truck. We need you to go get help."

Mose finally took a good look at Stevie. Her face was pale. She held Marni tightly with one hand. The other she had pressed into a red bloom in her own calf. Marni's chest was softly rising and falling.

"I don't know if I can run, Mose. I don't want to leave her."

Mose wanted to kiss Stevie's hand and try to get Marni to wake up, but he was scared to bend down. He patted Stevie on the head.

"She's lost a lot of blood."

"Be just fine," Mose said. "Promise." He didn't know where the words came from, but they came, low and soft. He could not take them back, so he wobbled onto the steps. The sound of oil being brought up from the ground clanged around him.

He checked the ignition of the beat-up old car for keys, but it was empty. The cat stood in the road looking back, waiting. Stepping into the dust, he began to walk. Then he began to trot, slowly at first, keeping ragged time with the pumping units. A fire burned in his shoulder. One arm hung limp, cradled by the good one. The cat stayed a pace ahead, stopping to wait every few yards.

Near the bottom of the hill, gravity yanked at him, and he tumbled heels over elbows, dust coating blood. Gravel stuck to his forehead and cheek. Mose rolled onto his back. The night sky shimmered, in and out of focus. The cool earth soothed him, and he did not have the courage to fight such a force.

The cat appeared again, purring. Just above her, Mose saw that Orion was finally making his appearance low in the summer sky. His belt pointed higher into the heavens, and his bow was drawn, ready to fend off creatures Mose couldn't make out.

Mose tracked the cat over his shoulder. She skittered over the steps until she sat on the porch of his house. The wind blew over him, moving the insulation that hung from the hole Mose still hadn't patched in the house that was empty, all corners and rectangles. He looked back up into the sky, where everything looped into being, never beginning, never ending.

Mose imagined his mama up there, stars for eyes, healthy, and smiling like she was in the picture that hung in the hallway, the one that showed her caught somewhere between woman and girl, squatting before a tiny snowman in a yard that showed the patches of dirt where she'd rolled the snow away. He imagined Marni, ringlets of fire for hair, moving beside his mama, talking with her, on and on forever, looping back around when they went out of sight, always coming back.

Mose sobbed into the ground and cursed himself for being a weak man. He fought himself onto his hands and knees and almost fell back down. His arm was done. He let his head hang between his shoulders and closed his eyes against the dizzy sick feeling pulling at him. Pushing himself upright, he faced east and began to move down the road past home, where the horizon was beginning to glow and Orion was already fading.

He moved in unsteady, chugging steps that scattered gravel. Morning birds stirred on the fence posts and called out to one another. The stars were growing dim, but he knew they were still there up above, watching. He kept moving. Mose swung his head to fight the darkness and gravity. Ahead, a bobcat and two lanky kittens ran halfway across the road and paused to watch him approach before gliding into the weeds.

He picked up speed. Forces began to move inside him that he now knew he'd saved up. In their rise and fall, his legs felt hollow, grew lighter than air. Where his heels had been, wings seemed to sprout. Dust plumed behind him, and the sounds of the birds and the oil field that had always been his home faded. All he had to do was lift one leg at a time, and the glow on the horizon got closer, burned brighter. At the end of the road was another dirt road, and down that one, a highway where just on the edge of town lived Justine Barnes in a house with a phone. This time, Mose knew he could make it.

You'll Be Honest,
You'll Be Brave

Justine pulled into Lula's as the morning sun began to glow behind the hills. She sat in her truck trying to massage the feeling back into her legs after the long drive, as sleepy birds chirped from the power line on the far side of the gravel road. After being on the Cherokee Nation's list for so long that she forgot she was on it, Lula had finally gotten her dream house in the country. The small three-bedroom rancher with green shutters overlooked Little Locust Creek, where a cloud of fog wafted into the humid air, leaving a dreamy haze over everything. Under different circumstances it would be a peaceful place to come home to.

Sheila already had her purse on her arm when Justine stepped stiffly inside. Sheila's eyes looked tired, but her bun, teased and sprayed at the back of her head, didn't betray a single stray hair. She gave Justine a long hug.

"Sorry I have to get to work, Teeny," Sheila said. "I wish I could stay with you."

"Don't know what we'd do without you," Justine said. She looked toward the closed bedroom door. No matter how Justine tried to square things in her mind or heart, coming home broke her open. She was not accustomed to being unable to contain what spilled out. "How is she?"

"Sleeping now," Sheila said, leading Justine into the kitchen. "She hasn't had a spell since right after I got here yesterday." Sheila opened the fridge and pulled out a big mason jar of brown liquid. "I made her some bone broth. That might perk her up some."

Justine hugged Sheila again and began to cry. She could rest her head on Sheila's, so she did.

Sheila, tiny and full of movement even at rest, always made Justine think of Reney. Sheila had gone back to the church—and Samuel—after Justine and Reney moved back to Texas that last time. With baby crow's-feet in the corners of her eyes, Sheila could have been nearly any one of the women Justine grew up with, perpetually on the verge of middle age and capable of anything from banging out a hymn on the piano to tying up her skirt and tacking a shingle back in place to making a pot of beans for sick neighbors with a baby on her hip.

Reney, meanwhile, was aging in reverse, it seemed. After she'd left that prick, she traversed the country picking up work as banquet waitstaff wherever she decided to pass time. Now she was a college student in Portland, Oregon, of all places. *Finding herself.*

"We've got to trust the Lord," Sheila said. "All we can do."

"Y'all go to the doctor now, don't you?" Justine said. "Can't you talk to Mama?" She eased herself into a chair at the same kitchen table she'd eaten at as a girl, picked up a packet of syrup from a bowl, and began to fiddle with it.

"She's old-time Holiness like Daddy. Plus . . ." Sheila said with shrug, "she's too ornery." She smiled. "She'll be happy to see you. She talks about you, Josie, and Dee all the time."

"I don't know why she won't go to Tennessee and live with them. There's Holiness churches out there. Beautiful country. Two daughters who love her."

"Whoa, sufficient unto the day!" Sheila said, smiling and waving her hands to show she wanted no part of that argument. "Samuel went and got her car. Amazingly, it's not much worse for the wear. Muddy mainly, a couple of scrapes, but fine."

"That's about right," Justine said.

"I know, isn't that something!" Sheila laughed and shook her head in wonder. "God is good." She gathered her keys and headed toward the door. "Samuel will bring the car over later today."

"Wish he wouldn't."

"I'm not brave enough to fight that battle either," Sheila said as she closed the front door and left them alone.

Justine stood in Lula's doorway a long time before going in and sitting on the edge of the bed. When Lula woke up, she smiled.

"Miss my baby." Lula ran her tongue around her dry lips. "I suppose they told you I had a spell?" She looked toward the wall. "Sheila said my car isn't here?"

"No, Mama," Justine said. "Your car isn't here."

Lula patted Justine's hand, closed her eyes, and said, "We will get it tomorrow."

When Justine had gotten the call from Dee, her oldest sister, she'd been on the phone with Reney, putting another new zip code in her address book so she could send the old photos Reney'd been asking for. Justine clicked over, and before she could get out a hello, Dee's voice cut in.

Lula had the seizure while she was out on one of her countryside drives, taking in scenery she'd seen a million times—probably on her way home from McDonald's. Thankfully, she'd only run through somebody's barbed wire fence. No one was hurt, though she was still having the seizure when a man stopped and called 911. Lula came to in the back of the ambulance and demanded to be brought home.

"When can you get up there?" Dee asked.

Justine closed her address book, put fifty dollars in Reney's card, and sealed it shut.

"Teeny?"

"This is why I wish she'd come out there with y'all," Justine started in. "Or at the very least, let them take her to the hospital. At least we'd have time to figure out a couple things."

"You know we can't make her do anything she doesn't want to do," Dee said.

"The bank's going to come get my truck if I don't get their check mailed," Justine said. She could hear Dee tapping on computer keys.

"I'm looking for tickets for me and Josie, but I don't know when we can get there."

"I don't know how long I can stay," Justine said, but when she got off the phone, she set about doing all the things she needed to do: leaving a message for her boss, shoving Reney's pictures and card into a box to mail later, writing Pitch a list he'd ignore, grabbing the bills that most desperately needed to be paid, running deodorant across her armpits because she just got off work and didn't have time to shower, slinging shit into a bag, running by the Smokehouse to grab some brisket and beans since Lula ran the roads too much to stock a cupboard, and, finally, driving through the night.

Now here Justine sat, back in Beulah Springs, propped up on a pillow next to Lula, reading her the Gospel of John as she dozed. After Samuel dropped off the car, she had hidden the keys behind a dusty can of commodity orange juice in a kitchen cabinet. By evening, Lula was up, pouring herself

Mountain Dew and wanting to ride to McDonald's. Justine microwaved her a plate of brisket and beans and told her to be thankful she wasn't wrapped around a telephone pole. Feeling bad for that one, she'd then taken her for a drive to watch the sun set over Tenkiller.

Justine was sitting in the living room flipping though a *Reader's Digest* when Dee and Josie showed up late that night. They came in dragging suitcases and bag after bag of crap. They'd already stopped by Walmart and bought the store. Josie carried in a television with a built-in DVD player.

"You know Mama's going to lose her mind when she sees that thing," Justine said.

"I told her." Dee dropped her purse beside the couch and plopped next to Justine.

"I'm not showing it to her, are you?" whispered Josie, as she heaved the box into the other bedroom and closed the door.

"How is she?" Dee asked. "The car doesn't look so bad."

"You know," Justine said. "Still slow and groggy but getting back right." She tossed the *Reader's Digest* aside. "Whatever that is."

Dee ran her fingers through the short hair she kept dyed strawberry blonde. Bracelets on her wrist jangled. "Bless her heart," she said finally. "And yours. She driving you crazy yet?"

"Asking for her keys," Justine said. "That's all she's really worried about. She knows she shouldn't be driving."

"Can't nobody tell that woman what to do," Josie said, forgetting to whisper as she walked into the kitchen. She had already dressed in her satin pajamas and had a sleep mask propped on her forehead. "About like somebody else I know, huh, Teeny?"

Justine and Dee shushed her at the same time.

"I'm just saying, the woman's hardheaded. She's going to do what she's going to do, whether it's run the roads or flush her meds." Josie had come back into the living room with a plate of cold brisket. "I don't know how we lasted sixteen or eighteen or however many years with her." She sat on the other side of Dee and sawed on the meat with the side of her fork.

"You both left my ass as quick as you could," Justine said. She was trying to make a joke, but it didn't come out right.

Dee put an arm around her and pulled her closer.

"Mama did the best she could," Justine said. "But the way we were raised up . . . it's kept us from . . ." She had that feeling again. She wanted to get in her truck, point it south, and turn the radio up so loud she could not think. She could point it west for all she cared, as long as she got gone.

"At least Granny was here," she said, finally. "For my sake and Mama's." She was crying again, and now so were her sisters. "I'd handle being beaten every day better than what went on inside my head." She wiped her face.

"Mama tried that too," Josie said.

Dee whacked her with a pillow.

"Hell," Justine said. "I don't even know what goes on inside my head."

By Sunday, Lula was back to herself, or so the sisters thought. She threw them a curve and skipped Sunday school. After exchanging a round of looks and whispers, they took her to McDonald's for her beloved flapjacks and then piled back in the car and drove her to Brushy Mountain. Lula didn't say much unless she was pointing out a bird or a rock formation she probably could have mapped. Dee and Josie oohed and aahed, pretending the scrub hills were as majestic as Lula thought. Justine did her best to keep quiet.

By the time they got back to the house, Justine's back was on fire. Since she'd hurt it slinging a broken pallet into the dumpster at work, she couldn't sit long, and the drive up had just about done her in. She did best when she kept moving, so she decided to work in the garage, which was stacked with boxes they'd hauled over from the attic of the last rent house. Dee and Josie got busy in the flower beds, and when Lula wasn't dozing, she stood over them giving directions.

It was a fight to get Lula to let anything go. Ketchup packets and McDonald's napkins bulged from kitchen drawers; stacks of Styrofoam coffee cups lined the counters. The garage wasn't much better. Half the crap was junk, useless stuff that lacked even sentimental value. The other half: photo albums and Lula's old artwork that had been left in the heat. If Lula didn't care any more about it than this, Justine figured she could clean it up and take what she wanted for Reney. She told herself she was saving the trouble of having to do it later, with the added benefit of getting to it before her sisters. She told herself she wasn't worried about getting caught.

When she leaned her ear to the thin door that separated Lula's bedroom from the garage, she heard nothing from inside but the pull chain clinking against the light in the ceiling fan. She adjusted the box fan whirling in the heat of the open garage door. Then she wiped sweat from her forehead and dug into a dusty cardboard box with DREFT stamped on the outside. Pulling out a warped photo album, she listened for Lula one more time. Then she dusted off the cover and started flipping.

She stopped at a photo of Reney, who couldn't have been more than two, sitting on Granny's lap. Reney was doing this thing she'd always done to whoever was holding her: pinching and rubbing elbow skin. But Granny, of course, was wearing long sleeves, so it was really polyester that Reney was rubbing.

In Portland, Reney was taking on debt to study books she could have read for free, as far as Justine could tell. Her Reney, who after high school had become such a hard woman, so cautious with money and closed off. Sometimes it seemed this kid she'd more or less grown up with, the girl she'd loved and fought with and rocked in the night—her daughter, her very soul—was a whole different person.

Reney called whatever it was she was going through her *rebirth*. She lived in a communal house of some sort and dated two different men that she called feminists. She'd taken to asking questions about her "Cherokee heritage" when she called home, wanting to hear old stories. Justine had stories aplenty; few that she cared to tell. Nonetheless, she found herself telling them all.

It was often late at night when Reney called. She asked for Justine's advice, something she'd never done back home. They could talk for hours now that she was gone. Justine wondered what Reney was doing right then. She thought about calling her.

Justine jumped when she heard footsteps. She shoved the album into the box she'd set aside for Reney and felt relieved to see Dee standing beneath the garage door.

"We're about to go to Walmart. Need anything?"

"Again?" Justine said. She stood and stretched her back. "Josie better take that damn TV back."

"I told her, but you know—"

"You know what?" Josie said, peering over Dee's shoulder. She was the middle sister but had always behaved more like the baby.

"Mama finds your devil box, all hell's going to break loose," Justine said, going back to her sorting.

"She finds my TV, I'm directing her to the ice chest full of Coors Light in your truck."

"You can't even get any channels out here," Justine said.

"I've got a whole season of *ER*. Clooney's an Oklahoma boy, you know. We're the same age. If I'd played my cards right and not run off with old whatshisname, maybe we would have got married."

"Bullshit," Justine said. "Bring back bleach. Did you see the bathroom? I swear Mama's eyes are slipping. Her nose too."

"Well her ears aren't, so you two better pipe down," Dee said.

Justine was in a groove when Lula opened the door leading from her bedroom into the garage. She wore house shoes, but her hair was neatly braided. She held bobby pins in her mouth as she wrapped her braid around itself on the top of her head. Justine noticed a piece of paper stuck to her cheek. It looked like a tiny curled tail growing out of her face. Justine was compelled to go wipe it away—she knew it would embarrass Lula—but she was feeling annoyed at her own fear over nearly being caught.

"You need your rest, Mama," Justine said.

"I get lonesome for my girls. Thought you all might like to drive to McDonald's."

"Dee and Josie went to the store," Justine said. "I'm sorting through all this junk."

"Those folks behind the counter love me," Lula said. "They treat me like a queen." The paper stuck fast to Lula's cheek as she spoke. It looked like it had come from inside the ring of a spiral notebook.

"I know, Mama," Justine said. "Maybe later."

She thought Lula was about to go back inside and leave her be, but then she stepped down into the garage. Lula scanned the boxes and garbage bags and then peered into the box Justine had been working in before moving to an untied kitchen trash bag.

Using her index finger, she shifted the trash bag open and pulled out a little Indian doll. The braided hair had come undone and matted. The faux buckskin dress came apart at the touch, and the nose had been chewed away to white plastic. The most intact thing about it was the bold lettering spelling CHINA on the doll's underparts.

"Mama, that thing's been in a box for twenty years. Mice got to it."

"Well, I'd appreciate you not throwing away my belongings," Lula said. She carried the doll back into her bedroom.

Justine was so relieved at not being accused of stealing what she wanted before Lula died that she ignored the urge to barge through the now closed door and argue. Instead, she dug the album out again and flipped back to the picture of Reney and Granny.

It struck her that unless Granny was caught in a moment with one of her half sisters, she rarely smiled in photos. Even in this picture with Reney, who Justine knew was one of Granny's secret favorites, her lips turned downward in a soft C.

The Granny of the photograph—old Granny—was a gentle woman who tucked her laughter into all of the places in their house that lacked. But "old Granny" had been far from a pushover. When it had gone bad with Lula, Granny acted as Justine's and her sisters' buffer.

Justine turned the page to a faded picture of Uncle Thorpe and his gang of kids—her cousins. The boys wore long pants and long sleeves and crew cuts. The girls were in long cotton dresses and pigtails. Most of them were barefoot— they'd probably been playing outside before whoever had the camera rounded them up and told them to freeze. She wiped a smudge over John Joseph, the cousin who'd been closest to her in age and her best friend. She smiled at the thought of the two of them fighting over who got to memorize "Jesus wept" for Sunday school.

In the picture, John Joseph stood off to the side a little, caught midstruggle, leaning back trying to hold a full-grown German shepherd. His hands hardly met around the dog's barrel chest, and the dog's outstretched legs were planted firmly on the ground. The movement must have caused John Joseph to be out of focus. There weren't a lot of pictures of him, and this one was out here, ruining in the garage.

Justine shook her head and stood up to rub her back as she scanned the garage. She set the album back into Reney's box before moving to another corner. There was no telling what had been lost.

She knelt before a new box and pulled out another picture of her granny. She was young in this one, her hair still

black, her skin dark brown. She stood in a wooden wagon full
of watermelons with Justine's grandfather, a severe-looking
white man in a cowboy hat and rolled-up blue jeans.

Justine squinted into the photograph, trying to imagine
her grandmother so young. She had been a maid in a big
ranch house when she'd met Justine's grandfather, a barn
hand who Justine knew had been a terrible drinker. It wasn't
hard to imagine Granny's strength. She was kind, but she was
not soft. That's where Lula got it, where Justine got it, and
Reney, too, Justine figured, though she'd done her damned-
est to keep Reney from ever having to access that kind of
strength. Granny had been brought up in Indian orphan-
ages and, later, Indian boarding schools. She'd never taught
her grandchildren the language beyond basic greetings. She
simply said that life was harder for those who spoke it.

Justine thought of all the times she'd bought herself or
Reney language tapes and materials at the Cherokee Nation
gift shop. You could probably start a library if you gathered
up the books, flash cards, and tape sets that she'd purchased
over the years, only to stash them on a bookshelf until they
made their way to boxes in the heat of her own garage.

This time, she didn't even peek over her shoulder as
she slid the photo inside the album in the box of thieved
treasures. She took out a manila envelope with folded pieces
of paper inside. From it, she pulled one of Lula's charcoal
teepee drawings. She marveled over her mother's talent.
No matter how many sets of pastels or pencils Justine sent
her, Lula would not—said she could not—draw any longer.

Justine put the teepee in Reney's box, too, and set the manila envelope to the side. In the bottom of the Dreft box was
a leather journal, stiff with age. She thought it was one of
Lula's diaries, which Justine always felt bad about reading,
though she could never help herself. Filled with Lula's perfect
cursive, the diaries spoke of deep loneliness and sorrows. It
was a side of Lula that she didn't reveal to anyone, as far as
Justine could tell. Justine checked the door and opened the
book. She nearly gasped when she saw the writing inside.
She hadn't seen her grandmother's sweet scribbly handwriting in years. It looked like Granny had used the book as a
record of their days, no matter how mundane.

*May 25—In Hominy with Celia all week. Caught perch and
catfish—big mess. Celia's baby son graduated high school
today.*

*May 30—Sweet Service tonight. Bro. Buzzard came and
preached good.*

*June 2—Sister Irene picked us up for church but had to leave
early for a sick little one.*

> *Thorpe gave us a ride home.*

*June 3—Lula made a cowgirl cake for Reney's birthday, so
pretty. Reney is always sweet and precious. She stayed all
night here again.*

At that entry, Justine set the book down and cried so hard she
had to pinch the top of her nose to keep quiet. After Reney

divorced, she'd started calling Granny her soul mate. She said Granny came to her in dreams and had ever since they'd moved to Texas when she was a little girl. In taking Reney to Texas, Justine knew she'd taken her away from Granny, who, it turned out, had been Reney's buffer too.

Reney had tried her best to follow in Justine's footsteps in her sorry choice of men, and the more Justine pushed her to do better, the more Reney dug in. Until she let go and drove off without a word.

"Are you ready to go to McDonald's?" Lula stuck her head out the door, surprising Justine again.

Justine jerked her shirt over her eyes and pinched them dry.

"Teeny?"

"McDonald's is disgusting," Justine said. "You need to take better care of yourself."

Lula leaned heavily on the doorway to ease down into the garage. "Is everything okay?" she asked.

"Mother," Justine nearly shouted. She took a breath then continued: "I'm fine."

Her mother cupped Justine's cheeks, as if Justine were a little girl and Lula were checking her face for cake icing. Justine wouldn't meet her eyes. Instead, she studied the piece of paper, still stuck to Lula's face. Lula must have fallen asleep studying her Bible and drooled.

"Mama loves you, Justine," Lula said. "But only Jesus can make it all better." She turned to go but came back and said, "Please don't throw away my belongings." Then she passed through the open garage door and climbed into the dented-up Pontiac.

"Where'd you get those keys?" Justine asked.

"I can rummage through my belongings too," Lula said. Then she settled into the driver's seat and started down the hill.

Justine picked up the box she'd been filling with treasures and sat with it in front of the fan. She pulled the rest of Lula's artwork from the manila envelope. There was a smaller envelope inside, too, labeled "Teeny" in Lula's looping letters. It was her High School Equivalency Certificate, lost nearly as soon as she'd gotten it all those years ago after Reney was born. She'd always been embarrassed to say she had only a GED, but right now, she felt proud of the yellowed piece of paper, saved all these years by Lula. She remembered what it meant when she got it. She was sixteen, but she could get a good factory job, a job with benefits. She could take care of Reney. She could help Granny and Lula.

She wiped the sweat from her face and pushed her hair behind her ears. Then she spread her GED on the floor before her, smoothing its creases. She placed a rock on top to keep it from blowing away. She added her grandmother's journal and Lula's drawings, all of them she could find. She placed the old pictures around everything, too, finding stones and knickknacks to place on each one. A pressed cardinal feather fell from an album. Justine sat there for some time, smoothing the feather between her fingers, letting the wind blow heat over her and her makeshift altar.

She looked back toward the road, where dust from Lula's car was still settling. Justine knew she should have taken her mother to McDonald's, where Lula was certain the pimple-faced kids saw her as royalty and not as the strange woman in a long dress who overenunciated her order and huddled over her flapjacks. Now it was too late. But maybe tomorrow.

You Will Miss Me
When I Burn

I spent my morning at the Dairy Queen with the idlers and
the cattlemen who get their feeding done before first light,
a typical Ferrell morning my Indian daughter-in-law would
say. It was a sparse crowd nonetheless; we didn't know yet
what the wind was going to do. People left their tables and
crowded around the television set hung in the corner. Smol-
dering houses and charred land all over the Red River spoke
to the notion that man can't do much to change the course
of nature.

Hank Marshall had an expert in fire behavior on his
show discussing "The Great Fires of '06." The man stood
on the tips of his loafers drawing a triangle and explaining
concepts a fool would be born with: a fire needs fuel, heat,
and oxygen—things we had in spades. "Our goal," the man

said, "is to manage one of the three elements, but fire exclusion has led to an excess of fuel, and drought conditions have exacerbated the problem." They went to a commercial, and the old boys and blue hairs set to talking smart, trying their best to act regular.

"If the air ain't so humid you swim in it, it's so crackling dry it burns you up," Elsie the big-boned waitress said, passing a cup across the counter. I winked at her, and she rolled her eyes.

"At least the wind let up last night," Liza Blue said. I eased into the bench next to her, setting my hat crown-down on the table. She leaned over and said she forgot how to sleep without the wind banging that iron gate against her fence post. Liza Blue was always bringing talk around to her bedroom.

"Maybe they'll get it put out," she allowed, and the way people nodded at the floor, you'd think they was in church. People with something to burn get real nervous when they start thinking about the off chance that hellfire and brimstone will come to pass in their day.

Crazy old TomTom Tompkins sat in the corner with a Big Chief tablet taking notes on everything with a pencil nub. TomTom fancied himself a big author because he printed up two of his books and had them in the trophy case for fifteen dollars apiece. When somebody walked in or out, he smashed his fat palms onto his tablet and hunkered over his coffee to keep the wind from blowing it all away. After the door sucked shut from the latest exit, TomTom looked up from underneath his green visor and said, "That dry bluestem is sitting on the Caddo Field just waiting for a spark like a lover listens for the sound of a truck door in the night."

I bent over laughing and slapped my boot against the tile just as hard as I could. Liza Blue jumped clean out of her curls. She spilled her coffee in her lap and cut her eyes until I put my arm around her and whispered.

We grew up together at the country school outside town. When my wife, Nina, died, Liza Blue showed up asking me if I wanted to get married "like we should have by-God done in the first place." She had the trouble with her voice that Katharine Hepburn had, so every conversation took too long, and that one was no exception.

"We'll make your homeplace over," she'd said. "Patch the barn, put a roof on the house, new pipes and wiring, fix the whole foundation. Dig a new well if need be. Even better," she said, "load your mare and come saddle up with me." She had a hundred acres and plenty of oil money coming in from her dead husband. Just like that, problems solved. I told her I was mourning and needed some time to think on it. That's what that daughter-in-law of mine kept whispering in my ear: "Don't make any decisions for at least a year, Ferrell." For once, her yammering was useful.

The clock was ticking on my year, but truth be told, I didn't need time. This is going to sound bad to some of you, but Liza Blue was too old for me. It wasn't the years on her driver's license that got me, per se. It was how she showed them on her face and in her shoulders—damn, how they wore her down. And besides all that, I already had somebody in mind.

"Elsie, you better send me that rag, honey," I said. "We got Hurricane Katrina here in Liza Blue's lap." Her case of the shakes was contagious. Before you knew it, somebody else had spilled coffee and another one knocked an ashtray onto the floor. "Terrible Tuesday, aisle eleven," I yelled and went behind the counter to help myself to a new rag. I kept it because it didn't look like we'd seen the last catastrophe. Before I wrung my rag out and hung it over the sink, I got through the Big Chinese Flood and worked my way to Exxon Valdez. Finally, I yelled out "Hindenburg!" just for mean-ness. Despite what the Indian might think, I can always tell when I'm wearing thin on people, so I put on my hat. I had a couple of things to take care of.

I'll be the first to tell you: it wasn't lack of concern that kept me fooling around the DQ that morning, and it wasn't that I expected some miracle to part the Red River and put out the flames. I had a strong feeling TomTom was right about the wind pushing the fire back toward Oklahoma where it came from and going through the Caddo Field, with its pumpjacks and tank batteries, to get there.

On the northwest corner of the Caddo sat the last five acres of my old homeplace. You could throw a rock and hit the Red River. I figured it would all go to the fire. All I had to do was load up that little mare of mine—Elsie, I called her, after that waitress, and sometimes just Fat Mare. The money I'd made from the sale of her mama was about gone, and with the fires on the horizon, I could see that today just might be the first of the rest of my days.

At Pitch's house, I clamped my hat down on my head and intended on walking straight to the door but ended up going around his truck because that's where the wind blew me. I banged on the front door once and pushed it open. "Fat Mare needs shoeing, Pitch," I yelled, going on in. I knew him and that wife of his would be sleeping because they work the night shift at the factory down the road. I called for him again, and he came out of the bedroom, pulling a long-handle shirt over his head and stomping his foot down into his boot.

"You'll break the back of your boot like that," I said, but you can't tell that boy nothing. I tossed him a sausage biscuit I brought, and he grabbed a Dr Pepper from the fridge, opened it up, and took three long swallows without coming up for air. With his head tilted back like that, I could see where my boy was losing the hair on his head, and I felt proud to have a full head of my own, proud I didn't work indoors under fake lighting on another man's schedule. But it got me antsy.

He swallowed a belch, blinking at the light coming in through the blinds, and said, "Fires still moving?"

"I reckon if it's fire, it's got to move," I told him. "Fat Mare threw a shoe last week. It don't matter if there's a fire coming or a tornado. She needs shod. Follow me and you can get back on duty when you're done."

Pitch rubbed the sleep out of his eyes and sighed. Then he grabbed up the biscuit and headed for the door. I had no more than pulled the front door to when that Indian started yelling out the window about a leaky sink. Pitch just looked at me and shook his head and slid into his truck.

I sat up close to my steering wheel—not because I couldn't see the road before me like the Indian might say—but because the wind was pushing me from side to side, whistling through the windows despite their being rolled up tight. I had a good strong grip on the business end, but I leaned down to adjust the cassette player and swerved off the road. Gravel peckered up my tailgate and fenders. In my rearview, Pitch was waving his arm out the window pointing to a turnoff, flashing his lights at me.

I slowed it down enough to pull into the country school's parking lot, and Pitch fought the wind to slam his door and make his way to my window. He is small like his mama was. He won the World Wide Futurity riding my brother's Appaloosa when he was just a kid. Sat atop that stallion like a man while his classmates were building forts and swinging at baseballs. Standing there squinting against the wind and sun, his face full of lines, he looked tired and old. When he was born, you could cradle him in one hand.

"You alright, Daddy?"

"Looked down is all," I told him. Sand caught him in the mouth, and he spit the other way, cussing.

"Scanner says looks like it's moving in on Ringgold. Wind don't change, could come this way. What do you want to do?"

"Just need the mare shod."

"Today, Daddy?"

"It won't wait," I said. He shook his head in the way he has of being confounded at the world and everybody in it. His mama did that a lot in the years after he came along, and she started seeing the world in terms of fat and lean.

"Well, pick it up a little," he said and pushed back through the wind to his truck.

I punched the cassette buttons some more, eased into gear, and turned it up when "San Antonio Rose" rolled around. I'm not ashamed to say my eyes got a little misty. I had my mind out West. I wasn't wanting to think about wind and heat and years of disrepair turned to kindling, but Bob Wills's fiddle was always Nina's favorite. The song mixed me up inside, made the drive home feel like a picture show I wasn't a part of.

I met the Wyoming girl at the San Antone rodeo back when Nina was hardly there even when she was awake. Sometime in the eighties Nina slipped a disk, and the doctors kept giving her pills until she ended up in the treatment facility in Fort Worth. Pitch was a newlywed, and the Indian had come with a little girl already in tow. When Pitch put up a trailer house on the other side of the pasture, there was new life around the place for a while.

Pitch set about pulling boards off the barn, and he'd build bonfires out of the throwaways. Big dancing flames.

We'd cook hot dogs on hangers and pull the brandy out of the cupboard. Nina would grab that little girl up by the hands and two-step around the fire like a fool-headed kid, cigarette sticking through between her grin.

When the Indian was at work, my wife took that girl all over the place. She was her bona fide sidekick. Nina even had her help fancy up the place, cutting contact paper and slapping it all over the kitchen, sending her up the ladder to reach where she couldn't. They about contact papered the whole house that year. Nothing was left out. Before it was over, even the fridge was wood-grained, which I had to admit was an improvement. Me and Pitch set about breeding a couple of mares, thinking about running some babies again. Things was looking better for all of us. Then Pitch up and moved to town for a job the Indian found him and left the barn almost as bad as before he started. The doctors were happy to oblige when my wife went down in her back again.

We brought in a hospital bed. She complained about not being able to sleep through the creaking of the pumpjacks that littered the pastureland around the house. She claimed she could hear the oil being sucked out of the ground, and it sounded like crying. It didn't seem to matter that those same noises put her to sleep when she was a baby.

To hear the Indian tell it, it was the piddly oil money my sister in Dallas got each month that did it. Everything fell back on me because I'd sold my mineral rights to Sis in hard times. The Indian cornered me one Christmas after she'd had too much drink. She wanted to paint the picture for me real good. She said Nina was holed up in the back room in the dark because I refused to get a job like a normal person, and her heart was broke from years of trying to hold everything together with contact paper and worry. Normal people work, she said again, as if I didn't understand the concept. You'd sell your ass if it wasn't attached to keep from an honest day's work, she said. I'll tell you one thing, I told her. I'll never ever be beholden to a woman I don't love. Or wear a chain around my neck like a dog. About that time Pitch walked up.

The Indian just stood there staring at me, her forehead cracking in two, trying to be sure she understood my meaning. They'd had troubles of their own since the day they met. It wasn't a secret either. Pitch stepped between us and took her by the arm and led her down the porch, looking back at me shaking his head. It was a month or more before I saw them again, and when I did, nobody spoke of what was said. The Indian barely said two words in my presence for a while, but good luck don't ever last. Nina added nerve pills and something else I can't call the name of to her close grip of back medicine and put cardboard over the window to her room because the sun gave her migraines.

By the time the Fat Mare came along, I was tired of moping around the DQ. I knew I had me the kind of horse my daddy had once, the kind that allowed him to buy the homeplace back from the bank when other boys was sitting in breadlines. I wasn't going to sell Fat Mare like I did her mama, just to make a payment. I swear that horse changed something in me. I ain't scared to get sentimental about it. I cut back to two fiber cookies and black coffee in the morning and sometimes wouldn't eat nothing but saltines and tuna for supper. Before I knew it, I was wearing the pant size I wore as a twenty-five-year-old man and could jump near as high. Soon as I had the Fat Mare trained up good enough to sit under a saddle, I loaded her for the biggest rodeo I could find, and that led me south to San Antone.

My song ended, and I hit the Rewind button and turned up the radio news. The newsman's voice came cocksure through the speakers. The wind advisory remained. He went on to say the fire was the fault of somebody throwing a cigarette out on the highway. One man, one instant he can't take back, and now families are packing up, leaving for the fire what they can't carry. What's done's done.

At the turnoff, feedbags were flapping against the barbed wire. A pumper leaned into the gale on top of a tank battery, likely trying to get a measurement before they shut it down in case the fire did what they thought it might do in the next forty-eight hours. I honked at him, but the sound got carried off. I could tell, because he didn't look up. I could smell smoke coming through the vents, but that didn't mean nothing. There'd been so many fires in the region you could smell smoke when the wind shifted for a week or more. The Rewind button popped out, and my song started up again.

* * *

Down in San Antone, that mare took in the grand entry parade like I expected, keeping a good eye on each flag we passed, never snorting or hopping to buck. After the man upstairs was prayed to and the country and the veterans got their due, I tied her up at the trailer, gave her some alfalfa, and figured on waiting around the bucking chutes for the dance to start.

Now, in the right conditions, a fire can exist long before you see a flame. I heard of Louisiana marsh fires that smoldered for years, waiting until everybody pretty much forgot about them before bursting into flames, jumping highways, and ripping through swamp shacks. Even water and wetlands sometimes ain't enough to stop heat and oxygen and fuel. Some things can't be explained away by a man in loafers with a string of letters after his name.

I'm here to tell you when I smelled smoke passing through the rodeo crowd, I thought it was my stomach I was listening to, so I followed my nose to an old-time chuck wagon outfit with a prairie schooner and a couple of draft horses. There, bent over the fire stirring a big kettle of beans, was the prettiest little gal I ever saw.

Of a sudden, I swear I must have grown two inches, and the years behind me didn't pile so high. This ain't going to sound right—but it don't make it not the God's honest—but when that girl looked up at me, smoke between us, my wife wasn't sick at home anymore, and I didn't imagine her happy or young again. In the face of that girl, she just wasn't. In that minute right there, the tin roof on the house wasn't rusted through and there wasn't more gaps than boards to the barn I built with my own daddy. Bills wasn't stacked ankle to ass. And there was one greater truth I knew for certain: That little cow horse I had tied at the trailer wasn't only the best-looking animal at the whole event. That horse was magic.

The girl wore her pants tucked into tall cowboy boots with blue tops in the way of cowboys out West. When I said, "Cookie, I been on the trail nigh half my days trying to get to your beans," she didn't roll her eyes and turn to the next customer like the worn-out waitresses back home. No sir, she pushed that long, straight, golden hair behind her ear and sparkled.

I eyed her full-on, taking my bandana out of my back pocket and wiping my mouth. "Damn my cats," I said. There'd never been a hungrier man of a sudden.

The wind shifted and blew smoke in her face, and I'll be damned if she didn't move around the fire next to me. "Smoke follows beauty," I told her, and she rolled her eyes and said, "If I had a quarter."

"You'd be mighty poor counting them from a man means it as much as me." I was feeling real horsey. I ain't ashamed to admit, real horsey for a man my age. She blushed and got back at her beans, and I took note of the ring on her finger and knew a girl of that caliber couldn't be so far from home without good reason. I pushed it. "Want to see the only other girl here near as pretty as you?" She looked at me sideways, getting wary, I could tell.

"Alright," she said. "But I got work to do here." I was shedding years by the minute, and she could see it.

Like I figured, when I walked up with Elsie, that girl took to her like a hobo on a ham sandwich. She knew good stock. She didn't need a leg up. I tied on the cook's apron, and that girl's little ass was, other than mine, the first and only one ever to sit atop Elsie. I stirred the pot, making a good hand while the girl rode circles around the wagon testing the mare's reverse. "You can drop the reins," I told her. "Hardly have to squeeze her at all." The mare was still green, and I knew she wasn't ready for a stranger to sit her, but the girl kept it between the lines, and the mare acted like she'd been broke for years.

In the late night, while we tended the coals and listened to the horses shift and stomp flies, I told her about my wife. I told her about selling Elsie's mama and how when I watched that trailer pull off I swore I'd never do it again. She told me how her husband ran a big ranch on the Wind River. She said busting ice for the stock and scrubbing floors was leaving her empty feeling and said how the husband—her high school sweetheart—didn't understand how empty was a bad thing when you could look up at sky surrounded by mountains and had plenty in the pantry. She was giving the business a year to make her money back, and if it did, she might give it another year. A real good listener she called me.

The circuit was taking them north, so I phoned home, stayed on, and made a good hand with the chuck wagon outfit. In Fort Worth, I let the Wyoming girl ride Elsie in the grand entry and had to turn down two offers from high rollers looking to go home with my horse. After the pots was washed and the utensils was packed, I invited the girl back to see the homeplace before they headed to West Texas. I hadn't told no stories, and I didn't have ill intentions. I never did.

When we showed up to the house, it was dark except for the orange streetlight Pitch had tacked on the side of the barn. We unloaded our horses and hayed them. When we turned them loose together, of a sudden my insides shifted, and for the first time I found myself wondering what in the world a girl like her was doing on my place, how her arm came to brush against mine and stay there.

"Let's go in," I said. "I want you to meet somebody."

I led her by the hand into the back room where my wife was laid up surrounded by her orange bottles and dusty cups. Stale smoke hung in the air. A cigarette burned to ash sat there, and the big console television bounced light off the walls, as it had for years. My wife looked up at us and pulled at her hair where the curls was pressed flat against the side of her face.

I wish I could tell you what she was thinking. I can't now, and I couldn't then. I sat on the edge of the bed and rubbed her foot and winked up at the girl who squatted down and told my wife she had a lovely home. "You should have seen that fat little mare work," I said. My wife always got a kick out of the babies that came off this place, and I wanted her to be proud again, like I was. "A man from Dallas offered me ten thousand on the spot," I said. My wife studied my eyes for a minute before she said, "Good night, Ferrell. Y'all have a good night." She turned the television off and turned over. She was twirling a curl around her finger when I closed the door.

There was nothing filthy in none of it, and if you call it so that's your own business. I don't figure a man such as me has time left to question good fortune or to wonder about love.

I put the girl's bags in my own room and asked if she was tired. She sat on the edge of the bed and smoothed the quilt. "Here's the bathroom," I told her, holding the door open. "If you want to wash the road off." She nodded at me, so I stepped in and turned on the water in the old clawfoot tub Mama had been so shiny on when Daddy brought it home.

She came in behind me as I was swirling the water with my hand trying to spread some cool in. I looked up at her and heard my voice quiver when I said it would take a minute to cool. She looked down at me and didn't make a move to step back out.

I reached out with unsteady hands and took ahold of her boot. She held the top of my head for balance, and I tugged it off. When they were both off, I rolled her socks down and stuffed them in the boots. She left her hand on my head and stood there digging her toes into the rug. The water dripped steady from the faucet behind us. I took her belt buckle in my hands and popped it loose. I looked up to make sure she was okay, and I could see her breath catch. I unsnapped the button with two hands, careful, and tugged at the zipper.

The girl shifted her weight from one foot to another when I pulled her pants down. I looked up again, and this time it was my breath that caught. I leaned in and pressed my face on the smooth skin beneath her navel. Then I took a deep breath and held her hips between my hands before I got up and left the room.

I stepped outside on the front porch where I smoked one of my wife's cigarettes, a pleasure I hadn't had in years. I leaned against the house, not thinking so much as I was out there trying not to think. It wasn't working, so I mashed the cigarette out and stepped back inside. Through the bathroom door I could hear splashing. I tapped twice and pushed in.

She smiled up at me, and I knew that the spell wasn't broken for her neither. I took the rag from her hands and rubbed soapy circles on her back. When she laid back to rinse, quiet as Sunday morning, I gathered up a thick towel and held it out for her. The girl stepped in it, and I wrapped her up and led her to my room. She stood there at the foot of my bed, blazing red nose to toes from the bathwater. I didn't know if she was waiting on me to stay or go.

I moved to the chair by the doorway and pushed a pair of dirty britches onto the floor. She flinched when the buckle clattered on the plank flooring. I said, "That buckle's the product of an arm jerker I drew in 1959." She didn't smile or sparkle or ask to see my buckle. Nina coughed in the other room, and the quiet after was big enough to carry us away, house and all. The girl pushed a hunk of wet hair behind her ear and unzipped her bag, real cautious to contort herself and stay covered. She kept a tight grip on her towel with one hand and started ripping a brush through her tangles with the other. I wanted to take that brush from her hand and work it through her hair gentle until it was smooth. Something wasn't letting me leave my seat, and she didn't come no closer to me when she was finished. I took a spare quilt from the closet and bedded down on the living room couch.

That's the long and short of it. Question it all you want. She left the next morning after brushing Elsie. Hugged my neck quick and promised to let me know when she was nearby. I got a postcard from Ruidoso. Later, a rodeo program from Calvary. She didn't ask nothing of me or give me a forwarding address. I was at the DQ when my wife called 911 for her own heart attack, giving the Indian one more thing to place on my head. Can't nobody say my mourning wasn't real.

When I pulled into the drive, a shutter had come loose and was banging against the house. Elsie ran up to the fence swinging her head. She didn't like the wind or what was behind it. Pitch flew in behind me, and the first thing he did was grab a piece of baling wire from his truck and go over and tie the shutter up. Sometimes I forget he was born here too. Born tiny as could be, squalling in the back room his mama passed in, but I didn't have time for recollections. I

Bonita

Whichever way the wind shifted that week brought in a different smell. You could close your eyes and imagine the Oklahoma prairie a distant campfire with marshmallows roasting over it, but the oil patches burning out in West Texas smelled like a grease fire. It hadn't rained since early September. With just one dusting of snow, the winter wheat wasn't nothing but squares of dirt and stems. Cows were skinny and bored, crowded around salt blocks, and feed bills were sending everybody to the poorhouse. Great big limbs broke off the oaks on account of the wind. To top it off, it wasn't even cold, and it was damn near February. Seemed God himself was turning North Texas into the Sahara right before our very eyes, and all we could do was sit back and watch, try not to blow away or burn up.

I told Pitch I smelled mattresses and teddy bears in smoke coming from Fort Worth. He said I was being dramatic, but the Red Cross filled whole gymnasiums with cots and fire refugees, as they called those poor people. It was awful. Hank Marshall from Channel 7 called the entire region a tinderbox, said the grasses were like matchsticks. I called Bonita one stop short of hell, but that'd been the case for years.

Other than the news on the television and the smell, it was business as usual, except I guess we were all a little on edge. On Friday, me and Pitch got into it before we left for the brick factory where we work the night shift. Business as usual.

We'd only been in bed a few hours when who but Pitch's daddy comes ambling in bright and early, not knocking, dragging his spurs across the kitchen floor and spitting tobacco juice all down the side of the trash can, like he does. Then he sticks his head in the bedroom and says, "Come on, Pitch, cock's crowed. Need you to shoe the Fat Mare."

I turn over to the wall. Of course, Pitch jumps up and jerks on some clothes and runs out the door, stepping over a pile of laundry, shoving his foot down in his boot. I sit up and yell, "Bathroom sink's filling that coffee can faster than I can empty it out." All I get in response is Pitch's truck coughing and kicking in the driveway. I throw the covers off and run to the window and yell some more, but he's already gone.

I'd been asking him to fix the sink for two weeks. It wasn't like we had the money to call the plumber, so I finally gave up and spent the morning on my back with a monkey wrench, twisting and turning, trying to replace the P-trap. Took me the whole morning to do what he could've done in thirty minutes, and I couldn't even get the new pipe back on right before I had to start getting ready for work. While I'm standing there at the sink putting on my makeup, here he comes banging in the door right before we have to go. He starts running water for a bath, on account of the shower was broke too. He smelled like hay and horse sweat, which isn't a new smell by any means, but that day it made me just about want to puke.

"We better hurry," he says and strips down, leaving his clothes in a wad like he does, his underwear and socks still stuffed down in his pants. I had the 7 News at Noon on for noise, and from the tub he says, "Hank Marshall calling for rain?"

"Hundred percent under the goddamn sink," I tell him.

"I'm sorry," he says, slapping his forehead like this was the first time in the world this sink or a million other leaks all over the godforsaken house slipped his mind. "I shod the Fat Mare for Daddy, then we got to working on fence—"

"He pay you?" I say, knowing the answer already. Pitch glared at me and started scrubbing shampoo into his hair.

"He's got plenty money to get his pants pressed and buy that two-hundred-dollar hat," I start in. "You could've helped me pick up this mess this morning, you could've fixed the sink, or you could've at least shod for somebody who'd pay you, Pitch." I wait a minute. "Or you could always sell that colt."

He'd been offered five thousand for it already. It didn't matter that I wrote the check for the feed bill every month—I didn't have a say. Since I got him on at the plant, he expected the money to be rolling in. Every Thursday I still raced checks to the bank to keep us from being overdrawn. He didn't count all those years of getting behind, when he was a roughneck or a jockey, not finding a new job when the rig moved or the horse came up lame.

"I guess I'm just a sorry son of a bitch for helping out my daddy," he says. Then he gets to going. "Justine, I don't drink, don't run around on you, don't hit you."

"Some standards to set for yourself, Brother Barnes," I tell him, like a thousand other times. But he lays under the water to rinse his head, so I go back to putting on my mascara.

And then I sneeze. I grab a Q-tip and turn on the water in the damn sink without even thinking about how there's not a pipe under there. Water starts gushing out, and all the while he's making all kinds of noise, pouring water from a plastic pitcher over his head, blinking like crazy, like he can't even hear me. I turn the water off as fast as I can, but not before half the floor is soaked, including two pairs of his jeans and underwear. My only pair of steel-toe work shoes are soaked through. My pants are wet. In the mirror I see the black all around my eyes, and then I really get to yelling.

"You're just like your goddamn daddy," I say. "This house is fixing to fall down around me, just like your mama's did. But you don't have to worry about it. Your ass isn't ever here."

He gets out of the tub, wraps a towel around himself, and starts moving his jeans around in the water with his foot, like he's doing a great big service, cleaning up my mess, sighing the whole time, peering around the corner, trying to see the clock because all the sudden time is real important.

I keep going. "I damn near had three nervous breakdowns trying to hold this house together with baling wire and duct tape and keep your underwear picked up. You leave your shit laying around. You come and go as you please. I'm not your mama, and I'm not about to end up like her. I don't want to die in this mess."

I've said all this before. It always gets him because he knows how his mama died, all alone in that rickety farmhouse on the river, doing without. When his daddy got too old to train horses, he started sitting on his ass all day at the DQ, bragging about all the runners from his glory days, showing off his trophy buckles to every traveler who stopped in for a bite. She was down in her back for damn near twenty years, waiting on him to come home and tell her about his day—who he saw, what they said, but mostly what *he* said. It was all I could do to take them a roast or stew a couple times a week. Hell, Pitch's daddy wanted applause when he brought in fish from the DQ once in a blue moon. Finally, her heart gave out and she died, all by herself in her little bedroom with a feed bucket sitting in the corner collecting water from the hole in the roof. To top it all off, his daddy still hasn't got her a proper tombstone. He said he couldn't afford it. Pitch made a cross out of cedar and sank it at the head of the grave himself.

This time Pitch drops his towel in the water on the floor, stands there stark naked, looks me in the eye, and says, "I'm his boy. I reckon that's who I am then." He stomps out, throws some clothes on, jumps in his truck, and drives to work by himself.

Used to be, when I called Pitch his daddy, he denied it or got real upset, and maybe we'd have a heart-to-heart, and he'd say he'd change his ways, because it hurt him to know how his mama died. But when he stared me right in the eye and said, "That's who I am," I knew then and there that things weren't ever going to change. Don't know why it took me sixteen years to figure that out, but it did.

We both worked the night shift, but he ran a forklift in packaging, and I sweated my ass off at the kiln. Our lunches were together, and that night when I saw him laughing and talking to the boys on the other side of the lunchroom, sneaking up to stick a tail he made out of duct tape to somebody's backside, like nothing in the world could be the matter, I thought to myself, *That's it. I'm done.* Driving home from work, looking at the fires glowing orange far off to the west, I set my mind to leave.

Reney was halfway across the country in school by then, smarter than I ever was to set her sights on gone. She'd met a nice man with soft hands and letters after his name. She said she could "go in a lot of different directions" with a degree in literature. I didn't know exactly what that meant, but I figured it was damn sure better than this. When she told me about her big plans or whatever backpacking trip she'd been on, she sounded happy. She sounded like a whole different person from the one that left here without so much as a hi, bye, kiss my ass. Now was as good a time as any for me to follow her lead. My hair was going gray, and my face was starting to sag in ways Merle Norman couldn't help. Talking about Reney and how proud she made us seemed like the only nice conversations me and Pitch ever had anymore.

This wasn't like when I was drinking, back when I'd declare religion and drag Reney kicking and screaming, hell-bound to Mom's in Oklahoma. It wasn't like when I loaded up mad and hit a straight shot for my sisters in Tennessee. I'd saved a couple hundred dollars from garage sales, and I thought I could stand to stay at Mom's until I got on my feet. Do it right, really make a life for myself. I figured with Chero-kee Nation's help, maybe I'd take some computer classes, see if I could cut it. Get in line for an Indian house with sid-ing you don't have to paint or maybe even something brick, have an extra bedroom for the holidays. I wanted someplace Reney wouldn't feel embarrassed to bring somebody home to. A place without all the yelling.

After work that morning, Pitch turned on Hank Mar-shall, and we went to bed without saying a word about what happened between us. I let that coffee can spill over and left the wet clothes laying on the bathroom floor. For the first time in ages, I slept just fine. When I woke up and—like always—Pitch was already gone, I set about packing.

I made neat stacks and labeled every single box. Things were going to be different back in Oklahoma. I'd stuffed my clothes in black garbage bags, had my knickknacks wrapped in paper and boxed, and I was trying to separate the cast iron his mama'd given me, God rest her soul, from what I had to steal from mine when she wasn't looking. I couldn't hardly see taking these little corncob molds, since his mama'd only passed a year or so before and he loved the things, but despite my better judgment, I couldn't stand the thought of some hussy-come-lately putting a perfect little corncob in Pitch's mouth, wiping the butter off his chin with her pinkie.

I'd just about decided to pack them, since it was me she gave them to, when I smelled the fires. They came blowing in the west window strong all the sudden, too strong. I ran out the front door. There I saw a great wall of smoke billowing up around Comanche Hill. The wind was blowing so hard my eyes were watering. All I could hear was the roar of the wind until the emergency siren went off, round and round, screaming.

Right about then, here comes Pitch's beat-up truck sliding sideways into the driveway. He jumps out and leaves the truck door open like he does—always in a hurry to get going again once he shows up—and then he runs up on the porch yelling, "Coming this way fast, you got to leave, where's my fire coveralls?" All in one breath, just like that, and he was gone into the house.

I'm standing there in the middle of the yard, dumbstruck, holding on to a cast-iron corncob. I knew there wasn't any telling in God's green Earth where those coveralls were, but Pitch is yelling his head off about where *I* put *his* coveralls, because today he decides he better really volunteer to be a volunteer fireman instead of just putting the sticker on his truck and gabbing at meetings. I come to my senses, spit the dust out of my mouth, and run into the house. When I get to the kitchen, all I see are shirts and pants flying from the bedroom door, a pair of underpants hanging on the kitchen chair.

"You seen my coveralls?" Pitch yells from the bedroom.

"Did you check the hamper?" I yell back, stuck to the kitchen floor, wondering if he's seen my boxes.

"Why would they be there?" Pitch says, huffing and puffing, holding his grandpa's pocketknife and his daddy's little .410. His race saddle is tucked under his arm, and he's wearing his first jockey helmet, the one his mama stitched the number 7 on by hand.

"Check the closet."

"What's all this?" he says, looking around at the boxes.

I do something I'm not exactly known for, think before I speak.

"It's your mama's cooking stuff," I say and drop the corncob into an open box.

"Just take what you need." He shakes his head and runs out to his truck like a kid with his toys. He has no idea this ain't the fire I'm running from.

Then it hits me. Reney's baby stuff. I run to her old room—which is just the way she left it except for the junk I've stacked in there—and start pulling stuff from under the bed, looking through Christmas decorations, witch hats, and dusty suitcases for the baby pictures. I find a box of brand-new jeans I was intending to sell that I got for almost nothing when the Boot Shop went under. I find two dog biscuits and a dream catcher made in China, one of Mom's teepee drawings, and a wooden keychain with my name on it that Reney made in eighth-grade shop. I shove that in my back pocket and get lucky again and find a little baby food jar with two silver-capped baby teeth rattling in it. But I cannot find the pictures or the birth certificate.

Pitch runs by the door with three more guns tucked under his arms, a beat-up felt Stetson stuck on his head, and chaps hanging around his neck that he hadn't been able to fit into since the year we met at the track. I fling open the closet door. It's stacked wall-to-wall, two deep all the way to the ceiling with boxes full of God knows what. I start pulling them down. Right off the bat I find a box of old photo albums—not what I want—but I throw them into the hall and yell at Pitch to put them in my truck when he runs by with the mounted deer head.

He's grunting picking up the box. Outside the siren is blasting, and the shutters are banging against the side of the house. "Why are you taking so much shit?" he says. He doesn't get it. He never gets it, and now's not the time to hash it all out again.

214

"Why do you need so many guns?" I yell back, but he's already gone. The siren usually only goes off for tornadoes, but the shutters are making so much racket that I wonder if there's not a damned tornado out there, too, so I start yanking down boxes faster.

Pitch comes in Reney's room. He's loaded everything important and wanting his coveralls.

"I don't know where your goddamn coveralls are," I say.

He's playing the saint, making a big show out of trying to be patient, shoving his hands down in his pockets, breathing deep. "Do you know where my old ones are?"

I ask him where he put them. That always stumps him.

"There ain't time for this, Justine," he yells, flinging his hands and kicking a hole in a box of eight-tracks.

And he's right. I start to cry, kneeling in front of the boxes full of everything and nothing at all.

"We need to go," he says. "Now."

"I can't find her baby pictures. Her birth certificate, the baby book. I looked everywhere. I can't find them." I cover my mouth and look around at the tapes and the wrapping paper and the mismatched socks. My hand smells like iron and Crisco. I smell the smoke in my hair already, on my clothes, on Pitch standing over me. "There's so much shit," I say, wiping my eyes, trying to straighten up.

"Move," Pitch says. He steps around me and starts hauling down more boxes. "They ain't in these?"

I shake my head, and he kicks them away, pushing them to the middle of the room.

"Hurry up," he says.

I open up a box, still sniffling. Outside, big trucks are tearing around the block. A police siren blasts over the noise, and Sammy Boyd, the rich prick turned cop who went to school with Reney, announces in his official voice that "the mayor has issued a mandatory evacuation. All residents must leave immediately. Drive east on Eighty-Two or south on Fifty-Nine. Immediately." His voice trails off, making a bigger deal out of "mandatory" and "immediately" on the next block.

"Shut up, stupid-ass Sammy Boyd," I yell.

"No joke," Pitch says.

My fingers are shaking and snot's dripping out of my nose, but I keep digging to the bottom of the boxes he pulls out of the closet, finding nothing but old clothes packed away for a garage sale and more Christmas stuff, a whole Wrangler nativity scene done out of cowboys, the Virgin a barrel racer in tight jeans.

Pitch's got all the boxes out, and he kneels down beside me to go through the last ones. "Is this it?" he asks, holding up a book covered in blue quilting.

I snatch it from him and open it, dropping the Christmas goat I was holding. Pitch looks over my shoulder and sees where the father's side of Reney's birth certificate is blank. He doesn't mention it and never has. He just knows that whoever Reney's real father is, he isn't around. Pitch puts his hand next to the footprints.

"Tiny little thing, wasn't she?"

"Little?" I tell him. "You try squeezing eight pounds and nine ounces out when you're no more than a baby yourself."

"That's big?"

"Pretty big," I say, flipping through the book.

Pitch smiles. Then he stands up, his knees popping. He strokes my hair once, like he hasn't done in a long time. "Reckon we got to load the horses and dogs. See if we can't find that damn cat."

"I might've seen your old coveralls in the shed," I say.

"Come on." He pulls me up by the hand. We stand there for a minute and look at each other, and I try not to think about what comes after the trucks are loaded. Pitch leans in and kisses me, first on the forehead, then on the lips. "Sorry about all that," he says.

About that time, Sammy Boyd comes back around the block, hitting that damned police siren, saying "immediately" like he's the governor of Texas.

I follow Pitch with the baby box in my hands. He stands there, studying my boxes and labels, biting his bottom lip. "You pack pretty quick," he says. His lip's chapped and bleeding, and without thinking, I wipe away the blood with my thumb. I think he's going to say more, but he lets it go. "Wind's whipping out there," he says. "Reckon we ought to leave *immediately.*"

I don't laugh and neither does he. He picks up a box of knickknacks and piles a garbage bag on top of it, and I put a bag on top of the baby stuff and take off after him. He balances my knickknacks on his knee and has to fight the wind to open the door. He almost drops it all but grabs ahold just in time.

"Saw Daddy downtown with his mare," he yells. "From what I heard, probably going to get Mama and Daddy's place." We stack the boxes in the back of my truck, and he says, "Hundred-foot flames."

The wind carries away whatever I try to say.

"Daddy says he ain't leaving. Says he'll save the mare."

"With a water hose?"

"Hell, I don't know. He's sitting in the DQ parking lot with her loaded, wearing his spurs. He's got a bandana tied around his neck, poking around looking for a damn cup of coffee. Shit," he says. "I should've put the sprinkler on the house." He takes off running around the side of the house, and I go after him.

"Well," he says, screwing on the sprinkler. "Can you take our horses?"

"Maybe I should run check on Ms. Johnny." I look toward our neighbor's house.

"She's already gone. The horses?" he asks, aiming the sprinkler at the roof, wiping the grit out of his eyes with his shoulder.

"What about your daddy?"

Pitch just looks at me and sighs and then looks back to the roof.

"Help me get the trailer on," I say. "Then you go on and I'll get them."

He sets the sprinkler then backs my truck up to the rusty stock trailer, while I run out to the back lot with a gallon can of oats, a halter and lead rope looped over my shoulder, calling up the Paint mare and her little colt. When Pitch brushes her, he'll duck under her belly and come up on the other side to show off what gentle horses he raises. "That there's a Barnes horse," he'll say, rubbing her above her tail.

She won't even come to me. The colt's only a month or so old, and I guess the smoke and the banging tin have her spooked. She stays far back, on the other side of the lot, nickering real low, jerking her head up and down, stamping her feet in the dust, keeping herself between me and that colt. "Come on, Gertie, we got to take a drive," I tell her, shaking the oats in the can, losing half of them to the wind. She's not interested. When I take a step toward her, she throws up her head, wild-eyed, and runs to the other side of the lot with the colt following after her. I take another step, and she runs to the opposite side again.

"You just got to go up and grab her," Pitch says, out of breath. He takes the halter off my shoulder, walks up and loops the rope over her neck, patting her, saying, "Whoa, Mom. Easy, girl." Then he slides the halter over her head and buckles it easy as can be. She jerks her head once and settles in to be led wherever he wants her to go.

"The tin had her spooked," I yell. But he's already un-latching the gate to lead her to the trailer, with the colt trotting along behind.

The air is getting thicker, and you can see the big orange flames at Comanche Hill now. I load the two dogs in the cab of my truck real quick while Pitch wrestles with the cat. The sun's going down, and the wind isn't letting up. It's coming.

Pitch cusses at his truck until it starts, then asks me to fly by the DQ before I leave. He wants to talk his daddy into following me or at least into putting his mare in with the ones Pitch has all the sudden taken to calling "ours." I tell him why the hell not, that I don't have nothing but time.

At the DQ, I see Pitch has left his fire gloves on my dashboard, so I run them over to his truck while he argues with his daddy. Laying there on the seat beneath a tangle of bits and spurs is one of his mama's quilts bunched up, halfway folded. Reney's belt buckle from the Fort Worth Fat Stock Show is sticking out of the edges of the fold. Pitch and his daddy are still talking, shaking their heads, and throwing their arms up in the air, and I sit down in the driver's seat. I push the bits to the floor and flip the quilt back. He's got a couple of pictures of me and Reney fishing the summer he took us to New Mexico, and there's one of the winner's circle at the World Wide Futurity when he won on Miss Easy Pocahontas, his daddy's pride and joy. Pitch looks like another person sitting on top of that mare. His face is splattered with mud and he's small, but he looks like he could do anything. His daddy's standing there grinning ear to ear, holding the horse's reins, and I'm beside him holding on to his arm with one hand and Reney's head with the other.

I drop the quilt and run back to my truck, leaving Pitch's gloves on his dash. He looks over at me and shakes his head, then comes jogging over.

"Go on. Daddy won't come."

"I'm afraid I'm leaving something," I say.

"You got what you need," he says, jumping a leg into the coveralls. There's a rip in the thigh.

"Will those be okay?" I ask him.

"Love you, Teeny. Now get going."

"Be careful," I say.

A water tanker from the fire department comes by, and Pitch takes off running to catch up, forgetting his gloves.

I start my truck and head east with the rest of the Beverly Hillbillies, relieved Pitch hadn't put his daddy's horse in with the other two. I don't need that on my conscience too. Marni and Stevie, two ladies who moved here from Austin, and the boy they adopted stay right behind me the whole way. When the traffic stops, we get out and drink Cokes and ask if anybody knows anything new. Nobody ever does. We sit on that highway most of the night, hardly moving, ducking when the giant tanker planes fly over, watching the wind, listening to the radio and the mare stomping in the trailer. The wind changes while we sit idling, starts coming from the south, shaking the truck and trailer from side to side instead of pushing us from behind. We all hope the wind shifted in time.

When we get to Gainesville, Marni and Stevie go on to a gas station, and I stop in a church parking lot to check on the horses and let the dogs out. Gertie's happy to see me this time and nickers for me to hurry up while I put on some lipstick and try to stretch my back out. I find a waterspout, put the lead rope on her, and open the gate. Out both of them come, Gertie shaking her head and the little colt nervous at first, peeking all around before he bucks a couple of willies, running circles around us both, sniffing noses with the dogs. I give Gertie some alfalfa and lean back on the truck to watch the colt nurse. Even there in the half-light of the church parking lot I can see it: he's a good-looking horse.

When Marni and Stevie pull up, I haven't even noticed that the wind has died down, and I'm feeling halfway comfortable. Marni's sitting in the middle of the seat, her face all washed out and pale, leaning her head over on Stevie's shoulder. Their boy's asleep in a car seat in the back, fine hair pressed to his face. "They opened up Eighty-Two West," Stevie says. "Want to follow us back in?"

Mom's is another four hours north.

"They know anything yet?"

"It doesn't sound great, but I guess we'll see."

"Ya'll go on," I tell her. "I'll load these horses in a minute."

They take off to see if they still have a house, and I sit there listening to Gertie stomp gravel and the streetlight buzz until the sun starts warming the side of my face. I start thinking about the firefighters back in Bonita and about all those folks on cots. The cedar cross Pitch peeled and nailed for his mama. Reney's hair when it was fine and resting against a car seat on this very same road, me driving like crazy, headed to Bonita or away from it. I think about what those horses are worth, afraid of what I'm about to do. Scared of my new old life in Oklahoma, scared of the one passing me by. Then I get to thinking about those hundred-foot flames and Pitch's five foot, three inches. And I can't hardly stand it. It's all so much bigger than him and bigger than me, bigger than us together. I stand up and shake the blood back to my numb legs.

Gertie's chomping alfalfa and shaking flies from her ears. That colt stops nudging Gertie for milk and takes a step toward me. Gertie speaks up a little, watches from the corner of her eye, and goes back to her hay. I squat down and ease my hand toward the colt, and he nibbles at my finger, leaving a string of milky slobber trailing from my hand to his mouth. Then he walks back over to his mama, turns his face to the sun, lets his ears droop, and sighs. I know what probably I knew all along. The horses aren't mine, and I can't no more take them across the Red River than I could leave not knowing if Pitch is okay.

On the drive back, sunlight shows me what we missed the night before. Farmers had to rush to cut down their own fences, and there's cows all over the road. Some are orange from the chemicals the planes dumped. Some are half burned and paralyzed from the fear and pain. Calves bawl for their mamas, and black bunches of stiff-legged and hairless cows smolder, cornered into triangles of barbed wire that don't burn. You wouldn't believe the smell. The fields are giant squares of black, as far as a body can see.

But the fire is gone. A couple of farmers are already hooking up dead cows to ropes and hauling them off over the burned-out stubble, taking them to wherever you take the things that don't make it. I pick up Hank Marshall "live from 7," and he says the news is not all bad. Some homes made it on account of the flames being so big they jumped the houses that had been watered down enough and just went on, like the fire wasn't satisfied with the house before it and went looking for one that wasn't so much work. Getting closer I see a burned-out car sitting on the ground, all the rubber melted from the wheels. The fire was so hot it busted out all the car's windows and painted the thing in ashes, but right next to it, a little wooden swing set stands fine as can be. Hank Marshall calls the area a war zone.

The DQ sign, lit up same as always, is the first thing I see when I pull into Bonita. I let off the gas and roll down the window, spreading my fingers against the wind. The old Boot Shop building across the street is ashes. A man's standing there, talking in front of a camera, telling the world about our ruin. A couple of snot-nosed kids try to make him laugh, not a care in this world. A group of men stand around drinking coffee.

Pitch and his daddy sit on a tailgate in the sunshine, their feet dangling below them. Their heads hang low, but I can see them smile through their black faces, talking. Pitch looks over, and I put the truck in park. He wipes his face with his sleeve and spits on the ground between his legs, keeping his eyes on me. Then he shakes his daddy's hand, squeezes his shoulder, and walks over.

"It's gone," he says. "Skipped over Ms. Johnny's and burned ours clean to the ground. Nothing left but floorboards in the bathroom and the iron fence in the horse lot." He hangs his hands on the trailer panels and leans his head there.

"We tried to save it."

I slide down onto the wheel well beside him.

"Wasn't nothing we could do, Just."

Gertie stomps on the boards, ready to get out. Pitch doesn't move. He's still looking at the horses, biting his lip, holding on to the trailer. I lean my forehead next to his hands. They're rough and black, cut up from fighting fire. He smells like fire. I can still smell the mare and her colt, all their alfalfa, all their shit, their sweat and dust. I can even smell the milk from that baby colt.

"You really think he's a runner?" I say.

"All a man can do is put one in the gates, open them up, and hold on," Pitch says. He stretches his back and waves once to his daddy.

Pitch squeezes my hand, and then he gets in his truck, starts it up, and drives down 82 with his arm hanging low out the window. I stand there watching, feeling my insides swelling bigger, getting ready, trying to take it all in, and when he turns off on our road, I follow him to see for myself what's left.

Consider the Lilies

The Saints are huddled over Mama singing again, but Sheila can't get through "Consider the Lilies." Her voice catches midchorus, and she goes quiet, trying not to cry. Her husband, Samuel, holds on to Mama's hospital-bed rail with one spotted hand and rubs Sheila's back with the other. He lifts up his voice to cover for her. Little Sheila's hair is done up in one of the fancy Holy Roller buns, poufed and sprayed with way more worldly charm than Mama ever allowed.

Mama's sunk down into her pillow. It's not the seizures that she calls God's will that have brought us here. It's a stroke, and it was a big one. I imagine she's wondering why her pearly gates look like bed rails and whatever in the world a sinner like me could be doing beside her in heaven. Her eyes dart around the room like a coyote caught in a trap, which this hospital room must feel like for old-time Holiness like her.

Dee hums along and strokes Mama's hand. She always had the prettiest, strongest voice when Mama made us get up in front of the congregation and sing. Dee doesn't look the Holy Roller part anymore, but when she opens her mouth, I feel like that girl in church again.

Sheila keeps going in and out through her tears, but Samuel sings his part, carrying them over the awful beeping and whirring machines until she comes back in with her beautiful voice and hair. It seems they've been married forever—and I guess they have—but I still think of her as a girl. She's not much older than my Reney.

I turn my back to them, try to prop up Mama's painting they brought with them. The thing is almost as old as I am, but the sunset still drips blood orange into a just-right purple sky. All Mama ever painted was teepees or landscapes of Sequoyah County, the scrubby patch of hills she saw nothing but beauty in.

When I turn back around, Dee stands at the foot of the bed, wiping tears and squinting into a cell phone pointed at Mama. Dee keeps her hair dyed reddish blonde, but now she's added purple streaks like a damn teenager.

"You think Mama wants people seeing her like this?" I snap.

Sheila jumps a little but keeps singing.

"God's moving in here, Justine," Dee says. "Calm down." She puffs her bangs out of her eyes and shakes her head. Then she slides her phone in her pocket and starts singing again.

I wipe my tears quick. As much as I've worked to turn myself stone, I can't get my eyes to set. I'm not sure Mama deserves any more of my tears, though her fair allotment would've probably drowned her wing of this hospital and half the other. I've never seen my mother's mouth and eyes so sorrowful, like a movie mask come to life. I go to her, smooth her hair, and kiss her forehead. I can't help myself. She looks up at me from under her bushy white eyebrows and lets out a sorrowful moan, looking like the most pitiful, dear beast you can imagine. I rub her limp arm and straighten the gown, adjust her cords so they don't pull. We don't know what her brain knows anymore. She is crying, too, now, and I wish this room and everything in it would wash away for good.

Mama's finally fast asleep. I try to be quiet, but the vinyl recliner groans, and the footrest pops into place like a steel trap. The whole chair rocks, jerking my back. I stifle my whimper, but when I look up, Mama startles me. She's all blankets and IVs except for her big brown eyes reflecting the green monitor. She blinks a few times, and then the green goes out.

She sleeps in spurts, which is more than I can say about myself. Since the nurse's last check, I've had this footrest up and down and back up again. Years ago a doctor told me the connective tissue in my spine was shot. He said I'd see a wheelchair by fifty if I didn't stop working, as if there was ever a choice.

I left the doctor's office that day with a handful of prescriptions. Then I drove straight to a pay phone and got Mama praying first thing. I don't pray anymore, but I could never shake myself of asking her to. I was standing there in a parking lot with my eyes squeezed shut when she started feeling the spirit and speaking it over me. Warm tingles came out of that phone straight through my hand, into my arm, and down my spine. I went on back to work the next day and have damn near every day since. Of course, I can't bend to tie my own shoes. But I guess it's one of Mama's miracles. That's what I call them, the kind of miracle that might answer one prayer but leave you in need of a thousand more.

She's survived a lifetime of these miracles, which trace back to Daddy emptying the bank account and leaving her with three girls and half an art education degree to pay the bills. There were the nervous breakdowns. Forty years of loneliness and untreated seizures. The miracle of antiepileptic drugs she won't take because Moses didn't think to bring them up in Deuteronomy. And now this stroke. If she could talk, I know she'd say, "Count it all joy."

"Try to get some rest," I whisper.

She blinks. I brace myself and try to ease the chair back down. Dee stirs on the couch.

"Want me to call a nurse?" I say. My leg is numb, so I lean on furniture to make my way to her.

Mama turns her head to the wall when I take her hand. The right side of her face is drooped pretty bad. I cup it, push it up a little. Her skin is cool and dry. A whisker on her chin pokes me. She pulls away when I touch her, so I check her numbers on the screen like the nurses showed me and put the pillows back under her calves. I offer her the little oral sponge thing to moisten her mouth, but she won't open.

"Wish I knew how to help," I whisper. I stand there for a minute rubbing her good hand until she pulls it away too. "Remember how to call the nurses, Mama?" I show her the right button and lay the remote beside her, then go back to my chair and pop it out. By the time I get resettled, she's back to watching me.

"What?" I say, louder than I intend, but she doesn't answer.

I shut my eyes and get to rubbing the scar on my left hand between my thumb and pointer finger. All these years later, the X is still ropy and thick from the infection I got when I marked myself with a razor blade, thinking it was going to make me real cool or real different or real anywhere but here, but probably only marked me for the damn fool I was.

By the time I got ahold of the *Rolling Stone* that happened to have Charlie Manson on the cover, I was so sick of spare the rod, spoil the child, sick of having to go up to the front of the church in matching homemade outfits and sing with my sisters. I was already rolling up the waistband to shorten my Holy Roller skirt once I got to school. I kept my suede fringe vest with the BE COOL patch in my locker. Of course the bell-bottoms my neighbor's mom gave me were an abomination to the Lord, even though I was pretty sure Moses hadn't considered them either. I figure I was just the kind of disciple that lunatic Manson had in mind.

After I'd used the razor blade to pledge allegiance to the only family more jacked up than mine, Mama asked me what the bandage was for. I told her I'd burned myself making a cake. Maybe I was remembering the crisscrosses on the back of her hands, in those days after Daddy left and she tried to bake her way to rent and Bible-beat her way out of whatever it was inside that broke. She realized pretty quick how far-fetched my excuse was. Not that I cared. I was damn near daring her to catch me.

I ease the recliner upright and force my eyes open to try to stop thinking about things that nobody can change, things that don't matter anyway, especially when Mama is in such a state. I dig deep into my pocket and pull out one of my pills. When all that's left is a bitter taste, my mind pulls at me like it does. I look in my purse to make sure the little orange bottles are still there. I can't slow down for fear the wheelchair will catch me. I'm half afraid it has already but for the miracle pills that keep me living in a different time, one where I'm still a half step ahead, one where I can keep working.

Mama's looking at me again. She's moving her mouth, but no words are coming out. When I make my way back to her, she looks away. She makes me so mad I could spit, but I can't begin to imagine the strength it takes to refuse a pill that would give you a whole new life, one without seizures, without the embarrassment of waking up to strangers' faces and unfamiliar ceilings. Faith that moves mountains. Faith that keeps you from stepping into a hospital until, for one reason or another, you're rendered unconscious and some well-meaning person admits you against your will.

I adjust her bed to bring her head up and switch her pillows around again. I wonder about the pain she feels right now, where it comes from, where it ends up, how she would rate it on a scale of one to the rest of her heartbreaking life. I don't figure she would respond to my inquiries even if she could, so I don't ask. I lie instead, say, "Go on back to sleep, Mama. Everything's going to be okay."

"I'm going to run out and get her some short-sleeve shirts for therapy," Dee says. She sniffs her pits. "Probably ought to find a shower too."

When the doctor explained how important the first two weeks are to recovery, Mama set her face and looked through him to the wall. She wouldn't budge when the therapists came into the room. It's hard to know if this is the stroke or her usual meanness, but I do know a thing or two about Mama despising short sleeves.

"She won't even realize it," Dee says. Mama is asleep, and she's talking about the shirts again. "You know it's not wrong, and so do I." She bats her eyes and runs a hand up her arm, acting stupid. They think Mama is going to pull through, though in what shape, they will not say.

"I'm not buying her clothes she wouldn't be caught dead in right-headed," I say. I almost take it back because of the "caught dead" part. It bothers Dee too. She shakes her head, picks up her phone.

"You do what you want," I say and go on organizing the flowers on the far side of the room, throwing out what's going stale, putting the brightest in the front. I haven't had the time or gumption to do any sort of throwing out or arranging in my life back home in months.

North Texas is light-years from here now. The godforsaken storms and flashes of lightning are so constant down there they almost make up for the dark brought on by power outages. Of course, Pitch stayed home, muttering he better keep the animals fed and the place buckled down. I didn't say I sat with your daddy and wiped his ass every day until he passed. He knows.

I don't think there's anything holding him to this Earth anymore with his daddy gone. I saw him standing in the pasture watching the horses work a round bale before I left. A gust of wind came that whipped up a cloud of dust and hay and grasshoppers so thick I lost Pitch. After it settled some, the horses were running wild around the fence line, but Pitch was standing there with his arms out, like he was waiting to be carried away. When it passed and the horses wandered back up, I could see Pitch's shoulders droop from the kitchen window. He hung his head and shuffled his way to the barn.

I tell him to get over it. Buck up. This is the way of things. Kids grow up. We either end up just like our parents or do our best to turn out nothing like them. If we are lucky, we by-God make a little better of all the things we can. Short of some terrible interruption, parents go first. That's the way of things. Of course, we work ourselves stiff in the meantime and cry ourselves dry, but maybe we get to have some little something that fills us up in our time. Our mamas and daddies? We don't have long to get over the loss—or celebrate the release, as the case may be—or our time here will be gone, too, and our own kids will be burying us. I told him some version of this for about the four-hundredth time before I left, and he stared through me like I was a piece of hay blowing in the wind. Reney says it hasn't been very long, and I need to let him work through it, that he's depressed. To that I say, who the fuck ain't?

Dee comes back from her shower with three-quarter-length sleeves and yoga pants for Mama so you won't see nothing sinful if Mama's skirt rides up.

"Look, Mama," Dee says. She's wearing a big jewel-crusted cross around her neck. It dangles over Mama as

Dee leans down. "The fabric is quick dry," she yells. "So if you really go to getting it, you won't be sweaty against your skin." She shows her the lady on the tag who's running and smiling with little dumbbells in her hands. "Might be you before long, Mama. We just got to get started."

"I've never seen one soul so happy to be running," I say. Dee looks hurt. I shrug and make a face at Mama. I swear she grins or tries to. The right side of her mouth stays down, but the left side comes up just a little. I think she nods her head at me. She was never much into bullshit either.

"Mama," I say. "These people ain't going to leave you alone until you do their therapy." Mama sort of grunts, so I go on. "Your choice, but if you want to get back home to your Sequoyah County hills, you better get your butt up and do what the doctors and nurses say."

She doesn't like it one bit, but we use the gait belt the nurses gave us to shift her forward. The therapist told us it's best for her to start getting herself dressed every day, as much as she can, so we untie the gown and try to help her pull the shirt over her head. We maneuver her onto the edge of the bed and slide the pants up. We put her long denim skirt over the pants so she feels holy. I put the skirt's waistband in her good hand.

"Pull it up, Mama," I say. She holds on to the skirt but doesn't do anything with her arm. I start to cry, because for all I know she don't even know how to get her arm to do what we're telling her to do. "Like this," I say and work the arm up for her. Her hand relaxes, and the skirt falls to the floor.

Dee has ahold of the belt from the side to keep Mama from sliding into the floor. I can hear from her sniffles that she's crying too. This keeps happening. We're trying to get some simple thing done, and the weight of what Mama can't do and who she is or isn't any longer and might not ever be again strikes us hard, and the next thing you know, the air is thick with our bawling. We try to hide it from Mama, but if she knows anything, she knows.

We finally get her half-decent and put brand-new white Target tennis shoes on her feet. We've just got her settled in the wheelchair, ready for therapy or whatever the nurses throw at her, when Sheila knocks at the open doorway. She presses her face to mine, and her cheek is already wet. She sniffs and smooths her blouse real fast and starts to pray over Mama before she sings. All of us are crying by the time she finishes, but then she offers to sew fabric beneath the V-necks of Mama's therapy shirts "so Aunt Lula is as modest as she'd want." I love little Sheila with all my heart, but there's always a step beyond what you think is good enough with these people. You'd think we would learn.

Mama's first word comes later that afternoon, as I'm combing through a tangle in her hair: "Don't."

Before long, she's ordering us around like servants. Never says please. Yells at us if we are too slow or fast or move her wrong. Asks me to close the blinds, but I close them too much. Tells me to open them back up just so, and I go too far. When I say, "Mama, I ain't sure where you want them," she says, "Oh, you *ain't*?" and gives me a real satisfied glare.

I know what she's doing, just like she knows quitting school embarrasses the hell out of me. She knew it before the stroke, and she knows it now. There's no reason she'd say that but meanness and an aim to hurt.

Of course I don't linger on it. I run down to the nurses' station and tell them she said a three-word sentence. When the doctor comes in, she goes back to staring at the wall. Not a word. After talking to her a bit and running her through some quick checks, the doctor sighs deeply and pats her on the leg. Then he takes us outside the room.

He listens kindly but looks at us with pity, like we are wishful thinking, wanting our mother to heal despite the terrible evidence before us. They don't know the extent of her meanness, and I tell him as much. He says, "A stroke of this magnitude often makes a person combative who never was before."

"It must be a miracle," I say. "Because Mama has come through this as mean as ever."

When Mama pulled the bandage off my hand that day, I stood there waiting on her palm, ready to tell her once and for all she wasn't going to hit me ever again. Unlike Mama, I knew where Daddy had got off to. I was ready to pack a bag and head for Texas whether he wanted anything to do with

any of us again or not. And if he didn't, I had just about decided I could find love in the leftovers of the Manson family
somewhere in the desert.

When she kissed the top of my hand and started to cry,
I didn't pull away. I don't know what it was that let me stand
still while she got close and pulled my hand to her breast
that morning.

"Oh Justiney," she said. "My sweet, sweet Teeny."

Her voice was familiar but I didn't know it anymore. I
don't know how to explain it except to say that things I'd shut
out a long time before kind of washed over me. A little girl
with two black braids flashed through the screen door with
a puppy named Chief. This was from before Mama started
chasing strays off with a broom and drowned that bunch of
kittens because they'd do nothing but get us attached. There
was a mother at the table, up late of the evening working on her
paintings. She could be distant, but when you had her eye, you
felt like you must be the luckiest girl in the world. She wasn't
sick. She was the most beautiful woman in Beulah Springs.
On the edges of it all was her husband. You could see it on his
face: he'd been waiting all day to get home. There were short
sleeves. Bare arms jutting all over the place! And makeup!

Her voice was familiar that day. But I didn't know it
anymore.

She kissed the top of my head—she still stood almost
a foot over me then—and pulled me into her, smelling like
butter and the rose-scented Avon powder puff us girls went

in on for her birthday. We stood there like that, me breathing her in, feeling like a lost world was re-creating itself in my chest, her breast heaving.

Then it stopped. She bent low to my eyes and said, "I can't make you pray, Justine. I can make you go to church and make you dress for the Lord." She wiped my hair from my face. "But I can't love you to Heaven, honey."

She turned to the piano where she kept the bottle of Pompeian olive oil, said a quick prayer over that, too, and poured some into her palm. She wiped her hands over my hair and over my heart and eyelids and over the X I'd carved into my hand the night before. She pulled me over to the couch, and she got down on her knees and sank her face into the cushions and began to speak her prayers low at first. Presently she began to moan and then to shout.

I'd been prayed over more times than I could count by then, so this wasn't something to take note of. I'd seen exorcisms and sign readers and all sorts of wonders in our little wooden church. What had me was the tenderness I caught in my mother's voice, the soft way she'd held me. That wasn't anything I was used to, not since before Daddy left. I was knocked so sideways that I forgot my fear.

"I'll tell you something else you can't make me do anymore, Mama," I told her. "Sing in church. I hate it." I took a deep breath. "And I don't need your prayers." I was out on a limb. I'd worried the thought deep in the night, sure the devil was winning my soul. But you couldn't tell it that day.

"We're all going to die, Mama. But I want to live. Some ain't in for illusion."

Mama raised her head from the couch cushion and wiped snot from her nose. She rubbed her eyes and blinked, probably trying to find her way to this all being a simple misunderstanding.

"Don't need your prayers," I said again.

Mama's eyes went vacant, and she began to beat me with her oily hands. Here I was, a hillbilly half-breed of the Oklahoma hills trying to deal with some kind of drug-addled maniac's theory of unified existence or some bullshit, while my mama lost her ever-loving mind upon my head and shoulders. It's not any wonder I gave up on schooling so early.

I kept trying to hold on to Manson's words from the crinkled *Rolling Stone* that was presently shoved deep under our mattress. No good, no bad, beauty in the totality of existence. Submission is a gift, and all sorts of horseshit that at the time spoke to something in my tortured insides. I tried hard to accept the force and weight of her palms, and for a good little while, I struggled.

"The light-colored spots are damage to the brain from the stroke," the doctor says. Then he moves his finger all across the image of my mother's brain. "See here," he says. "She's been having them for months. It looks like fireworks all across here." By *here* he means her entire brain, as far as I can tell.

He leaves, and me and Dee go into the waiting room to call Josie, our middle sister in Tennessee, to relay this sorry news. Together we cry and cry and cry. The two of them have started going to church again. They've recently settled on a church they're calling *charismatic but not crazy!* They won't have a drink with me anymore. They claim it's not wrong, *necessarily* they add, but that they just feel called to *not*.

Here in the bright-lit waiting room, I close my eyes while they pray with each other over the distance. Even I have to admit those old sounds of desperation and certainty stir something in me, so I say, "Some God she serves."

The only other person in the waiting room is a full-blood who is dabbing his eyes with a red bandana, and all I can think about is the sad Indian in that old commercial who cries over trash and traffic. Maybe I've been away from Indian Country too long, but I swear this man looks just like the guy from the commercial except his belly is big and his hair is bleached orange and standing up every which way with gel and he's wearing a sleeveless jean jacket with a middle finger patch on the breast instead of a buckskin shirt and braids. I think about me and my sister holding each other crying a minute ago and think we probably look just like the sad Indian, too, and that Mother, in her two white braids, probably looks just like him too. Everywhere in this whole hospital are sad Indians crying but nobody thought to make a commercial to save our lives, so we keep playing different takes on the same scene nobody watches but us. I want to hug the man in the cutoff jean jacket. I want to wrap my

241

arms around his big middle and maybe never go back to North Texas and its godforsaken storms and sad cowboys and never come back here to this waiting room or Mama's waiting-for-deliverance room. Never go anywhere but home with this man who might be crying but is by-God here.

Dee takes my hand after she says amen and a bunch of thank you, Jesuses. She squeezes it and leads me away from my destiny and back to Mama. Mama is sleeping so peacefully now that you can't tell her brain is full of fireworks. There's this joke that's been going through my head since the doctor told us the news. All the sudden, it strikes me as the saddest shit I've ever heard, so as we settle into our nests, I start to tell it.

"Okay, so an atheist lives next to an old-time believer, an old widow lady on a fixed income, I guess."

"You can't be real," Dee says, and I wave her off.

"Every morning the old Christian lady walks out onto her porch and smiles into the new day and shouts, 'Thank the Lord for this day!' Now from the outside, she don't have much to be thankful for. Half her windows are covered in plastic and the porch isn't nothing but a rickety roof over a dirt floor. She probably has cancer and suffers untreated seizures, if we are being realistic here."

"Teeny," Dee says.

"No, now every morning the crotchety old atheist—you probably forgot about him. Don't. He wears rainbow suspenders and smells like piss and yells out his window over his coffee, 'There ain't no Lord!'"

Dee shifts on her love seat. She picks up her phone and starts swiping, clicking her red nails on her screen.

"Well, this goes on for a while, as things do in jokes. And one day the atheist decides he's going to get the crazy old Christian good. So he limps to the grocery and buys a few things. Before sunup, he puts them on her porch and waits behind the old oak tree that separates them.

"When the lady steps out to take in the day, she sees the groceries. Well, she kneels down and begins to pull out bread, cookies, a whole bird. She gets to crying and getting happy with the Lord and cries out, 'Thank Jesus for this bounty in my time of need!'

"The atheist waits for her to get good and worked up and then jumps out yelling, 'I told you, there ain't no Lord. I bought that!'"

"What a butt," Dee says. Her phone is back in her lap.

"Asshole," I correct her. Then I add, "An'it?" practicing, I reckon, for when I go home with the man from the waiting room.

"Anyway, the old lady isn't fazed. She goes right on dancing for joy. 'Thank the Lord for providing me these good, good groceries,' she says. 'And for making the devil pay for it.'"

"That's it?" Dee says.

"I don't know. Maybe they get married and get their own TV show."

"God does have a way of providing," she says and picks her phone back up.

"Except when he don't or won't," I say, digging into my purse. I try to ease back the recliner, but it springs open and rattles my neck, sending hot pain all the way down to my numb-ass toes. "There ain't never been a time when Mama wasn't in need," I say. "She's dedicated her life to God for forty-some-odd years, refused medications for seizures on faith, and claimed her healing despite years of chewed-up tongues, wet beds, and car wrecks as evidence to the contrary. What does she get out of it? One hell of a testimony and a bed in a hospital that specializes in stroke recovery."

Dee gives me one of her "I'm the older sister" looks that burns me up inside. I guess I've raised my voice because I look over and Mama is glaring at me.

"Mama?" I say, not sure what she's heard. Just like that, I'm a girl waiting to get into trouble all over again. I feel myself getting madder and madder at how Mama, even laying on a hospital bed, can make me feel. My phone buzzes in my pocket, so I take it out and find a message from my sister, not the one in Tennessee, but the one sitting right here that's damn near sixty-five. I open it, and there's a dancing cartoon version of my sister saying: YOU MAD BRO???

Something weird happened when Mama beat the hell out of me that day. Things went underwater for a minute after she closed her fists. Then I guess everything I'd been trying to understand clicked. Finally, all of existence and life came together and everything really was the totality of the now. An'it! Me and Charlie Manson understood what it meant to submit. I think I smiled a little. I know I held my palms up to her and said, "Jesus on the cross, Mama." And I meant it. I was going to let her kill me, and not even out of spite.

This is when things get a little fuzzy. She shouted, "Get thee behind me, Satan" and threw me into the old beater piano someone had given us. The next thing I know, I am coming to in my big sister's arms. Mama is laying on the couch quivering, Josie pressing a rag to her face.

The other girls were smart enough to put the Mississippi River and a thousand more miles between her and them. I settled for the rusty Red River, among my other shortcomings. If I was a dweller, I'd be as incapacitated as Pitch waiting on a cloud to take him up out of the pasture. So I take my medicine to grease my spine and soften the nerves that carry the pain and go to work and do a man's job better than half of the assholes I work with. I can drink and dance them under the table at the casino when I get tired of going home to a ghost. You've got to keep moving, whatever you do, but when I get around Mama, my movement's all in reverse.

No matter. When tragedy in the form of seizures or strokes or car wrecks strikes, I load my shit in my truck and make the drive north. By the looks of things, the stroke is probably going to end these trips. When it does, I'll be left with no place to aim these stories, and I reckon they'll go wherever all the hurt with no home goes. And what will be left then?

Mama's having a good day. Dee has gone to Mama's house to shower and tidy up the place. With no one else around, Mama is letting me work her right hand. I'm putting a rolled-up washrag in her hand and opening her fingers and letting them close themselves around the washrag to remind the muscles how to work.

I learned all kinds of tricks taking care of my father-in-law when we had to watch him wither for one year and twelve days. That wasn't so very long ago, and here I am putting my terrible knowledge to work. Beautiful by-God circle of life this is.

I work the right leg, starting at the hip and moving the whole leg up. She's not a small lady and gives me a run for my money, always. I rest her calf on my shoulder, the one with all the knots in it, hoping to get a little massage out of the deal, and raise the whole leg as high as I can. After I do that a bunch, I move down to work the knee and eventually work all the way down to her toes.

My neck is killing me by the time I'm done, but I've promised her a bowl bath. I get a new rag and fill her plastic bowl with hot water and wipe it over her head until her hair is wet enough to put in the special no-rinse shampoo. Then I get the vitals: face, pits, under her breasts, and everything else.

Mama's always been so modest with her body that I almost can't do it. I figure I've seen and done way worse, but when I stop and think about it, I'm pretty sure that's a lie. But like damn near everything else in my life, I grit my teeth and separate myself from what I have to do. Keep going. It strikes me that me and whoever else has cleaned her up at the hospital are probably the only ones to see this sight in forty years. I'm so embarrassed that I almost get to laughing, but then I start to cry at the thought of her saving herself for Daddy and now this. *That* is the saddest shit I've ever heard of.

After I've got her cleaned up, I comb and rebraid her hair. I dip the comb in a little Styrofoam cup of water and can't help but think about how we found her out of her mind that morning after Daddy left, leaves in her hair, humming "In the Garden." Mama was always listening to the Mahalia Jackson orchestra album then.

Before she settled on cakes, she tried to sell the landscapes she painted of Sequoyah County. Turned out, not many people were as enamored with those hills as her, so she sold her brushes and unused canvases. She sold everything we could part with and traipsed around town looking for someone to hire a near forty-year-old woman with three daughters and no husband. She was breaking all the while, I reckon, until she ended up in the yard at 3:00 a.m. in her nightgown, hair wild all over like the Choctaw woman who lived down by the creek and cut feed sacks into kid-sized dolls.

Her two braids are snow-white now, thinner than they used to be, but with some water they are smooth and neat.

They fall down her chest almost to her belly button. Even with her mouth drooped, she is a striking woman. It seems like just the other day she was the powerful, fearsome presence she had to become, and now here she is.

I'm standing over her, sort of taking her in when she reaches across her body and takes my hand with her good one. She squeezes me and rubs her thumb across the inside of my palm.

"Sweet Justine," she says. "My Teeny."

I look to the door, hoping to see Dee or one of the nurses walking in, but the doorway is empty.

She smiles, and the left side of her lips curls upward. The right side stays down, and I think of the two movie masks again, the happy one laid overtop the sad one.

"The smart one," she says. "Strongest too." She pulls me toward her, and I'm surprised—even though I know I shouldn't be—at her strength. "Me and you," she says and bonks our foreheads together hard enough to hurt. "Always love you, though. My baby."

Her voice is full of air, strange.

She kisses my hand, and I wipe the drool that's always creeping out the right side of her mouth with the washrag. She blows stinky air from her mouth, in exasperation I guess, and slobber strings across my hand.

"Want you to listen," she says and pushes the washrag away.

"You're getting better, Mama. We're going to be taking you home before you know it. Dee went to get your house ready."

"Listen," she hisses and squeezes my hand so hard I think I might cry.

She doesn't gently whisper "I'm ready to go home" like I've heard that some sweet old Saints do on their deathbeds. There's no peace in my mother, faithfullest of servants, as she whispers, "Help me."

I pull away, but she won't let me go.

"Justine," she says. "I can't." She's starting to cry, but her right eye won't work so the tears are only falling from the left side.

"Doctors say if you do the therapy there's a good chance you'll be able to walk with a walker. Dee's talking to some guys today about putting a ramp on your porch."

"No ramp. No walker," she says. "I'm tired."

"You are strong as an ox and stubborn as a mule. You can beat this."

As I say the words, I know I'm full of shit. She might be able to leave the stroke unit, but she's eighty-two years old. She can't beat that. And even if she could, to what end? The way she looks at me, burning through my eyes with her good one, I know she knows that, too, and I get the feeling she knows I know I'm full of shit.

"Wanted you to go to Heaven. Couldn't lose you girls," she says. "Always loved my babies."

The truth is, I never doubted Mama loved me. She loved us fiercely, even as she beat the hell out of us. When I was in a jam, there was not a thing I'd do before I'd make my way to a phone and call my mama. By the same token, there was not a thing I could do or any word I could fling at her that would cause her to refuse prayers on my behalf. A gentle hug after I bombed a test or some understanding that certain kids are going to have to run wild, so meet them somewhere in the middle and let them feel like they are getting away with something by wearing short sleeves, well, we can't have everything.

"Please," she says. She can't bring herself to say sorry, but I understand how a mother can go too far and regret it as soon as it happens. I understand how desperate it feels to lose the thing you've created that has become your only life. I feel myself think about forgiveness because I don't know if I'll have another chance. I'm real afraid of what that forgiveness looks like here in this hospital room on the fourth floor in Tulsa, Oklahoma.

I look around and see a pillow on the recliner. I lean down and bonk her back on the forehead, and then I kiss the red spot.

"Hurts, don't it?" I say, and she just looks up at me from beneath those eyebrows. I swear I see a kindness in her eyes that I thought got killed a long, long time ago. It hurts to not know if Reney ever saw this kindness in the eyes of her grandmother. Like a big old baby, I hurt for the little girl I was and wonder who she could have been without the Bible, without sickness, without so much by-God loss. But without the things that make us who we are, we're nothing, I reckon. Pitch standing in the pasture without his daddy, waiting to get carried away with the dust.

I crawl onto the bed beside her and lay on my side along her. I get up under her bad arm and position it across me like she's holding me herself. I put one of my legs over her leg. I close my eyes and can smell her again from all those years ago. Rose-scented powder and butter.

"You made me strong, Mama," I tell her. "You did what you could."

"I'm ready to go home."

"I know, Mama," I say, but what I know is I'm full of shit. I'm not strong, not as strong as she thinks, never strong like her. I'm afraid that every day that Mama suffers from now on is my responsibility.

"You can't give up now, Mama," I whisper in her ear. She doesn't answer.

"God will take you when he's ready. Granny will be there. Uncle Thorpe will be there. There'll be a rejoicing, Mama."

I feel her breathing with my body. Our breaths even into one another until hers catches and she lets loose a ragged, empty cough.

I start to hum so soft I don't even know if Mama can hear it. I rock her until I don't even recognize songs in the sounds I make. I think maybe she joins me, but when I finally stop, it's just hospital noises I hear.

"Mama, are you okay?" I ask. She still doesn't answer, but her hand finds mine around her waist. She squeezes once and lets go.

When Sheila and Samuel walk in the door, I've already got my backpack zipped up, and I'm strapping my pillow to the side. Mama's eyes shift from me to sweet little Sheila, who's rubbing on her arm, asking if she'd like a song. Dee comes in just as I'm saying goodbye.

"You're leaving?" Dee says.

"I've got to get back to work," I tell her. She stands there looking confused, still holding on to her purse, but she hugs me back when I squeeze her neck.

I go to Mama and bend down and wrap her up. She feels so small, like a tiny bird. I press every bit of her into me for as long as I can.

"Teeny," Mama whispers. "Thank you."

"I'm sorry, Mama," I say. Then I go. As I make my way past the nurses' station to the elevator, I hear the Saints' voices starting up. Dee joins them. The harmony they make is beautiful. I feel it moving along my arms and into my spine and down my legs.

For a long time, I thought harmony was just people using air and vibrations at the same time. I thought that once the singing stopped it might as well have never even started. But when the heavy hospital doors close behind me, there is a ringing in my chest like a song. When I close the door to my truck and later when I cross the state line, I can still feel the voices. They carry me home.

PART III

Near Future

What Good Is an Ark to a Fish?

1.

I pad around my house in the morning, turning on faucets and lights to assure myself that the apocalypse is still self-contained over a thousand miles away at my mother's doorstep. Texas border states have already begun rationing plans. Through their television noise, scientists and preachers scramble to understand such centralized tragedy, use incantations and formulas to predict where this may go if it ever leaves Bonita. Some claim aliens.

2.

To be clear, I'm not speaking in metaphor when I tell you the end of the world began on my second wedding day, more than a year ago. Leaves littered my mother's lawn. Dried bits the grasshoppers left behind turned Bonita parking lots and roads a pale green ocean. A case of wine left too long in a truck exploded. Trees stood naked, bare arms raised to the sky as if seeking answers.

My mother's temperature gauge read 112 that day, but I was in love, if sweaty, in my sundress. Outside, grasshoppers crunched underfoot. We kept a broom handy to push them outside, letting three in for every one swept out. Mother, embarrassed, ran her well dry trying to turn brown grass green, as if the weather and bugs were a reflection on her and her housekeeping, not a sign of what was to come.

3.

I fill the bathtub each night. When the faucet squeaks to life come morning, I water the plants, fill the dog's bowl, and empty the tub, watching the clear water swirl away to nothing. Plant stalks swell and leaves droop. I wander out to check the sky for dangerous cloud formations, kneel and place both palms on the ground. Neighbors wave, keep walking. Leaves shift in the breeze, lazy and unconcerned. My Idaho sky is blue for days. Rainbows come and go in the sprinkler's twirl.

I don't know if a thunderstorm would make me feel better or worse at this point, so I turn on the television. Bonita's apocalypse is growing old for the rest of the country. No news for almost a week.

4.

It's probably true that we all have our own self-centered versions of when this started, when we decided to believe or stop believing in coincidence. The tornado that ripped off a section of my mother's roof, causing her to box her sequined tops and fall upon her knees, was weather and nothing more in my mind. Her fundamentalist upbringing wouldn't allow her the luxury. She heard the roar of the wind twisting metal and dislodging bricks. The sky took her bobtailed cat and left her half a home. That same sky later took Pitch, and that is not a metaphor either. At least I don't think so anyway.

Mother was chastened by the rain that pelted her carpet, only to watch the clouds dry up with not a drop of relief for months on end. When it seemed she could not take one more loss, she lost Lula. She looked to God for answers. He wasn't speaking, so she looked behind her, made a list of transgressions, hoping to balance some divine equation. She underlined "mother" in red.

I thought I had run far enough away to be sure I saw things back in Bonita clearly. I couldn't have known that, in my flight, I would forever keep one eye over my shoulder, and in doing so would circle back again and again. When the second earthquake hit, shortly after the first round of fires I'd called plain old bad luck, I knelt in my closet and tried piecing together my own prayer, unable to remember anything beyond "thy kingdom come." Disaster close to home had not given the words new meaning, so I left the quinoa to burn on the stove and called Mother.

5.

I work her every way I can from my Idaho kitchen to hers, our voices ones and zeroes pinged through space satellites. I tell her we'll load the horses, haul them across the canyons and mountains, and put them in the backyard. Bring your chickens. Just brick and wood, I say of the three-bedroom home she's scraped for, the patched-up house whose mortgage will probably outlive her. I hear her switch the phone to the other ear, bang a door shut. I brag on the depth of our town's reservoir and the snow-tipped mountains you can see in August. A preacher buzzes radio noise in the background. I've never even heard of a tornado in Idaho, I say. You can carry your gun on your hip in the grocery store! She sits there, jaw set in silence I can see. Then: You know the story of Job, she says. What if God picked the wrong person for the job?

6.

NPR finally runs a story, a color piece on Bonita's Riders for Christ—a group that takes its message almost as seriously as its method of delivery. Before all of this, they opened rodeos performing cowgirl tricks against a backdrop of fireworks and

"God Bless the U.S.A." Now sword-packing Riders sit sentry at each of the cardinal directions outside town, certain the Four Horsemen will gallop down from the heavens any day in need of spangled escort. Steve Inskeep says a few have liberal enough interpretations to pack rifles, which has created something of a rift. Those Riders man only the Southern outpost, where the group's leadership think the Horsemen are least likely to appear. Steve outlines stories for tomorrow's program in the event the rapture doesn't occur overnight. Then he cues Blondie. I pick up the phone to make sure my mother hasn't found herself a sword.

7.

Every day before she died, Lula bowed her head and prayed for Mother's cussing and carousing to stop. She prayed for Mother to humble herself before the Lord and care about what good Christian people thought. She prayed my mother would get out of that mess she was in, as she referred to Mother's marriage to Pitch. Adultery in Lula's eyes, though my only real memories of my mother's first (and God-recognized) husband are the blue welts he made of her eye; the way the bruises bloomed purple, then yellow on her chest and back; how we both missed him when he finally left. Lula prayed for God's love to rain like fire from the heavens. I wonder if this strange apocalypse is what she had in mind.

8.

There will always be those ready to don a cowboy hat and ride the bomb down with a yippee-ki-yay, those who sell hats and work the levers. While the Bible church holds twenty-four-hour prayer meetings, sinners filter into the casino and the VFW, filling up the dark places, no need to conserve, no need to conceal pent-up desires. Faithful to no end the time is nigh.

My mother refuses to step into a church, but she's taken to covering her head, wearing long dresses. I find myself in the unexpected position of suggesting she go to the casino to keep some semblance of normalcy. She won't hear of it. Mysterious are the ways.

9.

I get an all-networks-busy recording and punch End and Send until I get a crackly ring, and she picks up. I don't tell her I'm half believer. I insist that while surely some kind of geoseismic shift has occurred beneath her very feet, this does not necessarily mean that the Christian God of Fire and Fury has returned. I tell her it probably has to do with all the oil Texans sucked up. Arrogant Texans messed up the tilt of the Earth, perhaps. Somehow altered weather patterns, I say. I was never good at science, and she reminds me of this. Then she tells me my ex-husband, Wes, leads AA meetings now, that his twin boys both accepted offers to play football at Texas Tech. I duck, jab. Ask if she's taken up embroidery or churning butter, ask if Laura Ingalls is the First Saint of the New Apocalypse. She sets her jaw. Okay, the end of the world *maybe*, I say, but show me this God.

10.

Can I love anything the way that I used to love the mystery of my mother, her strength in suffering?

11.

Today I ask if she wishes she'd left before it got so hard, come to live with me and my husband in the high desert where we could listen to the end of the world over the airwaves and cook frittatas still. This is what we do when there is nothing new to report and the line goes quiet. This is how we push back at the distance and the catastrophe. She says, Do you wish you'd stayed?

12.

CNN runs a segment on a newly discovered Mayan calendar. A reporter goes around interviewing people in front of the Mall of America, asking for views on the Texas Apocalypse and the End of Time. I wonder what the Mayans had in mind as they toiled, fashioning stone chink by chink: a twenty-four-hour news cycle, complete with a running Twitter ticker of the apocalypse?

An African American woman claiming Mayan and celestial ancestry speaks. She wears a purple tunic with strange lettering. Says this whole Mayan hysteria is a big misunderstanding. The Mayans didn't create calendars, and there isn't an End of Time. They were measuring divine light, outside time. I make doodles on the back of a Chinese take-out menu. In the end, it all looks like lightning bolts and cyclones.

The anchor seems relieved until the Mayan woman places a hand on her polyester sleeve and explains that just because the ancients weren't concerned about our modern world, it doesn't mean the events in North Texas aren't indicative of what's to come. We must practice seeing with our eye-eyes, she sighs, before we can see with our mind-eyes. And then: North Texas is now. When she smiles into the camera, she seems sad for us. I hear my husband's key in the door. He's home from giving a final, so I turn off the television, fold the menu into a tiny square, and cram it into my back pocket.

13.

My husband is a skeptic. He thought the grasshoppers last August were a nuisance, nothing more. Of the heat, he said, It's Texas in August. What did you expect?

When I speak to Mother, he opens the computer, goes quiet. As soon as I hang up, he closes the laptop, and his sigh misplaces the rest of the air in the room. I don't think he does this for my benefit. I think he does not appreciate what he cannot tie down with reason. I think this is why he loved me in the first place: I am a good challenge.

14.

At first nobody danced at the wedding, or Mother's Event, as I began calling the night. The Legion hall filled, scattershot, with my aunts from Tennessee and a few Bonitans, mostly Pitch's relatives. Few friends made the trip to Texas, and when I bemoaned the fact, Mother knocked back her white zin and said, Yes, it's too bad you have a family that loves you.

I ran off and cried in a storeroom stacked with cases of beer. Not because I had traveled around so much that I didn't really have friends or because of what Mother said but because without Pitch there, the wedding felt like a funeral. He faded so slowly that I hardly noticed when I lost the only real father I ever knew. Idaho is so far.

Mother said that by the time he disappeared into a dust storm, she could almost see through him. I'd been told stranger things that turned out true, and I couldn't find a record of him anywhere. Still, I looked, hoping someday I'd find a number and he would turn up fat and happy, living out his days in the mountains of New Mexico, catching trout or raising runners. But mostly, I knew. He wasn't coming back.

I dried my face and rejoined the ladies in tight jeans and men in broad-brimmed straw hats. People brushed one another's backs as they came in, checking for grasshoppers, and made quick for cold Dos Equis and napkins to dab sweat.

The swan-carved melon soon sat empty, save the black seeds. My aunts fanned themselves and cried tears of joy when we recited the vows we'd written. Aunt Josie said she thought I was going to end up dying in the Bonita DQ for sure, but look at me, born again and brand-new.

Mother cocked her brow toward the empty dance floor, so I gave up on Rebirth Brass Band and put on the AC/DC that she had insisted I load on the playlist. As soon as the bells began to ring out and the guitars snarled to life, cowboys began setting down drinks, clasping hands with their women, marching bowlegged toward the rented speakers. I took a hard pull of my beer. She knows her crowd, my husband said.

I told you, Mother said and led us onto the sawdusted floor, "Hells Bells" echoing off the walls. My husband shrugged his shoulders, pushed up his glasses, and proceeded to get down, banging his head and bouncing his ass off Mother's as I clapped them on. In those sweaty three minutes, Mother was right; everything was, somehow, perfect. But soon I'd had two beers too many, and barefooted and half-cocked, I was out-Bonitaing the Bonitans. I woke up the next day as ready as ever to leave and never come back.

15.

I get the all-networks-busy signal for two days before I decide to go. My husband calls the plan hopeless and vague. He says we need to save our resources. He quietly reminds me of my job search. He asks me if I really think adjuncting for another semester will finally lead to a full-time position. I shrug, and he walks away. He comes back to say that my mother is a grown woman who can take care of herself and never has been inclined to listen to reason. That's easy to say, I blab, when it's not your mother living on the brunt end of the beginning of the end of the world, which is mean because his mom died years ago.

Being the man he is, he agrees to go to Texas if I wait for him to enter final grades and agrees to use his credit card to pay for the gas that has skyrocketed. Despite rationing, you can still travel freely if you have the money and don't live at the end of the world. He tells me I am about to put an end to that freedom on both accounts. Then he squeezes my hand hard and begins to pack.

I pack with one hand, work the phone in the other. Sending, ending. Sending. I fill my backpack with Ziplocs and wool socks. I check the tent for stakes. My husband packs a few shirts and some underwear and fills his bags with books on Greek philosophers whose names I can't remember how to pronounce. When I come in with the orange cat-hole trowel, he takes it gently from my hand and puts it back in the garage. I don't know how to pack for the end of the world, so I imagine a backpacking trip.

16.

Mother picks up as we're driving through the red rocks of Moab listening to a classic rock station. It's Don Henley's birthday, and every station seems to be in on the awful celebration. When I hear her voice, I punch off the radio and sit up. Everything is fine, she says. A trembler, not too big. She tells us to turn around and go home. Or head west—everyone should see the Grand Canyon, she says. She sounds tired.

Why don't we all go see it together, I say.

You know, she says, it's just a few miles from one rim across to the other. Imagine all that sky, she says and fades off before adding: People die all the time trying to get across.

We're coming, Mama, I say and snap the phone shut. I lean my head back and close my eyes. All I see are burned-out buildings and twisted metal. My husband touches the side of my face and pushes the car faster.

17.

A fierce wind greets us when we pull to the top of the hill outside town. A line of delivery trucks waiting to move into Bonita has us backed up alongside the roadside park. From the looks of it, the park was recently a happening place, but news teams have mostly abandoned their makeshift camps. My husband points out that Texans favor a liberal definition of the term "park." It's just a couple of cement slabs with picnic tables and a trash can off the highway, usually devoid of much else besides prickly pear or bluebonnets in springtime.

I point to the farthest table, tell him this is where Mother and I came to watch the sun set when I was a girl. I absorbed as much of that time as I could, that time after work and school before she reapplied her lipstick and walked through a cloud of perfume and out our front door, where she'd spend the night dancing the sun back up as I slept.

Now tarps pop and snap in the wind, strain at the lines holding them to Earth. One guy in a dingy brown suit huddles on a bench squinting into his phone. We roll down the windows despite the wind. A brown beer bottle rolls across the cement slab. Plastic bags flutter against the table legs, trapped just east of the freedom stretching ahead on the endless Texas prairie.

Toward town, things appear just about normal, aside from a gas well that billows orange flames and hazy, electric smoke. My husband is taken aback by the sight, but I tell him this happens from time to time in oil country, even when there isn't an apocalypse going on.

18.

Mother, speaking on good authority I assumed, had always told me nothing good happened after midnight. I have a feeling that's when I was conceived. I know it was sometime the summer before her ninth-grade year, not long after she started to sneak bell-bottoms to school, where she changed out of her Holy Roller dress and put on eyeliner she stole from the drugstore. I can imagine her scrubbing her eyes red to get the makeup off, rolling the jeans into a neat ball and putting them in the bottom of her locker, walking back home at the end of the day defiant but looking like the Holiness girl she was supposed to be.

Mother told me plenty, wanting to make certain I didn't follow in her footsteps. I mostly listened, until late one night my sophomore year when I let a stout little running back named Jett sweet-talk me into going to see a well fire that had erupted when drillers hit a gas pocket. We left a party around eleven, me peering out the back window every few minutes, sure that every set of headlights belonged to Mother. After parking his truck in a ditch, we followed the orange glow through pastures, carrying a bottle and blanket over tree-lined fences until we got to the flame.

I snuck into the house close to sunrise and tiptoed past Pitch's snores, and only after I was tucked deep into my bed did I smile to myself, excited at the new life that awaited me outside Mother's hypocritical rules. The next morning, I discovered a hickey the running back had left, like a badge. He told everyone except his girlfriend that he got further than he did.

He turned into a meth head, still in and out of jail. Mother always swore it was him who broke into the house and stole the change bucket. I was long gone by then, of course. Cause and effect, my husband says and inches the car forward.

19.

Two rangers lean against their Mustangs at the front of the line. Just beyond them, atop Paint horses, sit two women holding purple flags emblazoned with a golden cross and sword. The horses shift and stomp. The flags pop in the wind. Would you look at that, my husband says. They wear cowboy boots and white tunics gathered at the waist. Wide leather belts and giant gem-encrusted cross buckles hold their swords in leather scabbards. I hope they've got Gold Bond in Bonita, my husband says, but he doesn't laugh. I raise my hand toward them, but they don't seem to see. Over the wind you can hear the thrust of the gas-driven flames from the well fire. The women stare beyond us out toward the western horizon in certainty. One dismounts and kneels in prayer, her voice lost to the wind and flames.

20.

The rangers let us pass after we explain our purpose, sign a dossier, and complete a few forms. They assure my husband that the fire will burn itself out and that there's no reason to call 911. Don Henley's been running through my head since Moab, and as the ranger waves us past, I sing, *You can check out anytime you want, but you can never leave.*

Not funny, my husband says and accelerates past the snaking flames that dance high into the sky welcoming me home.

21.

On the last stretch into Bonita a hand-painted sign warns: WELCOME TO PRETTY. SLOW DOWN—ROUGH GOING. Mother warned

us that a small group of white locals have taken it upon themselves to expunge foreign words from the English language,
hoping, I guess, that the coming God is a white supremacist
too and that he appreciates their attention to detail.

Thanks for the heads up, assholes, my husband says as
we bottom out. He thinks the road could be buckled from
the heat, but I think earthquake. You can see where the earth
bucked and bowed, picking up the two-lane road and setting
it several feet off to the side, leaving the double yellow stripe
misaligned. Infinity broken.

22.

While we were busy packing tent stakes and books, it never
occurred to us to bring more than road food. The stupidity
strikes us at the same time when we see the beat-up grocery
store in the middle of town, which is really just the middle
of a highway. There never was much to Bonita, especially
before the casino. A few gas stations. The VFW and Legion
hall. Two drugstores. One or two grocery stores, depending
on the year. Plenty of churches and a rodeo arena. After the
heathens voted the town wet, there was never a shortage of
liquor stores, and the sign for one is half-lit just down the
road. That will be the next stop.

The gas station across the street is nothing but charred
rubble and bits of metal that skitter in the wind. Gas lines
ruptured in the last earthquake, and dust coats the cars in the
grocery store lot. A boy who can't be more than ten stands

in the back of a pickup holding a shotgun. His little brother is yanking on a kid goat's ear. Not that unusual, I say to my husband, who's gone quiet.

When I open the car door, my husband stays put. She's not going to leave, he says.

I nod at the boy with the gun, but he just shifts his feet and stares at me. I can't believe we didn't bring bacon, I say.

Fine, my husband says and follows me through the parking lot.

The checkout lady recognizes me, though to me she is only a face. She tells us that a few other places have reopened, but they'll rob you blind if you don't watch. Tell your mother we miss her at the V, she says. No sense moping around waiting on the big one. She smiles, and her teeth are stained from coffee or cigarettes, probably both. Her eyes are lined in dark blue, and you can see where the powder has settled into the wrinkles crisscrossing her face. She doesn't smooth her rouge, just leaves the circles be, like setting suns.

23.

When we pull up to Mother's, the place looks empty without her usual array of petunias and marigolds. A blue tarp still covers the roof on the east end. It's buttoned down tight with bungees in all directions, looks professional. Pitch's horses run up to the fence and nicker, toss their heads at us. They're skinny. Mother told me grain's hard to get and she's down to her last few round bales, but it's still sad to see them looking like the horses kept by people who aren't horse people—people who stake a horse to a lead in the backyard and cram three kids on the bony animal to ride through the streets unshod during parades. I wonder what those horses look like now. I wonder what those kids look like.

24.

Mother walks out and stops, as if we are a vision she can't trust. Standing there on her cracked concrete porch with sagging steps, arms crossed, she seems small. The bonnet covers her eyes. Then she bounds down the steps and shouts, My professors! When she grabs me up, she feels, again, whole and as big as the world. My husband stands back watching us. When we don't let go or stop our crying, he begins to unload camping gear. Bless you babies, Mother says, stroking my hair. Bless my sweet babies.

Those are my Lula's words, not Mother's. I pretend not to notice and hold on tight.

25.

I have my mother's hands. Our left central incisors each stick out just a hair, the loans she took out for braces on my stubborn teeth a waste of money. When I've drunk too much, my husband reminds me that I have more than Mother's hands and mouth.

26.

The wind knocks out the electricity at night. The tarps covering the unrepaired portion of the roof rumble across the ceiling with each gust. Mother's heeler burrows beneath a pile of quilts stacked in the corner. Mother doesn't seem fazed even though it's her night on the grid. She goes around muttering prayers and lighting candles. When she's not squeezing my hands and stroking my hair, it's almost like she's not even here. My husband fills the lantern I brought. I ask him if he'd like to play Frisbee with his laptop.

27.

It turns out the end of the world has been subsidized. We must, however, convince Mother to accept the food FEMA ships in. God will provide, she says. It's for us sinners, we say, and she gets a worried look, grows quiet.

When we pull in at the Tuesday pickup, my husband says in a big, booming voice, BEHOLD GOD FEMA.

Great, I say. On the seventh day God created formaldehyde trailers.

He says the end of the world is making us dumb and walks away to grab a box. I'm happy he's making jokes, and when he comes back I'm grinning. Hey look, two-by-two, I say, dropping cans of tuna and chicken into the box.

Why would a fish need an ark? he says. What good is an ark to a fish?

28.

Time moves slowly at the end of the world. Each day Mother cooks a breakfast to end all but won't eat. She's in there cracking store-bought eggs before we wake up. When we shuffle into the kitchen, she shakes her head at the pale yolks in apology. The hens have stopped laying her prized multicolored eggs with the hard shells and yolks like setting suns. With a clenched jaw, she flips the sizzling sausage that we splurged on when there was no bacon, plates the biscuits and the FEMA milk gravy, and sets it all out on the counter. When we finally sit down to eat, my husband and I exchange looks as Mother blesses the food and the day and gives thanks for everything from the table and chairs to the hairs on our heads. She only smiles when she's standing over us while we eat. We do our best to keep eating.

Mother spends the rest of the day in her room. When I'm not recovering from breakfast, I drive my husband crazy with my encyclopedic store of Don Henley songs. I don't know how I know so many or how to stop singing. He retreats to the garage to read. Or stares at the blue roof, his face smashed in concentration, muttering numbers and supply lists. I can see he feels bad that he's not a son-in-law who can swoop in with a hammer and make things right again. Sometimes I see him standing next to the barbed wire fence trying to work up the courage to climb over and pet the horses.

I go to the bedroom to lie down beside Mother while she reads the Bible. Sometimes I stand on the bed and sing: *All she wants to do is dance.* I remind her of her disco days and toss my hair like a stripper. I find her box of shiny outfits and play dress up. She doesn't get angry. She smiles and reaches out to pull my hand to her mouth where she breathes it warm and kisses it. We have to be ready, she says.

29.

On day four, my husband comes into the kitchen and plops down a grocery sack of toilet paper, pulls out a packet of powdered eggs. Fresh out of the real ones, he says. He starts to say something else, then trails off, smoothing the edge of the fake eggs as if what he wants to say can be found there and coaxed out.

People were talking about cattle dying, he says finally. The guy hauled them to a sale because he didn't have any grass or water left on his property. When he let them out, they trampled each other trying to get to the water. Within minutes, they all collapsed. Water intoxication. And if that isn't bad enough, he says, the bag boy says there's a sex room at the VFW.

I squeeze the toilet paper to my chest like an idiot and sing: *We've been poisoned by these fairy tales.*

It works because he hops onto the counter and sighs. Alright, which song? I shrug my shoulders and dance a little more. Then he surprises me and says that maybe we should just go to the V and have a drink.

Eyes Wide Shut II: Apocalyptic Cowboys and Hell-Bent Barmaids? No thanks, I say. Do you remember the lady at the grocery store? Do you really want to see her naked? He rubs his eyes, says things may be getting to him, says I need to think about what I want to do. Then he picks up a leftover biscuit and walks into the garage. The weather has been calm for two days, the sky blue. It's making us all a little crazy.

30.

Before all of this, my husband loved that Mother wasn't like his first mother-in-law, following him around tallying up his shortcomings, holding secret court with her daughter over the telephone. While he feared what harsh truth might come out of Mother's mouth, especially when she was on to her second red-eye, he loved that she was a let-it-loose kind of lady who did her lipstick every hour on the hour, even if she had to pull it from a dented-up lunch pail. Sometimes he walks back to her bedroom and stands in the doorway for a while before he turns and walks back out. I think he's starting to worry about that with which he cannot reason.

31.

I approach Mother with half a plan. She is lying on her bed with her hands clasped, Bible open beside her. The wind has picked up. You can hear it whistling through the small spaces and moaning through everything else. Out the window I see a dust devil moving across the pasture. The horses are running. A large limb cracks in the tree that stands bare in the front yard. I watch, waiting for it to fall. When it doesn't, I sit on the bed. Let's take a drive, I begin. I tell her we need to fill up the car. The corrugated gate is banging against a fence post, ringing out again and again. God wouldn't want you in here hiding behind prayer, I say, pushing.

The birds are all gone, she says. I tried feeding them, but the little things blew off. Tumbled away one after another when they gathered for the seed. I guess I shouldn't have. The ones that didn't catch on the fence rolled right across the pasture. Haven't seen a bird in two months or more.

I look out the window for a sign of something okay, something not terrifying. A yellow grasshopper thunks onto the screen. Mother begins to massage the top of one thumb with the other. Arthritis has turned the joints in her hands into balls of cartilage, just like Granny's before her. What if you're right, I tell her. What if God's decided, *Well, so much for Earth and all those little people down there. And you know, I think I'll stretch it out, make them suffer good.* If this is all we've got, then what? I want to hear you laugh. I want to hear you say, throw dirt on it, and fuck 'em, feed 'em fish heads to anybody who doesn't like it. I need you to fight. I need you.

She doesn't say anything, but her eyes fill with tears. I pull her hands apart, wrap them in mine. I raise her hand to my mouth, take her index finger, and run it over my sticking-out tooth. Then I run my finger along hers, feeling the bump of imperfection. Remember when you used to come into my room when I was dead asleep and do this, I ask, leaning my forehead against hers. Looking into her eyes is looking into my own. You'd open the door, say: *Are you asleep*, before barging in to lie down and tell me about your night.

You needed your rest, Mother says. I start to say something but she cuts me off, says, He'll come like a thief in the night. She picks up her Bible.

Well, I say. If he's a thief, he's not a very good one making all this noise.

32.

When I poke my head into Mother's room to tell her we are going to leave for a bit, she is sitting on the edge of her bed. Her purse is at her feet, and her head is covered in a silk scarf tied beneath her chin. She looks tiny there and older than I've ever imagined she could be. I wonder if she's been hiding these old lady purses and scarves beneath her bed for years, just waiting for the right moment to become this person I see before me. She smiles thinly and hugs her purse tight against her chest. The uncertainty I see in her eyes tells me it's not faith keeping her in her bedroom. This new religion is one of fear. Her only certainty, I'm afraid, is that she somehow deserves all of this sorrow, and I don't know that I'll be able to convince her otherwise here.

The wind has let up some, I say. Come with us. It'll just be a short drive.

Honey, she says. It's not the wind I'm scared of.

33.

The sun's close to setting, and as we pull out of the drive, the wind blows us onto the gravel shoulder before my husband yanks the car steady. I've left him up front alone so I can sit in the back with Mother, like the new moms I see on the road, unable to let the baby rest buckled behind their backs for a second. When she didn't fight the seat belt like she always does, my husband gave me a look that said, *we've got to get out of here* as plainly as if he'd written a note. I make soft cooing sounds and hear myself saying, There, there. We'll be just fine.

Remember our sunsets, I say. Remember how we'd pack an ice chest and go up to the hill and watch the sun go down? How it'd stretch for miles, lighting up the sky blood orange and blue and everything in between? Mother looks out the window, and I imagine that she smiles.

My husband fiddles with the radio up front. He pauses at a fuzzy news station long enough to hear that a tornado has ripped through downtown Oklahoma City. A big one. They're interviewing the police chief, who sounds confused. His voice catches. It's just gone, he says. I lean forward and punch it off. There's no sound for a while except the sound of the tires on the road and the wind. Always the wind.

Finally my husband speaks up. I know Oklahoma's close, and I feel for them, he says. But isn't this good news for Bonita, in a sense? I mean, climate change is terrible. Terrifying. But it's science.

Mother is praying to herself. Her whispers grow louder. I find his eyes in the rearview and give him the please-shut-up look. He jerks his head over his shoulder toward Mother, says, We need to talk.

I lean my head over onto Mother's shoulder and think about a new apocalypse unconstrained by precedent or the absurdity of town borders. Words run through my head: Mother and plenty of water. Safe haven and plenty to eat. Understanding and safety for the man driving us, love. I can't tell if I'm begging for these things or thanking something or someone or both. As if awoken from a dream, Mother looks down on me and says, It's been forever since I've watched the sun go down from the hill.

34.

When we pull up, the well fire still hasn't burned out. My husband just shakes his head, giving up on understanding anything, I'm afraid. One of the Riders is leading her horse toward a trailer at the base of the hill. Her head hangs, stiff from sitting on top of a horse for God knows how many hours. The wait can't be easy on the faithful either.

Two new rangers man the exit out of town and past the roadside park. My husband stops, and one of them sticks his head in and asks if we have everything we need. I lean forward and tell him we just want to catch the sunset. My husband doesn't protest when I say we'll be right back, but I know we're going to have to make a move quick. I can let you go, the ranger says. But they're shutting down unofficial entries. The man does not put up with any kind of reasoning or logic, so my husband puts the car in reverse and pulls perpendicular to the road. He puts it in drive, leaves his hand on the gearshift. Ahead, a horse trailer pulls onto the road. The Rider raises a weary hand. Finally, my husband speaks, but I have to lean in to hear him: We could just go.

35.

I turn to Mother. What do you think, I say. Let's just go. Somewhere things are better, somewhere things can still be okay? We'll visit the library, go to a restaurant. We can swing wide and see the Grand Canyon.

The animals need a new round bale, Mother says. And they'll need another one after that. My husband slams the car into park, and when he sighs, I have to roll down the window to get some air.

36.

Mother picks up her purse, opens the door, and steps out. I've never seen my calm, constant husband have a panic attack, but by the looks of things, I might.

We can't stay here forever, he says. I love you, and I'll help you tie her up and make her go, or I'll hold you when we leave her, but I've had enough of whatever you want to call what's happening here.

He grabs his hair with both hands and looks like a Munch painting.

Do you even know what you're asking me to do, I say. I hit the seat back with both hands and begin to cry. I need him steady. I can't be the steady one. It's not in me anymore.

Mother is holding a crumpled tissue to her mouth, teetering across the cattle guard, heading toward the well. I fling the door open and say, Do what you have to do. He's still sitting there when I look back.

When I catch up to her, she's standing at the base of the flame, close enough that when I take her hand it's already warm. You can't imagine heat, she says. You have to feel it for yourself.

37.

Flames dance, casting shadows across Mother's face. Heat vapors make the world look unsteady, dreamlike. Please, I say, but this close to the flame, its roar swallows the word. The pressure comes and goes, whips in and out, a giant blowtorch below the Earth's surface beginning to run itself dry. An orange ball billows twenty feet or more into the sky before the flames shrink down and snake wispy in the wind. The fire makes its own wind, and I feel it moving through my clothes, pushing back stray hairs. My husband crosses the cattle guard but stands back a ways watching us. He shrugs his shoulders and gives what smile he can muster. Mother offers him her hand, and he comes over and puts his arm around my waist, working to be the person I need him to be for a while longer.

38.

Above us, the new Riders keep watch on the hill, silhouetted by the setting sun. They step high in their stirrups and lean forward, bracing for something we can't see. We stand there, staring into the flame, until it begins to grow dark outside our circle. The wind picks up, whips the flame around, lighting our faces. Mother pulls my hands close, turns them over, studies them like she used to when I was a girl. I'm not crazy, she says. I don't think so anyway.

I know— I try to say, but she cuts me off.

To tell you the truth, she says, I don't know if it's suicide or salvation, but this is home. I don't even know anything else anymore. But you, she says, you were always my perfect angel. The wind shifts directions again and begins to roar. There is a loud bang, and people are yelling off in the distance.

I'm so proud of you, Reney, she yells. Then she wipes my hair from my face, leans her forehead against mine, and shouts, I'm glad you're not like me in the ways that count. I take her by the shoulders and hold her gaze, try my best to see past my own reflection, to see her as she is right now, as she must have been all those years ago, defiant but afraid. Space opens up, the sky goes soft. I see what's before us, I see what's been, and I see out past the sun where stars explode and life starts anew. I know she won't be in the car when we drive away. I don't know if it matters where we are when all is said and done. We are together, two parts of some unimaginable whole. When I've seen more than I can take, I give in, close my eyes, and feel the warmth of her skin. I imagine her as big and whole as the world, pretend her words were lost to the flame.

Acknowledgments

So many thank yous—

Adam Eaglin, for reading and rereading, for seeing the book even when I didn't, for making each story better, for your undying patience and generosity, for your belief.

The incomparable Elisabeth Schmitz, for your brilliance and spark, for giving *Crooked Hallelujah* and me a chance and doing all you can to make us shine. I feel so lucky to have found my way to you.

For Katie Raissian, Yvonne Cha, and Jazmine Goguen, for sharing your sharp editorial eyes and encouragement.

Morgan Entrekin, Judy Hottensen, Deb Seager, John Mark Boling, and the whole fantastic team at Grove, for working so hard and for putting your hearts and souls into the work.

Michael Adams, for your kindness and humor, for your generosity of spirit, for your love of Paisano Ranch and Texas letters, for being, always, you.

Scott Berg, Mike Scalise, and Nina McConigley, for writing back and picking up when I cried out from out of the blue.

Dick Bausch, for helping me believe I could do this, for doing all you can to teach us that *this* matters, for the cheers, for the stories and guitars.

Alan Cheuse, for being the voice in my ear long after you've gone.

Brandon Hobson, David Treuer, Erika T. Wurth, and Leila Aboulela, for being early readers of *Crooked Hallelujah* and responding with such generosity.

Steve Goodwin, Allen Wier, Peter Klappert, James Nolan, Chris Chambers, Mrs. Maddox, and Mrs. Flusche, for teaching me so much, introducing me to some of the greats, and for reading my early flailing.

The University of Texas at Austin and the Dobie Paisano Fellowship Program, The Native Arts and Cultures Foundation, The Elizabeth George Foundation, The School for Advanced Research, Writers & Books, and George Mason University for the gift of time that came in the form of financial support, space to write, encouragement, connection, and sometimes, roadrunners, and water moccasins.

The Editorial Committee of the Board of the *Paris Review,* The University of Central Oklahoma and Rob Roensch, and the *Missouri Review* and Elise Juska for reading so thoughtfully and generously supporting my work.

Bread Loaf, for the beauty, inspiration, and community—especially the Frost Farm Cats—and most especially Alix Ohlin for your generosity and insight.

The editors who gave some of these stories their first home and made each one so much better: Cal Morgan, Emily Nemens, Evelyn Rogers, Hannah Reed, K.E. Semmel, Paul Reyes, and Allison Wright.

Amy Amoroso, Kirsten Clodfelter, Carl Della Badia, Michael Noll, and Alexis Santi for lending my stories your brilliance and care.

Anna Habib, Matt Hobbs, and Gretchen Sullivan, for being such sharp readers and generous souls and for generally poodling out all over the place.

Annie Moore, Louise Liller, Cordy Meza, Jen Scott, Chris Sparks, Danika Myers-Hurwitz, Hannah Burgard, Rachel Nicolosi, Chantel Guidry, Chris Sheffield, Rachel Lettre, Amtchat Edwards, Katie Hart, Katie Billings, and Keena Galvan for all the love and words and music and mountains through years and miles.

Everyone back home who helped me with questions about the language, horse mane(s), old pickup-truck cassette decks, fertility, Beenie Weenies, gunshot wounds, and so much more.

My aunties, who have been a big, powerful circle around me from the time I was born, who still carry a weight and a presence that helps me know I'm home, who can tell a good joke, who don't care to say that we are the funniest sons of bitches we ever met.

My grandmothers—some by blood and some by kindness alone—for wrapping me up and carrying me on your wings, for saving me the last wild onions, for being my protectors, my heart.

Pop, for choosing us and holding on tight; for teaching me how to fish, ride, shoot, and drive a stick, all by the age of twelve; for keeping the freezer full; for fixing everything broken; and most of all for, loving.

Mom, for your strength and your heart that's as wide as the world; for sharing your love of books and a good wha-wha; for always knowing I could and making sure I did too; for making every game, even if you showed up in your braids and UPS browns at the half; for being Granny to Cypress Ann; for fierce, fierce love that won't ever quit.

Cypress Ann, for coming here and filling me with so much love that I can hardly bear it; for being you and only you.

Scott, for making me and this book so much better. Without you, none of this would be.

KELLI JO FORD's *Crooked Hallelujah* was longlisted for the PEN/Hemingway Award for Debut Novel, The Story Prize, the Carnegie Medal for Excellence in Fiction, and The Center for Fiction's First Novel Prize. She is the recipient of *Paris Review*'s 2019 Plimpton Prize, the Everett Southwest Literary Award, a Native Arts & Cultures Foundation National Artist Fellowship, an Elizabeth George Foundation Grant, and a Dobie Paisano Fellowship. She teaches writing at the Institute of American Indian Arts. She is a citizen of the Cherokee Nation.

GROVE PRESS

Reading Group Guide

by Yvonne Cha

CROOKED HALLELUJAH

Kelli Jo Ford

ABOUT THIS GUIDE

We hope that these discussion questions will enhance your reading group's exploration of Kelli Jo Ford's *Crooked Hallelujah*. They are meant to stimulate discussion, offer new viewpoints, and enrich your enjoyment of the book.

More reading group guides and additional information, including summaries, author tours, and author sites for other fine Grove Atlantic titles may be found on our website, groveatlantic.com.

QUESTIONS FOR DISCUSSION

Unstoppable forces of nature are always looming in the lives of Justine and Reney, to which Justine remarks, "It's all so much bigger than him and bigger than me, bigger than us together." (223) Talk about the symbols of natural disaster present throughout the book. How do they represent or relate to the other sources of chaos in these women's lives?

Violence is an ever-present undercurrent in these stories. Reney witnesses much violence inflicted on her mother, and she herself becomes a victim of such violence. Speak about how these violences are internalized by these characters, and how they are perpetuated or combated.

The deep affinity Lula feels for the land grounds them in Beulah Springs, with Justine and Reney continuously returning to Indian Country. What does home mean for these women? Where do they feel they most belong?

Faith is the source of much anger for Justine. And though she wonders "who she could have been without the Bible," (250) she eventually returns to the rituals of her mother's Holiness religion when

Lula dies. Why might Justine choose faith in her mother's absence? How do the characters' relationship to faith transform over time?

―――――

The mothers and daughters oscillate between being each other's caretakers and being cared for, resembling one another even as they vow to be different. Discuss their similarities and their differences. Do shared traits bond these women together or set them apart?

―――――

Animals also play a large role as companions. The book opens with Justine holding a stray cat. Reney sets her goldfish Binky free. In young adulthood, she feels a deep love for her mule, Rosalee. What role do animals play in the emotional lives of these characters? How do they function as symbols for human relationships, illuminating the nature of bonds, and their relationship to the earth?

―――――

The book is organized into three parts, with single stories bookending the collection. Why might these two stories be set apart? Are there ways in which these two stories serve as organizing principles to the rest of the book?

―――――

Justine remarks, "Without the things that make us who we are, we're nothing." (250) What are some "things" that define these characters?

―――――

After Pitch's father dies, Justine comments, "I don't think there's anything holding him to this Earth anymore with his daddy gone." (233) What are some differences between the role of fathers and mothers in this book? How are they portrayed differently, or held to different standards?

―――――

Reney says, "I used to love the mystery of my mother, her strength in suffering." (261) Discuss moments of strength exhibited by Justine throughout. What made her mysterious? What made her strong?

Much of the book is set during the oil booms and busts of Texas and Oklahoma. What are some ways that this economic backdrop shapes the choices the characters make throughout the book? How might American capitalism inform the choices available to the characters during these times? What are some ways that American capitalism has shaped how they view their worlds?

Justine's and Reney's family live in the Cherokee Nation of Oklahoma as the result of Indian Removal. How might you view their lives, their religion, and their home in the context of this history? How are these individual characters shaped and informed by American Settler Colonialism? What are some ways that these characters resist the forces of colonialism?

Justine says to her daughter, "Don't ever be like me." (97) Does Reney come to emulate her mother, even as she is repeatedly told to reject her mother's life?

"I'd met my soulmate as a girl and she was my great-grandmother." (100) Why does Reney call her great-grandmother her soulmate?

How does the story of Moses Lee relate to the recurring themes of grief and manhood that appear in the rest of the book?

Reney makes a big decision after suffering multiple miscarriages with Wes. Why might Reney decide not to ever become a biological mother, despite her fierce love for her own?

––––––––––

SUGGESTIONS FOR FURTHER READING

There There by Tommy Orange

Sing, Unburied, Sing by Jesmyn Ward

Sabrina & Corina by Kali Fajardo-Anstine

Where the Dead Sit Talking by Brandon Hobson

Love Medicine by Louise Erdrich

Sharks in the Time of Saviors by Kawai Strong Washburn

Milk Blood Heat by Dantiel Moniz

The Only Good Indians by Stephen Graham Jones

Everything Inside by Edwidge Danticat

Dog Flowers by Danielle Geller

Heart Berries by Terese Marie Mailhot